Outlaw
Bride

Eli swallowed hard. The strong scent of honeysuckle went straight to his head. She was too close. Too sweet. The night was too warm. And he was too worn down to resist her any longer.

Maybe if he kissed her, just once, he could get her out of his system. After all, this was merely . . . attraction.

A sigh combined with a faint moan escaped her, then she leaned into the kiss and tightened her grip on his neck.

A fire ignited inside him. His last dwindling thought was that a little bit of Annie wasn't nearly enough.

Other Books in
THE AVON ROMANCE *Series*

Avon Books are available at special quantity discounts for
bulk purchases for sales promotions, premiums, fund raising
or educational use. Special books, or book excerpts, can also
be created to fit specific needs.

For details write or telephone the office of the Director of
Special Markets, Avon Books, Dept. FP, 105 Madison
Avenue, New York, New York 10016, 212-481-5653.

Outlaw Bride

KATHERINE COMPTON

AVON BOOKS ◆ NEW YORK

OUTLAW BRIDE is an original publication of Avon Books. This work has never before appeared in book form. This work is a novel. Any similarity to actual persons or events is purely coincidental.

AVON BOOKS
A division of
The Hearst Corporation
105 Madison Avenue
New York, New York 10016

Copyright © 1991 by Katherine Compton
Inside cover author photograph by Johnny W. Demkowich
Published by arrangement with the author
Library of Congress Catalog Card Number: 90-93619
ISBN: 0-380-76411-3

First Avon Books Printing: June 1991

AVON TRADEMARK REG. U.S. PAT. OFF. AND IN OTHER COUNTRIES, MARCA REGISTRADA, HECHO EN U.S.A.

Printed in the U.S.A.

RA 10 9 8 7 6 5 4 3 2 1

In loving memory of J. J. Keim, Jr., aka: Bud, Joe, Outlaw, Pawpaw, and Daddy, who gifted everyone he met with tall tales, a smile, and a sense of humor.

Also, to my mother, Bernice Keim, whose strength and courage is the source I look to whenever my own falters.

To Betty, my sister, my dear, wise friend.

To Bubba, the knight in shining armor of my youth.

And to Jim, who taunted and teased me throughout my childhood (still does at times—just to keep me on my toes) and, inadvertently, taught me how to stand up for myself.

I love you all more than words can say.

Prologue

Summer 1883

The thunder of horses' hooves shook the ground beneath Annie. Nestled in the bushes, she squinted and covered her ears, but the shouting and gunfire seeped through her fingers. Her face was so close to the ground that she could smell the dust kicked up by the riders. A bullet whizzed by a few feet in front of her, forcing her to sink deeper into the underbrush.

Annie had been around gunplay all her life and knew how to handle herself during a shoot-out. Ordinarily, she skedaddled before the fireworks commenced. But she hadn't had a chance to run this time. The gang had ridden into camp with the posse just behind them.

Dang those Texas tin-stars, she thought. They must've chased the boys straight across the border and right into Indian Territory.

Annie pushed a leafy branch aside and peered out. She hadn't ever seen a lawman up close. They hardly ever came into the Territories. This posse was either downright gutsy, or not too smart. It was plain as day, they were outnumbered. Curious as to why the Texans would do such a fool thing, she studied the bunch.

Suddenly a big white horse moved into her line of vision, blocking all else from view. Her gaze traveled up the stallion's powerful legs and settled on the man in the saddle. He was too young to be a sheriff. Must be a deputy, she figured. He sat tall and straight on the prancing horse, his gun drawn and aimed. He was no more than a stone's throw away, and Annie held her breath, afraid he might look down and see her.

There were so many shots being fired that she couldn't say which one hit him. She only saw him jerk, then fall. He landed on the ground beside her, so close she could've reached out and touched him. But for a long moment she merely stared at his clean-shaven chin. Her gaze lowered gradually to the red stain soaking his shirt and tinting the edge of his cowhide vest that was dusty, but not dirty or worn.

Lawmen weren't so different after all, she reckoned. They might wash more often maybe, but their blood was clearly as red as any outlaw's. Was he dead? she wondered. His eyes were closed. But hadn't he just quivered slightly?

Annie took a deep breath and bit her bottom lip. He sure didn't look so fearsome now. Snapping a twig off the bush, she leaned forward and brushed the leafy part across his cheek. When his eyes moved behind his lids, then barely opened, she quickly dropped the stick and drew back.

For a short spell, he didn't seem to know where he was or what was happening. He had a wild, scared look about him. A tightness gripped Annie's chest. It was the same feeling she got whenever she came across a hurt critter in the woods. She hadn't never been able to bear the sight of something ailing.

Rubbing her damp palms together, she glanced about to make sure that none of the gang was watching. Paw was covering Frank while he reloaded, and everyone else appeared to be too busy dodging lawmen's bullets to take much notice of her. She fixed her gaze on the wounded deputy again, and her heart started to beat in her throat. Paw would nail her hide to a tree if he ever found out. But she just didn't have it in her to sit there and do nothing while the deputy died.

She swallowed hard, glanced up to check the whereabouts of the others once more, then crawled slowly, cautiously toward the bleeding Texan.

He focused on her as she approached him, opened his lids wider as she hovered above his face. He was wary. She could tell. White men didn't trust half-breeds any more than red men did. And anyone who saw Annie knew right away that she was a breed. Her blue eyes gave it away. Deadeye had told her that if it weren't for them, nobody would have been able to tell she wasn't a full-blooded Cherokee like her ma.

"I reckon it's gonna pain ya some when I move ya," she whispered, keeping her expression bland. "Ya gotta keep quiet till I get ya under the bushes. Ya hear me, deputy? Ya cain't yell out."

His brows furrowed above his pale green eyes. He ran his tongue over his parched lips. "You . . . you're just . . . a kid," he murmured, then winced. "You can't lift me."

"I wasn't figurin' on liftin' ya. I'm gonna roll ya." She stretched across him, caught his far shoulder, and tugged with all her might. "Deadeye says—" Her voice strained with the effort it took to turn him. "I'm strong as an ox, for m' size."

He grimaced, but never made a sound while she wrestled him into the cover of the bushes. Then, peeking through the branches, she noted that the gang had pretty nearly done away with the rest of the posse. "Got me this here special place, I do. A little cave close by. Ain't nobody knows about it but me. I'm gonna take ya there soon as it gets dark. And I won't tell. Cross my heart and hope t' die. I won't tell no—"

Annie's sentence broke off when she looked back at the deputy and saw he was out cold. Tentatively, she reached toward him and brushed a lock of golden hair from his forehead.

A fuzzy warmth rushed through her, as it had the time she'd held one of the puppies for sale outside the livery in Dregg's Flat. She'd wanted one of them pups powerful bad. Just wanted something all her own to care for. But they'd been priced at a whole nickel.

Cocking her head, she traced her finger over the shiny silver star pinned to the lawman's vest. This here, she reckoned, was even better than a puppy. Her very own deputy to care for. "I ain't gonna let ya die," she said in a voice a notch below a whisper. "Ya hear me, deputy? I ain't gonna let ya die."

Chapter 1

Early April 1888

"**H**ightail it, Annie!" Deadeye Pete shouted as he galloped past her, pushing his horse hard. "They're movin' up on us fast!"

Annie shifted in her saddle and looked over her shoulder. The sun had just slipped behind the hill, illuminating Indian Territory's dusky pink skyline. Thunderous hoofbeats preceded the cloud of dust that formed on the horizon. The silhouettes of four swiftly moving riders rose from the dark ridge like demons from hell.

Annie flattened her hand on the top of her well-worn hat, shoving it down more securely. "Dad-burn lawmen," she murmured as she swiveled back around and dug her boot heels into her mount's flanks. They sure were a persistent bunch. She had to give them that much. Tin-stars rarely ever chased the Calhoun gang this far into the Territories.

An explosion of gunfire came from behind. Annie ducked low and hugged her horse's neck. "I told Frank we shouldn't oughta hit

Bartlett Springs in broad daylight," she said to the animal's ear. "I told him, Ol' Blue. I told him I'd heard the sheriff there didn't cotton to nobody robbin' his bank."

A bullet whistled past her, and Annie urged Ol' Blue to run faster. But it seemed the only thing picking up speed was her heart.

Setting her sights on the line of trees ahead, she noted Deadeye lagging back again, waiting for her at the edge of the woods. Danged old fool was gonna get himself kilt someday if he didn't stop playin' nursemaid.

That fearful thought had barely settled in Annie's mind when she saw Deadeye jerk, then slump in his saddle.

She went cold inside.

Hastily moving up beside her companion, she reined her horse. The tired, weathered face he turned to her was god-awful pale in contrast to the black patch over his left eye.

"Annie," he rasped. "Go on. Get, girl! I'm done for."

"You *ain't* done for, Pete." She glanced from the blood seeping between the fingers he pressed against his shoulder, to the riders barreling toward them. "Believe I'll just show them lawmen a thing or two." She snatched the money bag from Deadeye's grasp and over his protests added, "Shucks, ain't no tin-star alive able to catch Annie Calhoun." With a whack to his horse's rear end, she sent Pete hurdling through the pass toward their hideout.

Annie held her prancing horse in place, took careful aim at the lead man advancing on her, then fired. With an old Indian war whoop, she lifted the money bag high and reared her horse, then took off for the cover of the woods.

Well acquainted with the area, she maneuvered Ol' Blue through the twisted maze of trees at a breakneck pace. The rumble of hooves behind her quieted as she raced onward. Smiling, she reached down and patted Blue's neck. "You may not be what you used to be, but you can dang sure outrun any horse bred in Texas, cain't ya, ol' boy?"

Fading shouts of *This way!* and *No, over here!* made Annie's smile widen. It was as fine a day as she could remember. Not too cold, not too hot. On the tail of winter, spring was commencing. The surrounding redbud trees, now bare, would be in bloom in a few more weeks.

She shot a smug look over her shoulder in the direction of her lost trackers, then frowned. Deadeye would make it to the hideout, she told herself. Camp wasn't far. And if she could just keep these yahoos busy a bit longer—

Still moving at a full canter, she turned back around and gasped at the fallen tree blocking her path. There was no way Ol' Blue could clear it. He couldn't jump that high.

She pulled back on the reins hard, but it was too late. Being the old war horse he was, Blue made a feeble attempt to leap over the sprawling branches, and Annie lost her balance. Before she knew it, she was flying through the air. Blue's shrill whinny resounded in her ears, and she lost her grip on the bank bag. Every ounce of wind she had gushed from her body as she hit the ground.

Then everything went black.

Annie awoke facedown in the dirt without an iota of an idea where she was or how she got there. She curled her fingers around a clump of dead leaves and raised her head a little, trying to focus her eyes.

She came to her senses abruptly when she felt the earth vibrate beneath her, signaling the approach of riders.

"There he is, sheriff!" came a nearby shout. "Right yonder. You see him? Just ahead there."

Annie laid her head against the cool ground, closed her eyes, and relaxed her breathing. There was nothing else to do but play possum, she decided. If she tried to run they'd shoot her for sure. No. It was best to stay right where she was and think this out. Dern Texans more'n likely couldn't find their backsides with both hands, much less their way out of these woods. Shucks, she'd slipped out of the grasp of lawmen before. She'd just bide her time.

The horses drew nearer. Annie heard the riders dismount. The carpet of dried leaves crunched as the four men moved toward her.

"Reckon he's dead?" Someone nudged Annie's rib with the toe of his boot.

"I don't know. It looks like he took a pretty

good tumble off his horse,'' came another voice. Something about the sound of it struck a familiar chord in Annie's brain. It was deep and strong and clear, yet it had the quality of being wrapped in a soft whisper.

One of the lawmen knelt beside her, took her gun from her holster, then rolled her onto her back.

Annie discreetly squinted one eye the teensiest bit open. Through the fringe of her dark lashes she spotted the kneeling man's holstered gun. A moment was all it took to gauge the distance and make her decision. She went for the Colt .45 Peacemaker.

Annie had a fast hand—lots of folks said so. But this stranger was faster. She had scarcely touched the handle of his gun with her fingertips before he'd straddled her and caught both her wrists, stretching them high above her head. Somewhere in the process her eyes flew wide open.

What she saw made her feel as if she'd fallen off her horse all over again.

Her vision darkened and coalesced around the face of the man sitting atop her. Sound closed off completely until all she could hear was the thumping of her own heart. Maybe she'd died and didn't know it.

The features above her grew dim, and Annie fought the faintness that threatened to swoop down and snatch the image from her. If he was truly there this time, she couldn't lose him. Maybe she wasn't dead. She could hear and feel herself breathing. Taking in deep gulps of air, she forced back the shadows that surrounded him and made herself focus.

It *was* him. *Her deputy.*

He was older. A man now. He'd filled out through the shoulders and the chest. The lock of hair that had escaped his Stetson and fallen across his forehead wasn't as pale as she remembered. It had darkened to a sun-streaked fawn color. Though he wasn't near smiling, traces of laugh lines that hadn't been there before were etched around his mouth and eyes. Oh, it was him, all right. She'd never forgotten those eyes . . . the cool green color of barley after an unexpected frost. She'd be willing to bet a whole silver dollar that she'd seen his face in her dreams more times than there were stars in the sky.

"Crazy blue-eyed breed," Annie vaguely heard one of the others say. "Is it just me, or does he look a mite like he's grinnin'? Must have bumped his head purty good."

"Ain't no more than a scrawny kid," another man said, squatting down and laying a hand on the deputy's shoulder. "Probably scared outa his wits. He *does* look a little moony, don't ya think, Eli?"

Eli. The deputy's name was Eli. Annie hadn't ever known his name. She'd just called him *deputy.* He'd never asked hers either, but had simply referred to her as *girl.* 'Course, a good passel of time had gone by since then, she told herself. It musta been . . . what? At least as many summers as she had fingers on one hand.

Eli. It was a right nice name. Closing her

eyes, Annie let it roll around inside her. It made her all warm, like a thick, cozy quilt on a cold winter's day.

"All right, boy," Deputy Eli said abruptly, interrupting Annie's blissfulness and prompting her to reopen her eyes. "We're going to get up from here nice and easy. You give me any trouble and I'll take a switch to your britches. You hear me, boy?"

Boy? Annie blinked, the references they'd all made to *he* and *him* just now hitting home. *Boy?* Eli thought she was a boy? She glanced down at her breasts. Well hell, it was no wonder they weren't showing the way he had her stretched out like a skinned rabbit.

Townsfolk had often mistaken her for a boy, since she'd always worn Frank's hand-me-downs and gone around with her hair tucked under her hat. The notion had never bothered her before. It did at the moment. In fact, it was suddenly *almighty* important that Eli knew she was female. Arching her back, she thrust her chest upward in a way she imagined he was sure to notice.

"I ain't no boy," Annie ground out between her teeth. Though she'd spoken low, the words had come out strong and fierce. She glanced from one man to the next, daring them to disagree. "And I ain't no scrawny kid neither." She softened her gaze when it rested on the man who sat atop her. "I'm a woman," she said with a lift of her chin. "A full-growed woman."

As he stared at the now apparent subtle curves of her breasts, Eli's brows formed a V.

He shifted his weight on her a little, then turned bright red and came to his feet, hauling her with him.

She didn't remember his being quite so tall . . . or his chest so broad . . . or his shoulders so wide. The last of the day's twilight glinted off the star pinned to his cowhide vest at eye level. As she focused on the badge, noting it was different somehow than the one he'd worn before, the verity of the situation seeped into her. He was a lawman. She had to be turning addle-brained to forget such a thing at a time like this. He was a lawman. And she'd just helped to rob his town's bank.

Annie lifted her eyes to his face, where she saw a mixture of puzzlement, disbelief, and irritation. His hard green glare threw a spook into her. Her gaze rose, jumping first to the brim of his hat, then to its high crown. The bullet hole there made her feel as if she'd just swallowed a pinch of snuff, and she grimaced. *Lordy.* She'd shot his hat. Done it on purpose. That was an unpardonable sin in these parts. This side of Pecos, there wasn't a body likely to forgive someone for putting a hole in his hat. She'd have hell to pay for that shot, she reckoned.

She was convinced the payback was commencing when Eli grasped her shoulders in a firm grip. She squeezed her eyes shut again, only to feel herself being moved an arm's length away from him. Squinting one eye open, she could see his mood hadn't changed for the better. He still wore a peeved expression and was giving her the once-over.

He'd been a good enough natured fella when she'd lent him a hand those few years back, she remembered. But then, that had only been nigh on her twelfth summer. She hadn't ridden with the Calhoun gang yet, and wasn't standing on the wrong side of the law . . . as she was now.

Eyeing the arrangement of his features, Annie decided he didn't look at all good natured at the moment. In fact, he looked downright mean. She swallowed hard. Lordy, maybe the years had changed him. Maybe he'd turned into the kind of lawman who took pleasure in making an outlaw sweat before he hanged him.

Just then one of the other men reached out and grabbed Annie's hat, causing her long, straight black hair to tumble past her shoulders. "Well, I'll be a fly on a donkey's tail," the man said, circling her. "She dang sure coulda fooled a genius in that baggy shirt."

Eli ran a hand over his face, stretched his eyes wide open, then narrowed them on his prisoner again. Maybe it was a trick of the lavender light that the evening played in these woods, but he felt a sudden, odd kinship to this self-proclaimed woman dressed in boy's clothing. It was almost as if they had stared into each other's eyes once before . . .

There hadn't been any sketches identifying the "Kid" mentioned on the Calhoun gang's wanted poster. No one, it said, had ever gotten close enough to see the Kid's face. Statements taken had all agreed that the Kid never entered the banks, but had always been

posted outside somewhere during the rob-
beries. Taking in the ragamuffin before him,
he could understand now why witnesses had
described the Kid as a boy of thirteen or so.
Even at this range, Eli himself was having
trouble believing she wasn't what she'd first
appeared to be. As she stood upright, her
oversized shirt hung loosely about her torso,
completely disguising her tapering waist.
And her dark hair, spilling over her shoulders, as it now was, certainly didn't help dis-
tinguish her from any of the half-breed bucks
roaming the Territories these days. They all
wore their hair long.

Eli flushed again, remembering the moment in which her breasts had strained
against the fabric, making it clearly evident
that she truly was of the fairer sex.

Quickly dismissing the image, he pressed
his lips into a tight line and nudged the brim
of his hat. He couldn't help but wonder what
a bath might do for her. Maybe cleaned up,
she wouldn't be too bad on the eye. It was
hard to tell at the present though. She was
such a miserable-looking little creature. Part of
him wanted to make a few threats that would
scare some sense into her, then feed her a
good hot meal and turn her loose with her
promise that she'd follow a straight and narrow path from now on.

But he couldn't do that. He was the sheriff
of Bartlett Springs. The last Larson in the long
line of lawmen. The good people of his town
depended on him to see justice done.

Without giving the idea of freeing the girl

a second thought, he glanced at his men. Their faces held unspoken questions. It was an awkward situation. The Bartlett Springs jail had never housed a woman prisoner before.

"Female or not," Eli said firmly, "the law is still the law. We're taking her in."

The short span of silence that followed was shattered by a half whinny, half human-sounding scream. The tortured cry turned everyone's attention toward the brush beyond the fallen tree.

"*Blue,*" Annie murmured, starting forward. Halted by a large hand that grasped her arm, she looked up into Eli's face and wordlessly begged him to let her see to her horse. After a moment's hesitation, he released his hold, but followed close behind as she climbed over the log and cleared away scattered branches.

Ol' Blue was lying on his side, his large round eyes wild and rolling until they settled on Annie. His hind leg was crooked at an unnatural angle. The lump in her chest rose to her throat as she knelt and stroked his neck. "Aw, Blue," she said softly, "why'd you have to go and try a fool stunt like that for? I knowed you coulda done it in your younger days."

Blue answered with a broken snort, his heavy breathing coming in labored spurts.

Annie laid her head alongside his. She was dying inside, near bursting with anguish. She desperately wanted to cry . . . *needed* to cry, but the tears wouldn't come. They never did.

Not since the day her ma had passed on. Excepting Deadeye, Ol' Blue was the only friend she'd ever had, and it pained her fierce to see him in such agony.

"Shh now, boy," she whispered. "Where you're goin' . . . well, I'll bet there'll be lotsa green pastures . . . shade trees for you to rest under . . . might even be a nice little filly a-waitin' for ya. You'd like that, now wouldn't ya?"

Annie flinched at the touch of a hand covering her shoulder. "Ma'am . . . look, miss—" Eli stammered. "What's your name, girl?"

"Annie," she murmured absently, her attention absorbed by Blue and her helplessness to do anything that might soothe him.

"Annie." Eli's voice softened as he repeated her name. He gave her shoulder a slight squeeze. "I'm sorry about your horse, truly sorry. But he's in pain. He needs to be . . . We need to put him out of his misery. You do understand that, don't you, Annie?"

Annie blinked. She nuzzled Blue's neck once more, then lifted her head and stared at the tall, sandy-haired lawman beside her. He was right. She'd known the moment she'd laid eyes on Blue that her faithful old companion was going to have to be shot. Another pitiful whinny sliced through her, and she nodded slowly.

As Eli helped her stand, her knees gave way and she stumbled against him. "It'll be all right," he said, grasping her arms to hold her upright. "Your horse will be resting easy in a short while. I'll see to it myself."

While Annie attempted to steady herself, she looked up into Eli's face. Something in the depths of his pale green eyes gave her the distinct impression that he felt her pain, knew her sorrow. Nobody'd ever done that before—just looked at her and known she was hurting. She'd inherited the ability to hide her feelings behind a blank expression from her Cherokee mother. Nobody had ever seen through it. But Eli did, was doing so now, and the notion that he was somehow sharing her anguish made her yearn to throw her arms around his neck and never let go. She was just about to give in to the urge when she realized that the others had joined them.

Eli handed her over to one of the men, and with a gesture of his head motioned for the deputy to take her away.

Though Annie was loath to leave Blue's side, she didn't have the strength left to struggle. Achingly aware of what had to be done, she started over the tangled mass of tree limbs, but stopped halfway across and looked back at Eli. Whatever it was she'd felt for him all these years suddenly grew in intensity.

Only yesterday, she would have called anybody a liar to his face if he'd said she'd let a lawman shoot her horse. But Eli wasn't just any lawman, she told herself. He was no stranger, either. Ever since the day he'd disappeared from her life, he had come back to her in her dreams. Whenever she'd been lonesome, or afraid, or simply weary of life, he had come to her in the darkness, seeming so real that she could almost reach out and touch him. There weren't many people she trusted, but she trusted Eli. She had no doubts at all that he'd send Ol' Blue on to peaceful pastures as quickly and as painlessly as possible.

Annie lowered her gaze to her ailing horse and wished she had a bit of sugar to give him. "It's okay, boy," she said gently. "Just close your eyes." Squeezing her own shut, she swallowed hard, then added shakily, "You were the best, Blue . . . the best horse a body coulda ever had."

Chapter 2

In the distance, a pack of coyotes howled at the bright full moon. Annie shifted her backside on the cold, hard ground. She missed Ol' Blue. Still, the way she saw it, he had done his chores on this earth and had earned eternal rest. Sorrows came, and sorrows went. She couldn't recall life being any other way. Wallowing in grief certainly wasn't going to bring Blue back.

What she ought to be doing at the moment, she figured, was thinking about how she was going to get out of this mess. With Eli sitting straight across from her, she was having a hard time keeping him from noticing the fact that she was working her ropes loose.

Everyone else except him and the deputy called Hollis had already bedded down for the night. They had been too smart to light a fire this close to the Calhoun hideout, so she couldn't make out his expression clearly. Peering through the darkness, she tried harder to see his eyes. Pale moonlight outlined his features, but the upper part of his face was shadowed by the brim of his hat.

Annie glanced down at her bound wrists and twisted her mouth to one side. She hadn't been too surprised when one of the deputies had called him *sheriff* earlier. She had figured as much by the way the others kept turning to him for answers. She just wished he could have been the sheriff of a town closer to the Mexican border—one she likely would have never ridden into—instead of the sheriff of Bartlett Springs, Texas.

Didn't make much difference anyhow, she reckoned. He didn't remember her. She supposed there was really no call for him to. She sure as hell wasn't nothing special. Uglier than mud, Frank had always said.

Focusing on a hole in the knee of her britches, she frowned. She had never truly expected to cross paths with him again, but she had often made believe that he came looking for her. 'Course, their actual meeting had been a far cry from the one she had pictured in her head. In her imaginings, he would come riding up on his horse, smiling. Sometimes he'd be carrying a bunch of wild violets. He would doff his hat—just like she'd seen the men on Main Street do when they walked by a gentle-bred lady. Then he would say, ''Annie Calhoun, I've come to fetch you to be my bride, and I'll just die if you won't have me.''

She closed her eyes and could almost feel the purple satin dress she should have been wearing, all soft against her skin, trimmed in black lace, same as what the girls who worked at the Four Corners Saloon wore.

An owl hooted somewhere nearby, and she opened her eyes slowly, letting the vision fade away. Fact was, she still had on Frank's old throwaways. No matter how hard she wished for it, she was never going to own no purple satin dress. And it would be a cold day in hell when Sheriff Eli fell down on his knees and asked for her hand. No amount of fanciful thinking would change who or what she was.

Something warm brushed Annie's arm. She turned her head, a little startled to find Eli draping a blanket across her shoulders. It was odd that she hadn't heard him approach. She wasn't usually so lax.

"Thought you might need this," he said, then settled on the ground next to her. "The days are getting warmer, but the nights are still cool."

Annie drew her knees against her chest and stared straight ahead. Her heart commenced beating a mite faster. She remembered how cozy and comfortable things had been between them when she'd tended him in the cave, then compared that easy feeling to the miserable one she was experiencing at the moment. She'd just as soon he didn't recollect who she was or know that she now rode with the band of outlaws she had once hidden him from.

Eli tilted his face toward the sky. "Yep. The rainy season will be upon us soon."

Annie slanted her eyes his way. Most generally when people talked about the weather, they were edging up on the porch to talk about something else. And that was just what he was doing, she figured.

She shifted her gaze to the horses, but watched him from the corner of her eye. Nobody could say Annie Calhoun didn't know when to keep her mouth shut. One outlaw never snitched on another. It was an unspoken law in the Territories. "I ain't gonna tell you where the hideout is," she said, then set her jaw firm.

Eli's short chuckle was followed by a smile. "No. I guess I didn't really expect you would."

"Wouldn't do you no good even if'n I did. The boys'd be long gone by the time ya got there."

The sheriff picked up a twig and snapped it in two. "I don't doubt your word on that account. I've been trying to catch up with the Calhoun gang for years. I was just wondering if your friends would come looking for you—"

"I ain't got no friends, mister. Nary a one, 'cept for—" She stopped just short of saying Deadeye's name. "I ain't got no friends," she repeated quietly.

Eli stuck part of the twig in the corner of his mouth and chewed on it thoughtfully. "I see. You must just tag along after notorious outlaws."

Annie stiffened her back. "I ain't no tag-along."

"Well now, if they aren't your friends, and you aren't a tagalong, you must be . . . what?" Squinting one eye, he took the stick from his mouth and pointed it at her. "Say, are you Frank's gal?"

Frank's gal? Annie looked at him as if he'd gone plumb loco. She tried to deny the ridiculous notion, but all that would come out was a choking sound.

"That's it, isn't it?" He tossed the twig on the ground and smiled more broadly. "You're Frank's lady friend or . . . something."

"Heck no," she blurted out after several attempts. Heat burned her cheeks. "Frank's my broth—" She closed her mouth abruptly. Tarnation. He'd almost tricked her again.

"He's your what?" Eli leaned forward, caught her gaze, and nudged up his hat. "Frank Calhoun is your brother?"

Annie cast her eyes down and got real still. Frank was going to tan her hide. Chewing her bottom lip, she tried to figure how best to proceed. What she'd said was done said, and she couldn't take it back. And shucks, the sheriff already knew Frank's name. What the hell difference would it make if she admitted to being Frank's sister? Coming to that conclusion, she nodded slowly. "He's my half-brother. We had the same paw."

"Harley Calhoun was your father?" Eli lifted a brow. "I wasn't aware Harley had a daughter."

Annie cocked her head his way. "You knew my paw?"

"No. Not personally, but there isn't a lawman north of San Antonio who hasn't heard of Harley Calhoun."

"They hung him some years back, you know."

Eli felt a twinge of pity at the hint of melancholy in her voice. The way she'd spoken the words didn't go with the matter-of-fact expression on her face. As he focused on the girl's moonlit features, something besides pity stirred within him . . . something that wasn't at all related to the present situation . . . something that teetered on the edge of his memory.

He'd seen the girl before, this exact expression on this particular face. But where? And when?

It was bound to come to him sooner or later. At the moment he had a more pressing matter to tend to. "Yeah, I heard they'd caught Harley trying to rob the bank in Fort Smith," he commented conversationally. "The Calhoun gang has sort of been a legend in these parts ever since the war. They're still giving the law a run for its money." Eli caught the flicker of a smile curving her lips. Friendly. He needed to keep it friendly. "Annie—you don't mind if I call you Annie, do you? If you'd rather I call you Miss Calhoun—"

She looked at him in astonishment. Nobody had ever called her *Miss Calhoun*, much less asked permission to. She ducked her head to hide her embarrassment and started fiddling with the hole in the knee of her pants. "Annie'll do."

"All right. Annie it is then." He cleared his throat. "Annie, you seem like a nice girl."

She looked directly at him, her fixed expression reminding Eli of a fox. Her eyes held a wisdom that stretched beyond her years. Regardless of her obvious lack of a formal education, she was quick-witted. She wasn't going to make this easy for him. He closed his eyes a moment in an attempt to gather the reins on his purpose. ''What I'm trying to say is that the circuit judge will probably go easier on you if you'll hand over the money. Just tell me where you hid it and I'll put in a good word for you.''

Annie pressed her lips into a tight line. Eli and his deputies had searched for the bank bag till daylight had given way to darkness. She hadn't been able to convince them that she had no idea where the money could be. She wasn't going to be able to convince Frank or Buck of that, either. 'Course, her half-brother and his so-called friend, along with pert-near everyone else in the Territories, usually thought she was storying even when she wasn't. And she reckoned they had good cause. She did tend to lie an awful lot, and was fairly good at it—especially among those who didn't know her quite so well. But how in the hell did you go about convincing somebody you *weren't* fibbing?

''I told you, sheriff,'' she said slowly. ''I don't know what happened to the money. One second I was flyin' through the air, and the next I was wakin' up on the ground. I musta let go of the bag somewheres in betwixt. I swear, that's the gospel truth.''

Eli narrowed his eyes on her, running his

knuckles along his jawline. "Lord knows why," he said after a spell, "but for some strange reason, I believe you."

Annie's lips parted slightly. She'd been ready with an argument. Now she couldn't think of anything to say. She could only stare at him while an odd sensation crept over her. It was a whole lot like the feeling she'd got last autumn when she'd sampled the elixir a traveling medicine man had peddled in Dregg's Flat.

"Well, I guess that's that." Eli slapped his knees and stood up. "Try to get some sleep. We'll be riding out before the crack of dawn." He made a slow inspection of the area surrounding camp. "I don't like being this close to your companions." Hooking his thumbs in his front pants pocket, he brought his gaze back to hers. "Don't get any foolish ideas. One of us will be keeping an eye on you all night." He gestured to the older deputy stationed by the horses. "I wouldn't try Hollis if I were you. He's meaner than he appears. Night, ma'am," he added, touching the brim of his Stetson.

Annie watched him walk across the way. He took off his hat and spread out his blanket, then turned and looked back at her while he unfastened his gun belt. "I hope for your sake, I'm right about you," he murmured, almost as if he was talking to himself. In the middle of wrapping the belt around his holster, he stopped and cocked his head to the side. "Annie . . . have you ever been in Bartlett Springs before today?"

She shook her head slowly, barely acknowledging the question. She wasn't really listening to what he was saying. She was concentrating more on the sound of his voice encompassed by the soft chirps of crickets. He spoke with a slight Texas drawl, but anybody could tell he'd had book learning.

Lying on the ground, Eli set his hat over his face. Annie stared at him for a short spell, then stretched out on her side with her bound hands under the blanket. *I believe you,* he'd said as plain as day. *He believed her.* Imagine that. The sheriff of Bartlett Springs had taken the word of an outlaw.

She shifted her gaze to Hollis and caught him yawning. He looked to her like somebody's granddaddy. Cradling his rifle, he sat down by a tree and leaned his head against the trunk. She figured she could pretty much count on him sawing logs soon.

Though her eyelids grew heavy, she forced herself to stay awake. While she commenced working her wrists free of the rope, she focused on the sheriff's unmoving form. She had a hankering to keep company with him just a little longer. She yearned to talk to him some more, maybe find out what kind of man he'd turned into. 'Course, that was a plumb crazy notion and she knew it. She wasn't likely to get a better chance to sneak off.

Quite some time passed before she got an inkling that old Hollis had indeed drifted off to sleep. His head lolled to the side, and his chest rose and fell with his even breathing. It was nearing dawn, and she figured she'd best get a move on. She would have liked to take a horse, but couldn't risk the fuss the critters would likely put up if she approached them.

After one last, lingering look at Eli, she started rolling as quietly as possible through the dried leaves, away from Eli and camp. When she reached the edge of the woods, she crouched, looked over her shoulder, then took off through the trees.

She ran hard, trying to gain distance before sunrise. The sky was already turning a soft gray. They'd be up and after her soon. If she could just make it to the pass before they found her, she could hide in the caverns.

Suddenly, shouts came from behind her. She strove to move faster, but her legs and lungs ached. Blackberry vines snagged her clothes, slowing her pace.

"There she is yonder, sheriff!"

"I've got her," she heard Eli yell.

The sound of hoofbeats came close on her heels. The sheriff's galloping horse moved alongside her. Leaning down, Eli snatched her sleeve, but she jerked free of his grasp. When he reached out again, he toppled from his saddle, catching her waist before he hit the ground.

The world tumbled. She fought like a wild-cat until he straddled her and pinned her hands above her head.

Taking great gulps of air, she looked up into his face. But in that moment, blinding sunlight crested the horizon and broke through the treetops. The brightness pierced her eyes, darkening his features.

Eli stared into the brilliant blue eyes illuminated by sunshine. A disturbing feeling rippled through him, overriding his initial uneasiness about wrestling with a woman.

The memory of a small half-breed girl overtook him with the same rush he got when he drank too much whiskey.

He had met Annie Calhoun before, by God.

The deputies' shadows fell across the little outlaw's anxious features as the three men gathered around. Eli blinked and his thoughts moved swiftly back from the past into the present.

"I say we go ahead and shoot her here and now, sheriff," one of the men said. "Won't cause so much trouble thataway. As I recall, the ree-ward for any of the Calhoun gang is good whether ya bring 'em in dead or alive."

Eli glared at the deputy who'd spoken, then watched the other two nodding in agreement with equal irritation. "We *are not* going to shoot her, Charlie." He came to his feet, reached down, and gave Annie a hand up. "Jim, fetch my horse. We're taking her in for a fair trial."

Chapter 3

E li held his silence for the better part of the morning. While they rode in the direction of Bartlett Springs, he stared at a strand of dark hair that had escaped Annie's hat and fallen into the hollow at the nape of her neck. She was subdued for the time being. Her mood gave him the opportunity to absorb the notion that she was no longer a child. Proof of that had been evident when he'd struggled with her earlier. As he tried to restrain her, contact with the soft curves of her body had been unavoidable.

Eli shifted restlessly in the saddle. He had looped his arms around Annie in order to hold the reins. Each sway of the horse caused friction between his biceps and her shoulders, but he told himself his uneasiness had nothing to do with the fact that she was female. What really bothered him was that the timid little girl who'd saved his life had grown up and taken a bad turn. Regardless, she was now a responsible adult. She had broken the law, and was going to have to face the consequences. And he was duty-bound to bring her in, not only by the state of Texas, but by blood. He owed it to his father, grandfather, and brother to uphold the Larson name. For them, there would have been no other choice . . . no quandary at all over apprehending the Calhoun Kid.

Eli listened to the sound of steady hoofbeats and the creaking of saddles for the next half hour or so. In the meantime, a strong compulsion built inside him. Annie had robbed the bank. Lord knew what else she'd done. But she had also aided him when he'd needed help. He had to let her know he'd never forgotten her kindness . . . had to tell her he was grateful.

"Annie, you and I have met before," he said at last, keeping his voice low and his eyes on the deputies who rode ahead. She acknowledged the statement by stiffening her back. "About five years ago, I was shot in a gunfight not far from here. You tended my wound. Do you remember?"

"I remember," she replied quietly, then ducked her head.

"I just realized this morning that you were the girl who helped me. I would have bled to death if you hadn't taken care of me. I . . . I don't know how to thank you."

"Ain't no thanks needed, sheriff." Without looking at him, she spoke in a quiet, even tone. "Hell, it's probably the only decent thing I ever done."

Eli stared at her battered hat, wishing he could see her face, wondering how she could have changed so much in five years. "Look . . . Annie, I owe you. I'd like nothing better than to put you off this horse and let you go about your business. But I can't."

She shrugged, but made no reply.

"I'm sorry, but I'm sworn by the state of Texas to see justice done. I took an oath." Eli sighed deeply, disturbed by her lack of response. "I'll see to it that you get a fair trial, though. I swear I'll help you all I can. I'll talk to the judge . . . tell him how you helped me. That's bound to count for something."

"I done wrong, sheriff. I reckon it's your duty to bring me in. I cain't bear no grudge agin' you for that. And you don't owe me nothin'. I didn't tend yer wounds just so's you'd be beholdin' to me." She glanced over her shoulder, not quite meeting his gaze. "I did it 'cuz I wanted to. So let's just leave it be."

Nothing else was said between them as the day wore on and they journeyed toward the Red River. Annie fiddled with the saddle horn, thinking hard about Eli's convictions, feeling the solid warmth of him behind her. She didn't know much about honor, hadn't been around too many honorable people in her time. *Sworn by the state of Texas to see justice done,* he had said. Those words meant a lot to him. She'd heared it in his voice when he'd spoken them. For a reason she couldn't quite understand, it made her powerful proud to be sitting on a horse with such a man.

In the distance, she could make out the sound of rushing water. The Red River was just ahead. On the other side of the river was

Texas. They'd be in Bartlett Springs before sundown. She fidgeted in the saddle, none too pleased about getting there. She had visions of the whole community of Bartlett Springs stirring hot tar and plucking chickens.

Along about suppertime, they rode into town. Annie leveled her chin and stared unblinkingly in front of her. Bartlett Springs, with its whitewashed storefronts and picket fences, wasn't any different than any other small town in Texas. From the corner of her eye she could see the good citizens lining the street.

Then the shouting commenced.

"It's one of the bank robbers!" someone yelled. "Sheriff Larson's gone and brung in one of the Calhoun gang!"

"Looks like you caught the runt of the bunch, sheriff!"

"Why, he's just a child," came a feminine voice.

"Old enough to rob a bank," countered someone else in a deep, gruff tone.

"Hang 'im high, sheriff!"

"Hang 'im! Hang 'im!" chimed a group of children.

Annie had been expecting the name-calling and finger-pointing, and had already decided to ignore it. She'd dealt with prejudice all her life. Then she felt Eli shift his weight.

Eli. Eli was sitting behind her, hearing it all, seeing it all. Somehow, that made it harder to bear this time.

The taunts burned her ears. Her face felt afire. She couldn't hold her lower lip steady or keep her limbs from quivering.

Annie closed her eyes. She tried to imagine herself getting smaller and smaller . . . crawling under a rock and hiding from sight. She wished . . . Hellfire, she wished someone would just shoot her dead and get it over with.

"All right, folks, that's enough!" Eli bellowed as he reined his horse in front of the jail. "This isn't a sideshow."

He dismounted and lifted Annie out of the saddle, holding her close in front of him while he made his way through the crowd.

"Smells like a stinkin' breed to me," commented a short, round, bearded man as they passed.

"It's the Kid! I'll swan . . . it's the Kid!" cried a young boy in overalls who scrambled out of the sheriff's path. "It's the *Calhoun Kid*," he whispered reverently, elbowing the openmouthed youngster next to him.

Eli reached his office and shoved Annie just inside, keeping a tight grip on her arm to prevent her from going anywhere. With furrowed brows, he turned to the sea of curious faces trying to peer around him.

He had always been proud of Bartlett Springs and its people. It was generally a friendly community. Women baked three-layer cakes to welcome newcomers. A pot of chicken soup could be counted on whenever someone took ill. The men were always ready to lend a helping hand fencing pastures or raising a barn. But Bartlett Springs shamed him this day.

"Y'all go on home now," he said vehemently. "Go on now. It's nearly suppertime. Go on home to your families."

Annie sat on the edge of the narrow cot, her hands folded tightly in her lap. The moon shone eerily through the lone window, casting the slanted shadow of bars on the plankwood floor. A god-awful terror, the likes of which she'd never known, had climbed upon her the moment she'd heard the clank of the closing cell door.

She expected the boys would have busted her out of jail by now, if they were going to. At least they might have gotten word to her about Deadeye. The old Confederate soldier had been more of a paw to her than Harley Calhoun had ever been. He'd once told her that fretting didn't change anything—just served to make a body sick. She reckoned he was right. Deadeye was generally right about everything. Trying not to worry, she took a deep breath and recalled something else he'd said. The way he had it figured, only the good died young. He had claimed he was too dang mean to meet his maker anytime soon. Annie had smiled when he'd told her that. Deadeye wasn't mean. He had to be the most gentle soul she'd ever known. What she had to remember now was that he was also sturdy. He'd been hit in the shoulder. She knew for a fact he mended fast.

She closed her eyes and tried to conjure up

a cheerful thought to keep her mind off things. But the usual visions of pretty dresses and fancy hats wouldn't come.

Opening her eyes, she focused on a knothole in the floor. She reckoned there wasn't much sense in pondering over such pleasantries anyhow. It appeared they were going to put her away for a good long time.

With a heavy heart, she thought of Eli. She hadn't seen him since he'd handed her over to Hollis. She couldn't calculate how long ago that had been. All she knew was that it seemed like forever.

The sound of the door in the other room opening brought her head up. "How's our prisoner?" she heard Eli ask. Coming quickly to her feet, she clasped the bars of the cell door and pressed her face between the cold steel rods in an attempt to catch a glimpse of him.

"Hasn't made a peep," Hollis replied. "She's been as docile as a lamb."

Annie's heart rose to her throat as Eli appeared in the narrow corridor that flanked the three small cells. Moving toward her, he smiled and lifted a towel-covered tray he carried.

"Thought you might be hungry," he said, and set the food on a small table behind him while he unlocked her door, then retrieved the tray. She stepped back and allowed him to enter, noting he'd removed his gun.

Eli sat down on the cot and patted the place next to him. "Maybelle's Cafe is just across the street. She's nigh and far the best cook in town. Her specialty is apple pie. Mmm-mmm, smells good, doesn't it?''

Annie made no move to join him. She plucked nervously at the outer seams of her baggy pants and glanced around the cell, never quite letting her gaze land on his.

"Come on, Annie," he coaxed softly. "Come on over here and sit down. You need to eat something. After you've had your supper, we'll talk."

She obeyed, hesitantly perching on the edge of the cot.

"Now let's see what Maybelle's fixed up for you." Eli set the tray on her lap, removed the blue gingham dish towel, and saw Annie's eyes go wide, heard her stomach grumble. "Look at that. Fried chicken, mashed potatoes and gravy, sweet peas, and biscuits. And there's that famous apple pie. Boy howdy."

"Is . . . is all of this here . . . for me?" she asked.

"Sure is. Hope you have a good appetite."

Ignoring the silverware, Annie dove into the meal.

While Eli watched in silence, he speculated about what could have brought her to her present situation. He waited until she had finished off everything but the chicken bones and was wiping her mouth on her shirt sleeve before he spoke.

"Annie, have you lived with your father all these years?"

She picked a crumb off her plate, popped it into her mouth, then nodded. "Till they hung 'im. I stayed on with Frank and the boys after that.''

"But where's your mother?"

Annie ran a finger around the edge of her mug. "She died when I was knee-high," she said softly.

"So Frank raised you?"

"Shucks, no. Frank?" She glanced at the ceiling and snickered. "He was always too busy to pay me much mind. Didn't put me out or nothin' though, after they strung Paw up. And he took me on as soon as I was old enough to ride with the boys."

At a loss for words, Eli studied her. He had an inkling it wasn't her fault that she'd taken the lawless path. Under the circumstances, she hadn't had much of a choice. Maybe if her upbringing had been different, if she'd had a decent family to take care of her, she might have turned out the same as any other girl her age—attending ice cream socials, enjoying the attention of some nice young man. Some who chose the wrong side of the law would never change. If given the opportunity, others mended their ways. Maybe it wasn't too late for Annie Calhoun. Corruption was something that grew like a weed in a garden, Eli figured. But if the seed wasn't planted too deep, perhaps it could be uprooted.

"Annie, I'm sorry about what happened today. About the way folks treated you when we rode in. I can't imagine what got into them. They don't normally act that way." He paused, checking for some sign that she accepted his apology, but she simply stared at her empty plate. "I suppose they all felt justified in what they did. People get mean when something they value is taken from them. Most of them had their life's earnings in that bank. That still doesn't excuse—"

"It don't matter," she said without looking up. "I reckon everything they claimed was true."

Eli took the tray from her lap, set it on the floor, then caught her shoulders and turned her toward him. "It does matter, Annie. What they did was wrong. We're all God's creatures, *all* created equally. Everyone deserves the courtesy of respect."

"Not me." She shook her head slowly. "I ain't sittin' in this jail for nothin', sheriff."

Eli crooked a finger beneath her chin and lifted her face. "You deserve as much respect as the next. The law says you're innocent until proven guilty. I intend to explain your situation to Judge Winthrop when he comes next Tuesday for the trial. He's a just man. He'll listen to me. I'm going to try to convince him to appoint someone as a guardian for you, maybe some nice family that can give you a wholesome home. Do you understand?"

Annie looked at him blankly. "You mean . . . I'd be livin' around here somewheres?"

"Probably," Eli replied after a moment's consideration, "if Judge Winthrop will see things my way."

Disengaging her chin from his touch, she dropped her head. "They . . . wouldn't let me," she murmured. "Folks, I mean. They wouldn't want the likes of me here."

"Aw, they'll come around, Annie. They're not bad people. Why, I'll bet two months' wages that the whole town is going to get an earful next Sunday when Reverend Perry gets wind of what happened today. Believe me, they'll be squirming in the pews when he gets through with them."

The corners of Annie's mouth quivered into a slight smile at the vision Eli's remark stirred up.

The sound of the front door banging open made both of them jump. Eli moved quickly to the cell door, his hand automatically going to his empty holster.

"It's all right, sheriff, it's only Henry," Hollis called out, then lowered his voice. "Hell, Henry, do ya have t' make so much noise when you come in? I was sittin' here relaxin' with my feet up and damned near fell outa my chair."

"Well, do-oo pardon me," the other man said, his words slurring together. "I'm sure if you had"—he hiccupped—"been tendin' your duties 'stead of sleepin'—"

"I was not sleepin'," Hollis insisted. "Just restin' my eyes, that's all."

"Was too."

"I was not."

"Was too," Henry said, stumbling through the doorway and into the corridor outside the cells. He stood swaying from side to side and pointed his thumb over his shoulder. "He was, sh-sheriff. He was sleepin'."

With a shake of his head, Eli left Annie's cell, securing the door behind him. "Come on, Henry, let's get you bedded down for the night."

Henry peered through the bars at Annie. "Whoo's 'at ya got in there?"

Eli caught the man's arm. "Henry Jennings, meet Annie Calhoun. She's going to be staying with us for a spell."

Henry frowned profusely. "Hmph. Hope to hell she don't snore," he grumbled as Eli maneuvered him through the adjoining cell door and plopped him onto the cot.

"Henry, why do you do this to yourself?" Eli asked in a sharp-edged voice, then went to work tugging off the man's boots. "You know what Doc Biddle told you. You know you can't go on—"

Henry rolled onto his side and grunted, signaling the end of the conversation. Eli stared down at the old man a moment, then mumbled an oath and left him to sleep it off.

When he stopped by Annie's cell to check the lock, she came up to him and curled her fingers around the bars. "Get some shut-eye, Annie," he said. "It's been a long day."

"Sheriff," she called, stopping him as he turned to leave. "Those folks out there today . . . well . . . they were awfully chafed. You reckon they'll try to lynch me?"

Eli resisted the sudden urge to wrap his hand around hers. "Nobody's going to lynch you, Annie. I wouldn't let them. You're going to have a fair trial. I'll talk to the judge like I said, and everything will work out just fine, you'll see. Now, try to get some sleep. Hollis will be here if you need anything. I'll see you tomorrow morning bright and early.''

Chapter 4

❦

The Bartlett Springs courthouse stood right in the middle of the town square, and was filled to the brim on this fine, sunny day. Citizens occupied every seat and lined the walls. Those standing in back lacked elbow room, while others flowed out the opened double doors. Children crowded outside the windows, shoving each other and craning their necks to get a peek inside. When news had gotten out that the Calhoun Kid was a girl instead of a boy as everyone had suspected, even folks from surrounding counties had come to the trial to get a closer look.

Annie shifted in her chair. The past week had been pure hell. Hollis had had to chase youngsters away from her cell window daily. They had come by every afternoon and stood outside behind the jailhouse chanting and throwing rocks. And the grown-ups had been no better. They had barged into the office, filing one petty complaint after another, then had come right out and asked if they could have a look-see at the Calhoun Kid.

Annie glanced sideways at Eli, who sat beside her at one of the tables situated in front of the rows of benches. She twiddled her thumbs, trying not to think too much about the buzzing of voices behind her. The judge probably wouldn't even notice that she'd washed her face and tied her hair back. Peering at the big, snowy-haired man in the long black robe, she still wasn't sure what to make of him. The way he frowned all the time made him appear awfully fearsome.

A hush fell over the room as Judge Winthrop called for the next witness, a lad named Joey Cox.

Dressed in his Sunday best, the boy strode down the aisle with his chest puffed out and his arms swinging. He edged his chin a notch higher as he approached the witness stand, raised one hand in the air, and laid the other on the Bible Hollis held out to him.

"Do you swear to tell the truth, the whole truth, and nothin' but the truth, so help you God?" Hollis asked.

"I do," the boy said with an affirmative nod of his head.

"You do know that you've just taken an oath not to lie, don't you, young man?" Judge Winthrop inquired, lifting one bushy brow.

The youngster gulped and appeared to lose a bit of his bravado for a moment, then answered, "Yes, sir."

"Very well then. Be seated and tell me everything you remember about the day the bank was robbed."

"Well," Joey began, then took a deep

breath, "Billy right yonder and Harold Finster there"—he pointed at the two—"and me was playin' a game of hide an' go seek, ya see. And I was it," he said, jabbing a finger into his chest. "I went round back of the bank lookin' for Billy on accounta he sometimes hides in the shed there—"

"Yes, yes," the judge said impatiently. "Go on."

"Well, I rounded the corner and what d' ya think I see? That outlaw right there." Joey indicated Annie with a jut of his chin. "It was the Calhoun Kid, it was. He . . . I mean she, was sittin' there on her horse holdin' the reins of a buncha other horses. They was the robbers' horses, I betcha. I'm fer sure they was."

"Now let's not speculate, son. Tell me what happened next."

"Well, sir, he . . . *she* told me to get. Real mean-like, she said, 'Go on, boy! Scat!' Then she up and chucked a rock at me." Joey made a face at Annie. "But she missed."

Annie jumped to her feet. "Why, you little pug-nosed, turtle-brained—"

"Order in the court!" The judge banged his gavel repeatedly on his desk. "Order in the court!"

"Annie," Eli whispered fiercely, catching her arm and pulling her back into her seat.

"Miss Calhoun," Judge Winthrop said with clear disapproval in his tone and on his face, "you will have your say in a short while. Until that time, I will stand for no more outbursts." Turning to Joey, he cleared his throat. "Now, young man, what happened after that?"

The boy glanced at Annie and shifted in his chair. "Nothin'. I ran home and told my ma, and she went for the sheriff."

The judge steepled his fingers against his lips and was thoughtful a moment. "You may step down, Joey. The defendant will now take the stand."

Eli nudged Annie. "Go on," he whispered. "It's time to tell your side. Don't forget to address him as *your honor.*"

Annie rose slowly. To steady her legs, she inhaled as much air as her lungs would hold. Then mustering up all the courage she possessed, she walked forward.

After Hollis had sworn her in and she'd settled herself in the witness chair, the judge said, "Well, Miss Calhoun, it seems you had some objection to something the boy said a few minutes ago."

"I reckon so." Annie glared at the youngster who cowered by his mamma. "He was lyin'."

"About you being behind the bank during the robbery?"

"No sir . . . I mean, your honor. I was there all right. He was lyin' about the rock."

"The . . . *rock?*"

"I didn't miss him. Hit him square in the bee-hind. When I aim at something, I don't miss."

Giggles and snickers rippled through the courtroom.

Judge Winthrop closed his eyes and massaged the bridge of his nose. "Miss Calhoun, how old are you?"

Annie frowned and twisted her hands. "I don't rightly know at the moment. Deadeye told me I was borned in the summertime. He said last summer was my seventeenth. It come up in conversation oncet."

"Don't you think you're a bit old to be throwing rocks at little boys?"

"I didn't want him hurt," Annie said. "If he'da been standing there when Frank and the others came out the back door, they woulda rode right over him."

"I see." Judge Winthrop settled back in his chair and folded his hands across his middle. "Where do you hail from, Miss Calhoun?"

"The Territories."

"Any particular area in the Territories?"

Annie shook her head. "We stayed in Dregg's Flat longer then anywheres, I reckon. But we moved around a lot."

"Who do you mean by *we?*" the judge asked with interest.

"Frank, Deadeye Pete," Annie said, then shrugged, "and the others."

"Outlaws?"

Annie looked at Eli, and when he silently gestured for her to answer, she nodded.

Judge Winthrop leaned forward, bracing his forearms on his desk. "Am I to understand you were raised among thieves and murderers?"

Annie drew herself erect. "They wasn't all murderers, your honor. Deadeye ain't no murderer. He's my friend. He always kept some of the friskier ones from—'' Feeling her face flush, she lowered her lashes and bit her bottom lip. ''From botherin' me. And Frank, he ain't never kilt nobody far as I know. He gets ornery now and then when he's had a few drinks, but Buck's the only— Well, Buck . . . now he's meaner then a cornered rattlesnake. I once saw him shoot a man just for snoring. Then there was another time that he took his knife and cut off this here fella's—''

Judge Winthrop stopped her with a raised hand. He had paled somewhat, Annie thought. ''I believe you've answered the question quite thoroughly,'' he said, then inhaled deeply. ''What about your parents, Miss Calhoun? Where are they?''

Pressing her lips into a tight line, Annie stared at her hands. ''Gone to glory, your honor.''

''I see,'' the judge said in a stolid tone. He paused briefly before going on. ''Miss Calhoun, are you aware that the bank teller was shot and killed during the robbery?''

Jerking her head up, Annie widened her eyes on Judge Winthrop.

''Understand, Miss Calhoun, that because you were a party to the crime and happen to be the sole member of the Calhoun gang who was captured, you shall be held responsible for the murder of this young man.''

Annie felt a sinking feeling in the pit of her stomach. She'd heard the gunshot, but nobody had said a word about having to shoot the teller. Her gaze traveled from one juror's face to the next. Their expressions held no mercy, and she hadn't any doubt what their verdict would be.

"I said, you may step down now, Miss Calhoun," the judge said sharply.

Hollis took her arm and led her back to the chair beside Eli. She closed herself off as the trial continued. More witnesses were called, but their testimony passed her by.

"The court will now adjourn for a short recess," Judge Winthrop announced at last, "while the jury deliberates on this matter."

"Your honor," Eli called out as the judge raised his gavel. "May I have a word with you in private?"

Frowning, the judge glanced from the sheriff to Annie, then nodded. "I will see you in my chambers."

While she waited for the jury's ruling, Annie tried to ignore the spectators' comments. As time ticked by, though, the cutting remarks got harder and harder to disregard.

"Half-breed," someone behind her hissed. "Gonna get what you deserve now."

Outside, children made up songs. Lyrics about the Calhoun Kid hanging from a tree drifted in through the windows.

Annie stared at her hands folded in her lap, letting the curtain of her hair hide her face, and wondered what in blue blazes was taking Eli so long? She'd figured the judge would have tossed him out on his ear by now.

It seemed like an eternity before the door behind Judge Winthrop's big desk opened.

Eli stepped out, and Annie anxiously watched him walk toward her, his expression unreadable. He sat down next to her, and after a moment reached out and awkwardly patted her hand. "I don't know, Annie," he said in a low voice. "I tried to convince him to give you a second chance, but—"

"All rise!"

Judge Winthrop entered ceremoniously and seated himself. The jurors trailed in behind him and took their places. "This court is now in session," he said. "The defendant will stand and face the bench." Directing his attention to the tall, elderly man who stepped forward from the jurors' box, he asked, "Gentlemen, have you reached a decision?"

"We have, your honor. We find the defendant guilty as charged."

Cheers, hoots, whistles, and applause burst forth from the crowd.

"Cease this nonsense this instant!" Judge Winthrop's authoritative voice dominated the others. He hammered his gavel furiously until every last whisper died down. Frowning, he let his dark glare travel over the assembly slowly, for emphasis. "If I hear one more peep," he said, holding up his pointer finger. "So help me, if anybody so much as sneezes, I shall not hesitate to clear this courtroom. Is that understood?" He lifted a brow, and was met with utter silence.

He straightened his robe, then pinned Annie with a gaze devoid of emotion. "Miss Calhoun, the state of Texas has found you guilty as charged. Do you have anything to say for yourself before I pass sentence?"

Annie's knees went weak. Her vision blurred. Then someone caught her arm, and she looked up to find Eli standing beside her, holding her upright. His presence fortified her, gave her strength to stay on her feet. Her head cleared somewhat and she focused on the judge. "I . . . I'd just like t' say how powerful sorry I am about the teller, your honor. Wasn't nobody s'posed t' get hurt. Frank promised me . . . nobody'd get hurt."

"Is that all you have to say?"

Annie nodded, unable to think of anything else.

"Very well then," Judge Winthrop droned. "It is my duty to inform you that the penalty in this state for the crime you have committed is death by hanging." He paused, allowing his statement to sink in. "However, the sheriff has brought to my attention a very commendable deed you once did him. His account of this matter has persuaded me to examine the possibility that you could reform yourself and become a law-abiding citizen. Because of what he has told me, and taking into consideration both your age and upbringing, I have come to a rather unorthodox sentence concerning this case."

Annie swallowed hard and waited for him to go on.

"Eli Larson is an upstanding citizen in this community," the judge continued. "While I value his opinion, I must disagree with his suggestion that I make you a ward of this court and entrust you to a guardian. You are, after all, a young woman, not a child.''

Judge Winthrop's warning glance put an immediate stop to the gasps and murmurs that moved through the crowd. ''I am of the mind,'' he went on, ''that if one desires to become respectable, then one should be awarded responsibility and not be coddled. Therefore, I have come to the conclusion that since you are of marriageable age, Miss Calhoun, a husband and family would provide such responsibility and would be of far more benefit to you than a guardian.''

Thoughts were settling on top of one another in Annie's brain. She tried to grasp exactly what it was that the judge was saying. The big words he used and the way he strung them together made her temples throb.

''I hereby declare,'' he said finally, ''that if any man in good standing within this community will offer you the asylum of marriage before I return on my regular circuit in two weeks, then you shall be spared, with certain stipulations, of course. Otherwise, I regret I will have no choice but to sentence you to hang by the neck until dead.''

Annie wrapped her fingers around the bars of her cell window and stared at the full moon glowing high and bright in the pitch-black sky. Faint piano music and laughter from a nearby saloon reached her ears. She must have been plumb dazed when she'd left the courtroom that afternoon, she reckoned. She knew that the crowd had exploded after the judge had sentenced her. But she couldn't recollect being whisked back to the jailhouse, wedged between Eli and Hollis.

As near as she could recall, Eli had been downright gleeful about Judge Winthrop's decision to marry her off. Annie sighed heavily. She supposed she ought to be rejoicing herself over the fact that the judge had opted not to hang her. But *marriage*? Good Lord Almighty. What in tarnation did she know about being a wife and raising young 'uns?

"Annie?"

The sound of her name spoken softly turned her from the window. Moonlight outlined Eli's tall form on the other side of her cell door. A great thumping commenced in the center of her chest. She had a powerful urge to run to him, beg him to stop the big pendulum clock in the outer office from ticking. Rather than doing so though, she swallowed the impulse. Stuffing her hands into her pockets, she acknowledged him with a nod and said, "Evenin', sheriff."

"Thought I'd stop by and check on you before I turned in." Eli nudged his Stetson a little higher on his forehead. "I was real pleased with Judge Winthrop's decree today, weren't you?"

Annie was silent. She merely shifted her weight and dropped her head.

"I know it wasn't exactly what we were after, but—"

"It ain't gonna work," she interrupted.

"Sure it will, Annie." He moved closer to the cell. "You'll see. This town is full of eligible bachelors. The word will get around, believe me it will. And when it does—''

Annie let go of a half snicker, half sigh. ''Yep, well, I reckon the mayor's son will be here in the mornin' just a-beggin' for my hand. Shucks, I might even have to choose between him and the preacher's nephew. Ain't that right, sheriff? Why, they'll be linin' up outside the jail here first thing tomorrow, now won't they?''

''Annie, this is no joking matter.''

''Yeah, well, I ain't laughin' too hard, am I?'' She stepped forward into a pale stream of light. Her gaze held Eli's steady for a moment, then she lowered her eyes and wet her lips. ''In case you ain't noticed, sheriff, I ain't exactly no county fair prize. Ain't nobody in their right mind, much less someone fine and upstanding, gonna come trippin' over themself to make me their wife.''

''Annie . . . I . . . well, I could probably rustle up a dress for you to wear. Maybe even a ribbon for your hair. And I see no reason why we couldn't string up some blankets and fix you up with a tub and hot water.''

Annie looked at him and tried to figure which one of them was more touched in the head—him for coming up with something so ridiculous, or her for actually considering it even for a single solitary second. ''Look, sheriff. Gettin' me all gussied up ain't gonna make a whole hell of a lot of difference. Ain't nobody respectable gonna be willin' to marry an outlaw, less'n he has chickpeas for brains. So don't trouble yourself none.'' She turned to stare out the window again. "You been more than kind to me, and I'm much obliged. But I ain't gonna truss myself up like a cigar-store Indian to catch a husband. It just ain't the way I do things."

Henry grunted, coughed, and rolled over on his cot in the next cell.

Eli took in her stubborn stance. There was more to her than met the eye, he realized. Suddenly he couldn't help but wonder what she would look like cleaned up.

"Sleep on this, Annie," he suggested in a quiet voice. "Maybe in the morning you'll see this ordeal for the blessing it is."

Annie glanced over her shoulder when she heard the front door close. With Eli gone, a sinking feeling overwhelmed her, a coldness that seeped into her bones. She was more keenly aware of the darkness that engulfed her. Searching the night sky, she spotted the North Star right off.

Most of the time, she kept her head about her as far as wishing was concerned. Saw it for what it was: a diversion from her troubles, an imaginary means of rising above impossibilities.

But there were moments, like now, when she *had* to believe that a body could honestly will things to work out the way they wanted. During these moments, desire crowded out common sense, and whatever it was inside that made her cling to life also demanded that she believe the path of destiny could be changed.

The secret wish she made in the next brilliant blink of the star was one only a dang fool would've made. Yet it lightened the heaviness in her heart and gave her something she needed badly at the present.

Hope.

Chapter 5

Annie was a mite surprised the next morning to hear that she had a visitor.

Hollis gruffly introduced the tall, gangly redhead as Delbert Phipps, then went about his business, leaving Annie alone with the stranger.

Delbert stood in complete silence outside her cell, blushing and rotating his hat slowly at his waist. Annie sat stiffly on the edge of her cot, feeling like a horse for sale at an auction. She half expected that at any minute the young man would ask to check her teeth.

An inner voice chided her, nagged that she ought to smile at him or something. *You ain't gonna have a fishpond full of choices,* the voice insisted. *Hell, he's a man, ain't he?*

To verify this claim, she made herself look directly at Delbert. She figured he was older than she'd first thought. Had nice features, he did, though at present he sort of resembled a kid about to get a switching. He was nervous as could be. Almost painfully so, she reckoned. Her gaze fell to the hat he held in hand courteously. Removing it had been a simple gesture, but it touched her and gave

58

her the gumption to rise and take a step toward him.

"Howdy," she said, then gave him a timid but genuine smile, mostly because he appeared to need a little encouraging. "Ain't much to look at, am I?"

Delbert returned her smile shyly. "R-r-reckon . . . I a-a-ain't n-neither," he replied with difficulty and ducked his head.

His stammering made Annie's heart sting, though she was careful not to let it show. She knew how it felt to be ridiculed or pitied for something that couldn't be helped. "Why, Mr. Phipps," she commented, moving closer to the bars that separated them, "you must be funnin' me. You're as fine-lookin' a man as I've ever seen. I'd bet my boots, if'n they was worth anything, that all the girls in this town go outa their way to catch your attention."

Delbert raised his eyes, which had just taken to twinkling. "N-n-nah, th-they . . . d-d-d-don't." He half snickered and shook his head.

"Well, then they must be either blind or not too smart." Annie stuffed her hands into her pockets and rocked back on her heels. "So," she said, not quite able to keep her gaze as steady as she would've liked, "you just curious 'bout what a notorious outlaw looks like up close . . . or"—she took a deep breath and forged onward—"could I be right in suspectin' you're the noble sort and might be here contemplatin' marriage?"

Though it didn't seem possible, Delbert

turned an even brighter shade of red, then nodded. His awkwardness was enough to tell Annie that he had indeed come on the second account.

"I-I-I," Delbert began, then stopped, appearing frustrated that his words wouldn't come out right. After a minute he tried again, this time spacing his words and speaking much more slowly. "Y-you're . . . pr-prettier . . . than . . . I . . . th-thought . . . you'd . . . b-be."

His statement nearly knocked Annie off her feet. *Her? Pretty?* The thought was one she couldn't rightly absorb. The feelings his flattery stirred up felt strange and foreign and a mite fearful because she wasn't quite sure how to respond. Embarrassment and confusion made her quickly decide to deny the compliment altogether. "Mr. Phipps, I . . . I ain't gonna lie to you and say I've actually ever seen myself in a mirror, but I've caught my reflection in a storefront window a time or two, and I'm about as plain as a pebble and as pretty as the back end of a sow. So let's not get off on the wrong foot here by bein' dishonest with each other."

Delbert started a deliberate shake of his head that became stronger as he spoke. "I . . . think . . . you're . . . pretty," he said slowly, but without stumbling over a single word.

The tilt of his chin brooked no argument, and Annie was reminded of a phrase she'd heard one Sunday morning as she'd stood outside the church window in Dregg's Flat.

Beauty is in the eyes of the beholder. Maybe in Delbert's eyes she truly was pretty. Leastwise she wasn't going to dispute the matter any further.

She smiled with an inner glow that suddenly filled her. "Mr. Phipps, what on God's green earth would make a nice fella like you want to get himself hitched up with the likes of me?"

Annie watched the knot in Delbert's throat bob. He hung his head and stared at his boots for a spell before he answered. "N-nobody else . . . w-w-would have m-m-me . . . 'c-cause I st-st-stut . . . st-st-stutter."

"Hell, is there a law against that in this town?"

Delbert cocked his head to one side and half grinned. "N-nah, but the g-g-girls in th-these p-p-parts . . . d-don't m-much . . . c-c-cotton . . . t-to it."

Annie could only imagine how much teasing Delbert must have had to take in his lifetime. She'd been poked fun at herself on occasion and knew how awful and sick inside it could make you feel.

Changing the subject, she asked him what he did for a living. He told her he helped his ma run the boardinghouse on the edge of town, but confided that he'd always wanted to try his hand at farming. He informed Annie with a certain pride that he had a knack for growing things.

Annie sat down Indian fashion on the floor and listened with interest. He grabbed a bucket from the corner, turned it upside down, and settled himself on it, telling Annie about the crops he'd thought about raising. They talked. They laughed. And somewhere during the course of the conversation, Annie noticed he wasn't stuttering anymore.

"I been thinking about that real hard," Delbert answered when Annie asked if he had some particular place to settle in mind. "Been thinking about striking out for the Territories. I've heard rumors about a land run. Folks say there's people lining up along the borders already, just waiting. Good rich farmland in some parts, I've heard. All you gotta do is stake your claim."

"Delbert Lee Phipps!" a boisterous voice broke in from the outer office. "Wake up, Hollis Downing! How could you allow something like this?"

The upturned bucket clanged and clattered against the jail floor as Delbert came to his feet. Annie jumped up and peered through the bars. Possibly the largest woman she had ever seen squeezed through the doorway and barged into the corridor outside the cells.

"Delbert Lee Phipps!" the woman repeated loud enough to be heard in the next county. "What in heaven's name do you think you're doing here? There's work to be done at home!"

Delbert's face turned the color of pickled beets. "B-b-but . . . M-M-Ma—"

"Stop that babbling and get on home. Go on. You heard me. Git, I said!"

Delbert glanced in Annie's direction but didn't quite meet her eyes, then left the jailhouse as fast as his long legs would carry him.

The woman turned a fierce expression on Annie that made her take two steps backward. "And you," she said, poking a finger through the bars, "you . . . you little *heathen*, you stay away from my boy, you hear?"

The breakfast crowd at Maybelle's Cafe was dwindling. Eli took a sip of his coffee and smiled across the small round table at one of his favorite people, Betsy Bruecks.

"So what brings you into town this morning, Betsy?" he asked.

The young woman tucked a wisp of light brown hair into the tidy bun at the nape of her neck, then gave him a serene smile in return. "Paw ran out of laudanum last night. I had to stop by Doc Biddle's to get some more."

"Is he worse?"

Betsy's smile wavered as she fingered the cameo pinned to her high lace collar. "Doc seems to think so, but I just know he's getting better, Eli."

Reaching across the table, Eli grasped her hand. "I'm sure he is." He traced her knuckles with his thumb and searched her warm brown eyes. He'd grown up with Betsy, played with her as a boy, then watched her turn into the graceful, intelligent woman before him now. Something about her reassured him that beyond all the violence and ugliness he saw in his work, there still existed a gentler, kinder world. He never passed up an opportunity to spend time with her. It was fairly common practice when they met in town, as they had in front of Farguson's General Store this morning, for them to stroll over to Maybelle's for a piece of pie.

"Whatever your reason for this trip into town, I'm glad you came. It's good to see you out and about," he said quietly.

She lowered her lashes. "It's good to see you, too. I missed having you to supper last week."

"And I missed your cooking." Eli leaned back in his chair and patted his stomach. "Hollis almost killed me with the concoctions he fed the posse in the Territories."

Betsy pressed her fingertips to her mouth and giggled.

Maybelle came by and poured them each another cup of coffee. "Y'all want some more pie?" she asked.

"No, thanks, Maybelle," Eli replied with a wink. "I think the three pieces I've had will do me this morning. How about you, Bets?"

"My gracious, no." Betsy shook her head. "I couldn't eat one more bite." She watched Maybelle mosey off to serve the next table, then leaned forward and narrowed her eyes on Eli. "What's she like?" she whispered. "The Calhoun Kid."

"Annie Calhoun?" Eli lifted his brows and stared past Betsy. "I'm not sure I know how to describe her. She . . . she's had a hard life. But I know there is good in her. She risked a lot to help me once. Several years ago, when I was a deputy, I got shot in the Territories.

She wasn't any bigger around than a fence-post and only half as high, but she rolled me into a cave and tended my wound.''

''I hear tell the judge intends to marry her off.''

''Yeah, well, that's the plan.'' Eli took a drink of his coffee. ''I figured since I owed her my life, I'd spread the word around. But not one of the eligible bachelors I've talked to over the past week has been willing to even set foot in jail to take a look at Annie. The sad part is, I really think she might make someone a decent wife if they'd just give her a chance.''

''Now don't you fret, Eli. Time's not up yet, is it? The judge is on a two-week circuit. You've still got a day or so.'' It was Betsy's turn to squeeze his hand. The bright, beautiful smile she displayed went straight to his heart. ''Things will work out just fine, you'll see.''

''I said turn around, girl! Let me have a look at ya.'' Each word the old man spoke held a razor-sharp edge.

Reluctantly obeying, Annie rotated slowly. By the time she came full circle and faced Mr. Jenkins again, her heart had sunk to her knees.

''Sure ain't got much meat on ya, do ya?'' he snapped.

Annie made no response. She merely slipped her hands into the pockets of her baggy trousers and stared at the cranky codger who stood outside her cell. Deep crevices lined his forehead and surrounded his small, closely set eyes, one of which appeared to be permanently fixed in a squint. His mouth was hidden by a scraggly white beard that fell to his waist. Annie figured old man Jenkins must be at least a hundred . . . maybe more.

"Ken ya cook?" Mr. Jenkins asked in a hateful voice that Annie was beginning to suspect might be his normal tone.

Pressing her lips into a tight line, she shook her head.

"Ken ya sew, milk a cow, or plant a field?"

"No, sir," she replied softly. "I ain't never done none a those things afore."

"Well, what in blazes ken ya do then?" Mr. Jenkins asked, puckering his face.

Annie would've liked to have told him where he could go, and came mighty near doing so. But it had been almost two weeks since Delbert's visit and not a single other suitor had shown up till today. Hollis had mentioned that the judge was due back in town tomorrow, and Annie didn't relish the thought of getting her neck stretched. Besides, old Jenkins didn't look like he'd last too much longer. She figured she'd be a widow in a year or two.

Taking a deep breath, she squared her shoulders. "I can ride," she said with a lift of her chin. "And I can shoot. I can hunt and fish. I can tend a flesh wound or cure an ailin' horse. And I can learn to do pert-near anything else, if'n I put my mind to it."

Narrowing both his eyes, old man Jenkins

scratched his jaw. "Well, I reckon you might do. Being as ignorant as ya are, I could train ya to suit myself straight off."

Annie closed her eyes. Her throat swelled shut and her stomach quivered. Wasn't no sense in harborin' these present feelings, she told herself. She could do all right by old Jenkins here. She just needed to buck up and picture herself swingin' from the end of a rope—

"Hollis!" Mr. Jenkins shouted, making Annie's eyes fly open, "B'lieve I'll just take this little filly off yer hands."

Hollis appeared in the doorway that led to the outer office. He hesitated a moment, glancing from Annie to the old man. A frown that clearly showed reluctance settled on his features. Then he shook his head resignedly and said, "There's papers you got to sign. Eli will be back directly, if you want to wait."

"Ain't got time to wait." Advancing on Hollis, Mr. Jenkins shoved him through the doorway and into the adjoining room. "If'n you want me to take this here troublemaker off yer hands you'd best let me put my mark on them papers now. I got cows at home bawlin' their heads off to be milked. Got things to tend to in the mornin', too. So I won't be wastin' my time comin' back into town."

Annie sank onto the edge of her cot, folded her hands in her lap, and tried to still her trembling limbs. She stared at the plank wood floor, wishing she couldn't hear what was going on in the other room, wishing she didn't know.

Eli whistled a soft tune as he strode down the boardwalk toward his office. The smile he'd worn for the past half hour or so still curved his lips. Betsy's company always made him feel good. It was as if she had always been there, patiently waiting in the shadows of his life, never pressing for commitments. She was perfect in every way. Warm, tenderhearted, understanding. A woman any man would be proud to call his own. He would've married her long ago if certain circumstances hadn't gotten in the way.

Eli frowned, weighing that thought. Someday, after he'd dealt with the man who had killed his family, things would be different. Then, and only then, could he ask Betsy to be his wife. But the fact that he *would* ask her to marry him was inevitable. He knew it. She knew it. Hell, the whole town of Bartlett Springs knew it.

As Eli approached his office, he heard a loud, argumentative voice coming from inside. He stepped through the door and found Hollis seated at the desk. Zeb Jenkins, an ink pen poised in his hand, stood next to the deputy. Eli's gaze went to the papers on the desk. "Zeb," he said with a curt nod, then shifted his attention to his deputy. "Hollis, you mind if I ask what's going on here?"

"I tried to get him to wait, Eli," Hollis stammered. "I told him—"

"I come to do my civic duty, sheriff," Zeb cut in. "Gonna rid you of that lawless half-breed. I aim to lay claim to 'er. Got lots of work fer her t' do. I'll keep 'er good and busy and outa trouble. I promise you that."

Eli narrowed his eyes skeptically on Jenkins. "If I recall correctly, Zeb, you married little Emily Dobbs a year ago."

Zeb snorted and tucked his chin. "She done went and run off, just like the others. I tell you, sheriff, them girls all had me fooled. Rotten to the core, all of 'em. And the laziest things you ever saw. I done filed desertion on Emily with the judge. Got the papers right here," he said, patting the bib pocket of his worn overalls, "if you'd care t' see 'em."

Pressing his lips into a hard line, Eli walked across the room and hung his hat on the wooden peg there. He'd been suspicious of Zeb Jenkins for quite some time. The old recluse had taken three young wives in the past three and a half years, all of whom Jenkins swore had left him of their own free will. The last young woman, Emily Dobbs, had just turned sixteen, when her father promised her to Jenkins. Eli suspected that money had changed hands, but had never been able to prove it. Nor had he been able to come up with positive evidence of any sordid goings-on at the old man's secluded cabin.

Evidence or not, Eli would be damned if he was going to trust Jenkins with Annie's welfare. He turned, picked up the coffeepot from the stove, and filled his tin cup unhurriedly. Then he took a sip, eyeing Jenkins above the brim.

Zeb squirmed under his scrutiny for a moment, then drew himself erect. "So if ya got no objection, sheriff, I'll just sign this here paper and be on my way t' fetch the preacher. Like I told Hollis here, I got things t'—"

"The girl's already spoken for," Eli said, quietly but firmly.

Hollis's jaw dropped. "But, sheriff—"

"Stay out of this, Hollis," Eli said in a tone that made the deputy clamp his mouth shut.

Zeb snorted again and lifted his bearded chin. "Ain't what I heared this mornin'. Folks is sayin' the only other that's even come to look 'er over was Delbert Phipps." Jenkins chuckled cynically. "And that sputterin' fool ain't gonna get far enough from his mamma's apron strings t' marry nobody." Zeb looked from Hollis to Eli, then sneered as if a thought suddenly struck him. "Know what I think, sheriff? I think meybe you just don't want me t' have that little Injun you got locked up in here, 'cuz you figure I mighta done something bad to them other girls. Well, I'm here t' tell ya they run off just like I said. And till you can prove otherwise, you got no call to keep me from layin' claim t' this 'un. Or meybe you'd just as soon see 'er hang than marry the likes of me."

Eli braced one hip against the desk, set his coffee cup down, and crossed his arms over his chest. "Someone has already offered to marry Miss Calhoun," he said levelly. "I think it would be best if you went on home now, Zeb.''

The old man visibly shook and bared his teeth. ''Who?'' he shouted, waving his arms frantically. ''I knowed for a fact there ain't been nobody else in the biddin' 'cept me and that dog-eared Phipps kid. If'n you ain't bald-faced lyin', you just tell me who?''

Eli ran his tongue over his lips and stared at the grounds in the bottom of his coffee cup. Taking a deep breath, he lifted his head and met old man Jenkins's gaze steadily. ''Me,'' he said, barely above a whisper, then cleared his throat and raised his chin a notch. ''Me,'' he said again, this time louder and clearer. ''*I'm* going to marry Annie Calhoun.''

Chapter 6

A nnie sat starch stiff beside Eli, her fingers clutching the buckboard wagon seat to keep from being jostled from side to side. Eli had told her his spread was just three miles east of town, but it seemed as if they'd been on the rutted, dusty road for so long that she wondered if it wasn't a sure sight farther.

She tried to concentrate on the scenery, the spring-green rolling hills dotted with budding trees. Any other time, she would've savored the sight, but she kept expecting to wake up back in her jail cell at any given moment.

She still couldn't believe what had happened in the past day and a half. She twisted the too-big cigar band around her left ring finger and gazed at the small bunch of daisies on the seat beside her. She picked the flowers up, laid them in her lap, and touched the petals. Her wedding posies. They felt real enough.

Her heart fluttered. This was truly happening. It was the wishing . . . the wishing had made it happen. She was Mrs. Eli Larson.

Annie glanced sideways at her husband.

Lord but he was handsome. She was lucky to have made such a catch. 'Course, she knew he'd only married her to save her from hanging. She aimed to do all she could to please him though, and reckoned that in time, he might learn to love her. Stranger things had happened. She wondered if he could tell that she already had feelings for him. He had his eyes narrowed on the road ahead. He hadn't looked at her or spoken a word since they'd climbed up on the buckboard.

Not that Annie could blame him much. The whole thing had been over and done with quicker than a body could blink an eye. They hadn't stood before no preacher. Instead, Eli had whisked her across the street to Farguson's General Store. John Farguson, bona fide justice of the peace, had performed the ceremony. Mary, his wife, had presented Annie with the hurriedly plucked daisies, then stood by, hands clasped to her heart, as the vows were repeated. Afterward, Annie had gazed up at Eli, thinking he was supposed to kiss her or something. But he had simply looked down his shoulder at her and said, "Let's go."

Eli sensed Annie watching him and sighed inwardly. His head was still spinning. There would be no avoiding a heart-to-heart talk with her. She kept looking at him with those big, mooncalf eyes. He had an inkling she already fancied herself half in love with him. And that flat-out wouldn't do. He had to find a way to explain in terms she could understand that this whirlwind marriage was only a temporary solution.

But he needed time to sort out this predicament himself. He hadn't yet decided what to do next. Truth be known, he hadn't actually even had a plan until the moment his mouth had popped open. At the time, claiming Annie had just seemed like the right thing to do. Once the words were out, he'd suddenly felt duty-bound to honor them. After all, she had saved his life.

Eli made a clicking noise and flicked the reins, urging the horses onward over the bumpy road. He'd had no choice. No one else suitable had stepped forward. What else could he have done—stood idly by and watched the Calhoun Kid dangle from the end of a rope? He owed Annie, by God. If it hadn't been for her help, he wouldn't be sitting here now.

Of course, the news had come as quite a shock to Betsy. But she'd listened carefully when he'd gone to her to explain how it had come about. He had assured her they would solve the problem of Annie. She'd said she understood his need to repay his debt, and that she'd do what she could to help him. Betsy had always been gracious, but Eli hadn't expected her co-operation.

He tugged down the brim of his hat. First off, he'd have to come up with future living arrangements for Annie, a suitable home with good people. It ought to be a simple enough procedure to ask the judge for an annulment after a spell—especially if the marriage wasn't consummated. And it wouldn't be, he vowed, glancing briefly at his new bride. Annie certainly didn't stir up any of those types of feelings in him.

In the meantime, maybe he could polish her up a bit. He hadn't missed the blank stare she'd given the marriage certificate, or the clumsy way she'd held the pen when she'd made an X where her name should have been.

Eli's heart lifted a little, and he smiled as an idea came to mind. He could teach her how to read and write, how to act more refined. He'd ask Betsy for help. His smile grew broader. He might even be able to place Annie in a girls' school in Boston after the annulment. That was it. He'd write Aunt Lottie first thing in the morning and ask her advice. She'd know how best to proceed.

"That's my place just ahead there." Eli pointed to a split-rail fenced pasture where a few cows grazed. Annie sat straight as the buckboard turned onto a long, winding dirt drive lined with white-blossomed dogwood trees. *Home.* The word floated around her heart, making her a little light-headed. Her life had been an endless string of moving on . . . *you cain't stay here* . . . always running from the law. She'd never really had a place to call her own.

Her eyes misted with visions of children playing, laughing, darting between fresh laundry hung on a clothesline. *Her* children. Eli's children. *Their* children. Their home.

She'd dreamed about it plenty of times, but it had always seemed hopelessly beyond her reach.

Annie pressed her fingertips to her mouth to hide a smile she couldn't stop as they crested a small hill and she got her first glimpse of Eli's homestead. Nestled between two huge elms, the house was far from large, and badly in need of whitewashing. But to Annie the spread looked as grand as any of the fancy hotels in St. Louie that Deadeye had told her about. A corral and faded rust-red barn stood to the right and farther back.

A passel of dogs commenced yelping and running from every direction as Eli pulled the wagon up in front of the covered porch that stretched across the front of the house. He hopped off the buckboard seat, then turned and lifted Annie down beside him. The tail-wagging dogs surrounded them, each vying for attention. The largest of the pack stretched up and placed huge paws on Eli's chest.

"Okay, okay, Bear," Eli said, dodging the big pink tongue aimed at his face. He scratched the beast behind the ears. "I see you. All right?"

Satisfied, Bear went down on all fours and backed away, making room for the others. Eli stooped and ruffled each mutt's fur affectionately.

Annie looked on, smiling inside and out. "I don't reckon I ever seen so many dogs in one place." She scooped up the pup that was tugging at her pant leg. "Where in tarnation did you get 'em all?"

Eli returned her smile as he straightened and nudged his hat up. "Just a bunch of strays," he replied. "They showed up one by one. Word must have gotten out that they could get a meal here."

Annie laughed as the wriggling puppy she was holding nipped at her ear. "What's this 'un here called?" she asked.

"Haven't named him yet, but this one," Eli said, nodding toward the little dog still hopping around his feet, "I call Chigger. Then there's Bear, Pooch, and Whitey. And that," he said, pointing to a basset hound lying on the porch, "is Snooze."

"I had a dog oncet. Part wolf." Annie rubbed her cheek against the puppy's soft fur, then set him on the ground and came back up with a frown. "But Frank shot him. Said he barked too much."

Eli's good humor dwindled as he met Annie's unblinking stare. An Indian's ability to control his inner emotions had never failed to amaze him—and Annie had mastered the skill well. Yet something that flickered in her pale blue eyes made him wonder if she was really as distant as she appeared.

Reviving his smile, he captured her arm and steered her toward the house. "Careful," he said, guiding her up onto the porch, "the second step is loose."

As Annie started over the board in need of fixing, a hissing commenced beneath the porch. She leaned to one side and saw the

face of a calico cat peering at her from the
dark cavity below.

"Never mind old Prissy," Eli commented
and tugged Annie along up the steps. "She's
a mite testy these days. In the family way,"
he whispered, as if he didn't want the cat to
know he was talking about her.

He opened the screen door, and the savory
aroma of something cooking made Annie's
stomach tighten. Placing a hand at the small
of her back, Eli ushered her across the
threshold. She staggered into a long hall that
apparently ran the length of the house, and
stood in awe of her surroundings. Through a
doorway to her right was an honest-to-
goodness parlor. The room had an unused
look and was sparsely furnished with a
threadbare sofa flanked by two small round
pedestal tables. Two large bookcases covered
the far wall, filled to the brim with books.
Directly across the hall from the parlor, a partially opened door offered a glimpse of an un-
made brass bed. Annie plucked at the seams
of her britches, thinking she oughtn't to
touch anything.

"Hello," Eli called out, then stepped
around her. "Billy? Betsy? Anybody home?"

"In here, Eli," came a soft, lyrical voice.
"I'm in the kitchen."

A tall, willowy woman appeared in the
doorway at the end of the hall, drying her
hands on the whitest apron Annie had ever
seen. Her hair—field-mouse brown, Annie
quickly determined—was pulled back into a
neat coil at the nape of her neck. At first, An-

nie couldn't see anything special about her features . . . but then she smiled. The woman's cheeks suddenly took on a rosy hue and her dark brown eyes sparkled, bringing Annie to the conclusion that she must have turned plenty of heads with her lips curved just so.

Betsy clasped her hands against her waist and stepped forward. Her gaze flickered between Eli and Annie, yet her beautiful smile never wavered. "Hello, Annie," she said politely. "I'm Betsy Bruecks, Eli's—" She glanced at the sheriff. "Eli's neighbor. I own a little place just down the road. It's so very nice to meet you."

"Ma'am," Annie replied and nodded, then felt mortified at the way her voice had cracked. No matter how hard she tried, she couldn't keep her eyes from roving over the older woman. Nor could she help wondering about the silent messages that Miss Bruecks and Eli were presently exchanging.

"Well, I do wish I could stay and visit," Betsy drawled and walked toward them. Stopping at the hall tree, she retrieved her blue cotton bonnet. "But I've left things unattended and need to get on home." Her gaze settled on Eli and she smiled all the brighter. "Billy's down at the creek fishing with Joey. He's already had his supper. I told him to be home before dark. I made a pot of stew, and there's corn muffins warming in the oven."

As Betsy edged around them and headed for the screen door, Eli caught her wrist. "Betsy—"

"It's all right, Eli." For the first time the woman's pleasant disposition faltered, but only for a moment. Pressing her lips into a tight line, she smiled again, then slipped her wrist from the sheriff's grasp and fussily fixed the bonnet upon her head. "I'm fine," she said. "Now y'all go on and eat your supper before it gets cold." Her warm brown eyes were soft and serious when they met Annie's gaze, and she added, "I do so hope we'll be good friends."

Annie dipped her head awkwardly and made a small circle with the toe of her boot against the scuffed hardwood floor. She searched her brain for some response, but found none. It seemed highly farfetched that this nice, law-abiding lady would truly want to associate with the likes of her. Annie figured Miss Bruecks was merely being mannerly.

"Oh, I'm sure the two of you will get along," Eli said, breaking the tense silence. "Here, Betsy, let me see you out." He took Miss Bruecks's elbow and opened the screen door, allowing her to go first.

From the corner of her eye, Annie watched them walk to the edge of the porch. Though they spoke quietly, Annie's hearing was better than most and she couldn't help but catch pieces of the conversation.

"No, Eli. We discussed this thoroughly," Betsy whispered. "You did the right thing. One good turn deserves another. That poor girl needs our help. It is our Christian duty . . ."

Eli tugged the brim of his hat and looked toward the house. Annie swiftly looked away, but, straining her ears, clearly heard his deep, vibrant voice—and the words broke her heart. "Betsy," he murmured, "you've got to be the most understanding woman God ever put on this earth. I'm going to talk to Annie tonight . . . explain how things are between us."

Annie felt hollow inside. She closed her eyes and bit her bottom lip to keep it from quivering. Her pulse pounded louder and louder in her head until all other sound stopped. Eli was sweet on Miss Bruecks. Annie had suspected as much when she'd seen Betsy moving about the place as if it were her own. Annie had at least been able to hope her suspicions weren't valid up until now. Now, she told herself, there weren't no doubt with the way Eli had been a-courtin', and a-cooin', and a-complimentin' the woman.

Annie jumped as the screen door clacked shut behind her. She turned to find Eli staring at her, his expression bland and unreadable. He stood thus for several long, agonizing moments before he looked past her.

"Let's go have us a bite to eat," he said. He sidestepped her, hung up his hat and holster, then started down the hall in the direction of the kitchen, leaving her no choice but to trail behind.

The evening hum of locusts filled the stillness while Annie sat across the kitchen table from Eli. A breeze fluttered the curtains of an open window. The last rays of sunlight slanted into the room through the window and back screen door, projecting dancing dust particles. Annie wasn't near as hungry as she'd been when she'd first smelled the stew. After a couple of bites, the food stuck in her throat. Lost in thought, she commenced nudging the potatoes, carrots, and bits of crumbled cornbread from side to side in her bowl.

Eli was *her* husband. *Her* husband, dadburn-it. Didn't make no difference how that came to be. *What God has joined together,* John Farguson had said, *let no man tear apart.* Leastways, that was the way Annie had perceived it. She reckoned that particular phrase applied to women, too.

Annie tapped her spoon against the rim of her bowl. She wasn't so ignorant that she didn't know the reason that Eli had married her. She knew he didn't love her. That was a fact, plain and simple. Hell, less than an hour ago, he'd been out on the front porch sparking some other gal.

Annie clenched her jaw, determined not to dwell on the notion that Eli fancied another. Didn't make no difference, she told herself again. She had loved the man for pert-near as long as she could remember, was so powerfully smitten that it hurt just to look at him. She reckoned she had enough love stored up inside her for the both of them.

And she aimed to be the best wife a body could ever want. Given time, Eli might grow to hold her dear. Maybe she could make him forget all about that Miss Bruecks.

Annie straightened, pressing her shoulders against the ladder back of the chair, and looked at Eli. Head down, he appeared preoccupied with his meal. Annie took the opportunity to assess him openly. She focused on his sandy, tousled hair, noting that it curled around his ears and was a mite longer than that of most other lawmen she'd seen. She admired the pale sun-kissed streaks woven in with the darker shades of gold and light brown, and marked the deep contrast between his hairline and tanned skin.

By a strange twist of fate, she had snagged herself a husband . . . caught herself the very man of her dreams.

And she'd be hanged if she would let some Sunday school teacher take Eli away from her. Why, if that Betsy came sashaying around here again, Annie would snatch her baldheaded. Miss Bruecks would wish to hell she'd never—

Another notion crowded in front of the unfinished thought. She knew how to fight. She'd tussled with the best of 'em. But fighting with your fists was one thing. Fighting just to stay alive was another. Fighting for your man was something Annie knew absolutely nothing at all about.

Furrowing her brows, she decided this predicament deserved some thought. She reckoned Eli wouldn't take kindly to her out-and-out walloping Miss Bruecks. That probably wasn't the way for a lady to settle things. Then it came to her that this might be one of those situations where a body had to fight fire with fire.

Upon reaching this conclusion, she attempted to recall precisely how it was that Betsy had set her mouth when she'd smiled. She also remembered that Miss Bruecks had had a fetching way of lowering her lashes. She was about to try her own version of Betsy's comely expression when the back door flew open and a freckle-faced boy of ten or so burst into the kitchen.

"Eli! Eli!" the youngster hollered as he skidded to a stop, leaving the screen door flapping. "I had 'im. Caught the granddaddy of Snake Crick, I did! He was this big." The out-of-breath boy stretched his arms as wide as they would reach, and his eyes got round and sparkly. "I did, Eli. I had 'im squirmin' on my line, but—" With a slump of his shoulders, his arms fell to dangle at his sides, and he pushed out his bottom lip. "But he got a—" Taking notice of Annie, he lowered his voice considerably. "He got away." Lip still puckered, his features moved into an angry frown. "What the heck is *she* doin' here?" he asked, pointing stiffly at Annie.

Chapter 7

❧

"**B**illy, this is Annie." Eli rose from his chair. "She's going to be staying with us for a spell." He started to lay a hand on the towheaded youngster's shoulder, but the boy shrugged and moved away.

"I know who she is." Billy puffed out his scarlet cheeks. "She's that no good, dirty, half-breed outlaw that claimed she hit Joey with a rock."

"Billy!" Eli took a step forward, then stopped. Annie noted a slight tic in the sheriff's cheek, and saw that his fists were tightly clenched at his sides. "Boy, you'd best mind your manners," he said in a controlled voice, "or else you and me are going to take a walk down to the springhouse by way of the hickory tree. You get my meaning?" He paused with a look that made Billy's chin tuck in. "Now, you apologize to the lady right this—"

"I won't!" Billy shouted, edging a tad closer to the back door. "She didn't hit Joey with that rock. Joey said she didn't, and I ain't gonna 'pologize t' no lyin', stinkin'—"

Eli lunged for the boy, but Billy shot

85

through the screen door and went running off faster than a jackrabbit.

"Billy!" Eli called out and started after him. "Billy, you come back! You hear me?"

Annie jumped up from the table and caught Eli's arm before he got all the way outside. He halted in the open doorway, still clearly furious.

She stood looking up at him, waiting for his bright green eyes to turn a cooler shade. From the distance came the tweet of a whippoorwill which seemed to catch his attention, and she watched the storm slowly pass from his face.

"Leave him be, sheriff," she said in a voice so soft and gentle that it sounded as if the words were coming from someone else. Startled by her odd tone, she dropped her gaze first to Eli's pulsating throat, then to her fingers clutching his shirt sleeve. It wasn't right for a woman to tell her husband what to do, she thought. Letting go of him, she trailed her hand down his arm, then took a giant step backward. "I ain't meanin' to be disrespectful." She glanced around the room that had now filled with twilight's purple shadows. "I just . . . well, there ain't no call to whup the young'un on my account. I'd be beholdin' if ya didn't."

Eli narrowed his eyes and pressed his mouth into a straight line. He stared at Annie for a long moment before he stepped back inside the kitchen and let the screen door bang shut. Swerving around her, he moved to a wide pantry across the room, took out a box of matches, then walked over and lit the kerosene lamp on the table.

The kitchen took on a warm, golden glow. Eli braced both hands on the edge of the table. He hung his head and studied the flaming wick dancing inside the glass globe. "That boy has been a real trial to me," he murmured. "I just don't know what I'm going to do with him. Most generally, we get along fine, but if I try to make him do right he flies off the handle."

Annie shuffled forth and hesitantly sat down in the chair adjacent Eli. His eyes slid to hers. "He's just a kid," she said in the same soft voice she'd used earlier.

"Yeah." He half laughed, half sighed, then seated himself and ran a hand through his hair. "He's a kid. That's the problem. I know diddle-squat about raising kids." He shook his head slightly. "Betsy's offered to take him, but I can't ask her to do that, not with her paw sick and abed."

Annie lowered her brows and tugged her upper lip. She was more than a mite confused about Eli's kinship to Billy. "Is he yourn?" she inquired, immediately wishing she hadn't asked.

Eli looked at her blankly. "Mine? You mean, my son? No. Thank the good Lord above us. I just ended up with him because the little devil terrorized the two other families he was placed with."

Annie nodded, but her expression must have conveyed that she hadn't really understood, for the sheriff launched into further explanation.

"You see, a couple of months ago his folks were killed in a stagecoach accident a few miles outside of town. I've finally located an uncle of his in Santa Fe. I wired him about his sister's death and informed him of Billy's whereabouts. I expect he'll be coming to fetch the boy soon."

Eli gazed out the screen door at the dusky sky beyond. "It's getting dark. I guess I ought to go look for him."

"Give him just a little while longer," Annie urged, stopping him from rising. "Boy just needs some time to himself to think things through, that's all. He'll come around." Annie saw a movement from the corner of her eye right outside the screen door. "You know, sheriff, Deadeye says it's a mighty important moment in a body's life when they first see the need to go off by theirself and mull things over. He says that's a sure sign of growin' up."

Eli disregarded the smudges on Annie's face. Her eyes were a clear, pale blue in the lamplight, and held wisdom far beyond her years. At that precise moment, he couldn't recall ever seeing a prettier pair of eyes.

The creaking of the screen door turned both of their heads. Billy lumbered into the kitchen with his chin tucked to his chest and his thumbs hooked through the suspenders of his faded overalls. "Miss Annie, I . . . I reckon . . . well, I reckon I'm sorry fer them bad things I said," he muttered, though he didn't sound all that regretful. He glared from beneath his brows at Annie, then shifted an altered gaze to the sheriff. "Eli, I'll take my switchin' now, if'n ya still want t' take that walk down to the springhouse."

Eli scraped his chair back, stood, and sauntered over to Billy. He laid his hands on the youngster's shoulders. The boy looked up at him with unshed tears glistening in his eyes. "Now that you've made your apology, I don't think that little walk will be necessary, do you?"

Billy sniffed and wiped his nose with the back of his hand. "No, sir."

"Then what do you say we go fetch Miss Annie some bathwater and make ourselves scarce tending to chores in the barn?"

Billy's mouth quivered as if he couldn't quite decide whether to smile or not. He finally settled on a very subtle grin. "I'd say that there might just be a fine idea, Eli."

Annie swallowed as she watched Eli pour the last bucket of heated water into the steaming brass tub situated next to the stove. She shoved her hands into her pants pockets and rolled a ball of lint inside between her forefinger and thumb.

"Cain't I just go down to the crick and wash up?" she asked, contemplating the vapor rising from the tub.

Eli set the bucket on the stove and began unrolling his sleeves. "It's too dark. You'd never find your way back to the house."

"You could hang a lantern out back and I could follow the light," she suggested.

Eli paused in the task of buttoning his cuffs. He looked from Annie to the tub and back again, then the corners of his mouth curved slightly upward. "Annie, you'll like a hot bath once you've tried it."

She shook her head slowly. "I don't think so, sheriff."

"Annie, you *need* a bath," Eli stated firmly.

"But I done took myself a bath not more'n a full moon ago."

Eli hooked his thumbs through his belt loops and cocked his head to one side. "I don't know how else to put this, so I'll just say it. Girl, you smell. Something awful," he added, wrinkling his nose.

Annie frowned. "I do?"

"You do."

She bit her bottom lip and considered the tub again, then took a step backward and shivered. "That there water looks hot enough to boil a chicken, sheriff. Hellfire, it's liable to scald the hide right off me."

Eli ran a hand across his mouth in an attempt to keep his smile from growing broader. He walked over to Annie, caught her wrist, and practically dragged her to the tub. "Here," he said, pulling her hand toward the water, "just test it. It's nice and warm, that's all."

She tried to wrench free of his grasp, but his grip tightened. "Trust me, Annie," he said, and her struggle ceased. She met his gaze, and her heart rose to the base of her throat. "Trust me," he repeated.

His pleading expression did something to her—made her weak-kneed and light-headed. Her normally sharp pattern of thinking slowed to a crawl, and she had the sudden disturbing notion that she would walk through fire if he asked her to. Taking a deep breath, she held it, then squeezed her eyes shut as he guided her hand on a downward course.

The water swirled through her fingers with the warmth of summer sunshine . . . soothing . . . nice, Annie thought. She opened her eyes and smiled at Eli.

The smile he returned was followed by a small chuckle that almost made her giggle, too. In fact she would have laughed aloud, had she not been so conscious of his fingers encircling her wrist . . . or so aware of the sensation that ran up her arm and caused a bittersweet aching in the center of her chest.

"See there. Now that wasn't so bad, was it?" Eli asked as he straightened and withdrew her hand from the bath.

Annie caught the dish towel he tossed at her and pressed it to her breast. She just stood there looking at him, admiring him, unable to reply, feeling full and lost and awkward all at the same time.

Eli took in the brilliance of her blue eyes. There was a sweetness about Annie that nearly took his breath away. He had a strong notion that he was going to enjoy teaching her, seeing her face light up with wonder every time she experienced something new. At the moment, he wasn't at all sorry he'd married her.

His smile faltered and he cleared his throat. "Uh, I almost forgot, Betsy left you something." He disappeared down the hall and returned shortly with a white bundle. "She said you might be needing this." He shoved the gift forward.

Bewildered, Annie took the crisp, neatly folded cloth. "What is it?"

"A nightgown," he said, and she could have sworn he blushed. He pointed to the back door, edging in that direction. "Um, I'm going to go out and help Billy in the barn. You have yourself a good soak." He stepped out the door, then poked his head back in. "And Annie, toss those old clothes on the stoop here. You can wear something of Billy's till we can get you some others."

Annie started to protest, but the door clapped shut, and he was gone. She focused on the bathtub again and grimaced.

Then John Farguson's words surfaced from the back of her brain: *Do you, Annie Calhoun, promise to love, honor, and obey . . . ?* That was what she'd vowed when she'd said *I do.* With a deep sigh, she began to unbutton her shirt.

When she'd shucked all her clothes, she stepped tentatively into the tub and lowered herself gradually into the water. To her surprise, it was the most pleasurable experience she'd ever had—better than lying in thick grass on a sunny morning. Heat soaked into the taut muscles of her back, making her all limp and lazy. By their own accord, her eyes half closed as she rested her head on the rim of the tub and let her arms dangle over the sides.

The conversation between Eli and Billy trailed off as they approached the house. A sweet melody came from within and drifted out the open window on the cool night air. "Ah-ah-mazing grace, hmm hmm, hmm hmm . . ." the woman inside sang softly, humming the missing words.

Both Billy and the sheriff stopped just short of the back stoop. They stood speechless at the sight of the stranger seated at the kitchen table.

A brand-new Annie sat finger-combing her thick, wavy hair over one shoulder, the damp ends curling about the waist of her white gown. In the hazy glow of the kerosene lamp, what had once appeared to be dull black, stringy strands now gleamed the true color of deep dark brown touched with red highlights.

"Gosh," Billy whispered amid the chirping crickets.

Eli glanced sideways at the boy, and was a little perturbed that the youngster's thoughts seemed to be running along the same lines as his own. "Come on." He caught Billy's collar, not quite as gently as he intended. "Gentlemen shouldn't stand out here and gawk like two old geezers."

Annie looked up as they entered the kitchen. She smiled brightly. "Feel this," she said, extending her arm. "I ain't never felt nothin' so wondrous. It's so clean and cool against my skin."

Billy reached out and ran his hand along her wrist-length linen sleeve.

"Boy, you need to get on to bed," Eli commented without taking his eyes off Annie.

"Aw, cain't I stay up just a—"

"No, you *can't*. The word is can't, not *cain't!*" Eli gave the youngster a meaningful look. "Miss Annie and I have things to discuss. Grown-up things. So you go on now and get ready for bed."

Billy slumped his shoulders and hung his head, and with a deep exaggerated sigh, shuffled down the hall.

"Night, Billy," Annie called after him, then turned back to Eli with her grin growing wider. "Well," she said and stood up, clutching the sides of her gown. "What do you think? Ain't this a hoot? I mean, me in a real store-bought gown." She chuckled and placed a hand over her heart. "I almost didn't put it on, you know, because that Miss Bruecks—" Her face momentarily lost its gleefulness. "But when I felt how soft it was . . ."

Eli lost track of what she was saying as he took in the way the light behind her shone through the fabric, silhouetting every slender, womanly curve. He had never imagined anything of the sort existed beneath her baggy clothes. His gaze roved down her body and slowly moved upward to her face. Without the grime, her skin was the color of warm honey and her features were more defined. Her high cheekbones slanted at the same angle as her dark brows. Her small nose was pert, her lips full and rosy. When he came to her eyes he broke into a lazy smile. They twinkled as she spoke.

"Oh, and sheriff, you just got to get a whiff of this." Annie gathered her bodice in both hands and brought the bunched linen to her nose. "It's like honeysuckles and fresh air and springtime all mixed up together. Here, smell this."

Eli stumbled backward as she approached him with her fists twisted in the front of her gown. He caught her shoulders and held her at arm's length. "I'm sure it smells real nice," he said, then spun her around and guided her back into her chair. He took the seat opposite her, folded his hands on the table, and made certain all traces of his former smile were gone. "Annie, there are a few things we need to talk about."

Her face took on the seriousness of his own. "I reckon you're right about that," she commented with a nod. "Before you say your piece, I want ya t' know I'm much obliged fer ya up and marrying me the way ya did. I mean, well—" she dropped her gaze to the table—"I knowed ya ain't fond of me like a man's s'posed t' be when he marries . . . and . . . and well, hell, I ain't all that easy on the eye." She made a little sound that might have passed for a laugh, then bit her bottom lip and looked at him from under her brow. Slowly, she slid her hand across the table and laid it over his larger one. "I aim to be a good wife to ya, sheriff. I'll make you happy." Sitting straighter, she lifted her chin a notch. "You just wait and see if I don't."

Eli opened his mouth, then closed it. While he'd tended to his chores, he'd planned everything he was going to say. Now, not a single word came to mind.

Annie squeezed his hand. "You look tired, sheriff," she said. "Maybe we ought to go on to bed and finish this here talk tomorrow."

Eli's gaze flew to her face. Her shy smile and the drop of her long dark lashes made him remember that this was their wedding night. Suddenly he realized that in all probability she expected—

He jerked his hand from beneath hers and came to his feet, almost toppling the chair. "Uh, Annie, the first door on the right there is all yours." He pointed down the hall and started toward the back door. "I . . . uh . . . have a sick mare I have to stay with in the barn tonight," he said, and tore outside.

Annie stood in the center of the kitchen, twisting the midsection of her gown, and stared through the screen door in the direction he'd gone. In a matter of minutes, light penetrated the cracks between the boards of the barn. She couldn't say how long it was before the big structure went dark again, and she turned, picked up the kerosene lamp, and started down the hall.

She didn't take much notice of the room as she blew out the lamp and crawled into the big four-poster bed. Nor did she dwell hard on the comfort of the goose-down mattress, other than to reflect that it was too soft and she would surely have a backache in the morning. She was preoccupied with more troublesome thoughts.

Cupping her hands behind her head, she focused on the darkness above her. Oncet, she had walked in on her brother and one of the dance-hall girls in the room round back of the Four Corners Saloon. They'd been buck-naked and all tangled together in an awkward position—and apparently in a great deal of pain, for Frank was a-groanin' and a-moanin', and the gal was a-wailin' louder than a preacher at a revival. Later, Annie had pestered Deadeye to tell her precisely what it was those two were doing. He had finally broken down and informed her that the activity that Frank and the girl had been engaged in wasn't torturous at all, but pleasurable. He had gone on to explain that it was something a decent young woman such as Annie mustn't take part in until she married—because it could cause babies. Deadeye had said these particular goings-on would most certainly commence upon Annie's wedding night.

Annie twisted her mouth to one side. Deadeye hadn't gone into detail, but she could pretty much figure that this pleasant activity took two participants. So it wasn't likely to happen. Leastways, not tonight. Not with her in here and her husband in the barn.

Maybe the sheriff was just a mite skittish.

Maybe he merely needed to get to know her better before they partook in this so-called pleasurable happening. The important thing was that they were man and wife. Hell, they'd have the rest of their lives to share a bed.

A peacefulness flowed over Annie. She snuggled deeper under the patchwork quilt and closed her eyes. A smile creased her lips as visions of babies, town socials, church picnics, and a happy family gathered on the porch filled her head and lulled her to sleep.

Chapter 8

A rooster crowing outside Annie's open window made her stir the next morning. She tossed from side to side and tugged the feather-tick pillow over her head.

What finally brought her to full consciousness was the aroma of frying bacon.

She sat up and glanced around the room, taking a moment to get her bearings. Clothes were strewn everywhere. A pair of old, weatherworn boots leaned against each other in one corner. The long mirrored dresser parallel to the four-poster held a stack of dime novels, opened letters, and an assortment of bric-a-brac, some of which Annie couldn't begin to identify. A small tintype in an ornately carved wooden frame caught her attention and drew her from the comfort of the covers.

She picked up the photograph and studied the four people therein closely. The man was big and resembled Eli, but was sporting a mustache. The woman beside him barely reached his shoulder and had sweet, delicate features. Though she wasn't smiling, she looked as if she was about to. Two boys stood in front of the couple, one taller than the other, obviously older. The set of his mouth told Annie the younger boy was Eli.

Her gaze rose by degrees to the tarnished silver looking-glass. All thoughts of the foursome fled as she stared at herself.

She reached up and shoved her hands through her hair, pulling it away from her face. She didn't have pretty apple-cheeks like Betsy's. Her own, she decided, were a mite hollow. Her eyes weren't dark and sparkly either. Still, she wasn't near as ugly as Frank had always declared. Plain maybe, but not out-and-out ugly.

"Annie!" Billy hollered, making her jump. She turned toward the thumping at her closed door. "Eli says you'd best be gettin' up if'n ya want some breakfast."

Self-consciously smoothing her hair, she hurried to open the door, but Billy was nowhere in sight. The smell of food struck her anew, and she followed her nose down the hall.

Eli was alone in the kitchen. With his back to her, he tended the contents of a cast-iron skillet on the stove. Annie admired his tall form leisurely, noting the way his chambray shirt fit snug across his wide shoulders and his Levi's hugged his lean hips.

"Mornin'," she greeted him from the doorway.

"Good morning," he responded, paying her little heed.

Billy burst through the back screen door, skidded to a stop beside Eli, and held up his hands as if a gun were pointed at him. "I washed up, see?"

Eli examined him briefly, gave a quick nod of approval, then returned his attention to the frying pan.

The boy sneered at Annie as he ambled over and took his seat at the table. She stared at him unblinkingly, without expression, until he dropped his head and commenced scratching something into the wooden table-top with his fingernail.

Somehow, she couldn't find it in her heart to be offended by the youngster's obvious resentment. Nor could she keep from smiling at the crooked part in his damp-darkened, slicked-down hair.

"Annie," Eli said, "will you get me that basket of eggs there in the cupboard?"

She brought the sheriff the eggs, and as his hand closed next to hers around the handle of the basket, he stilled and looked from the bodice of her gown directly into her eyes. He appeared to be about to say something of utmost importance when he opened his mouth and asked, "How do you like eggs?"

"I like 'em just fine, I reckon," she answered.

"No. I mean how do you like them cooked?"

Annie frowned at that question. Nobody'd ever asked her to specify her preference. In fact, she *had* no preference when it came to food. She'd always eaten whatever, whenever anybody'd offered. Perplexed, she lifted her brows, then just to keep from appearing ignorant about such things, replied, "Cooked. I s'pose I like my eggs cooked, sheriff."

Billy snickered from his place at the table.

Eli closed his eyes in an exasperated fashion and turned back to the stove. "Sit down," he ordered. "You're getting them sunny-side up."

Seeing that he was in no mood for questions, Annie opted not to ask the one that was on the tip of her tongue. She barely noticed Billy's scowl as she settled in her chair, propped an elbow on the table, and stroked her jaw thoughtfully. Attempting to figure out just how Eli could tell exactly which side of the eggs was "sunny" proved to be quite a dilemma and kept her occupied till the meal was served.

The menfolk took great interest in their breakfast. Annie didn't mind that there wasn't much conversation. She was fairly busy with her own plate of side pork and the best-tasting eggs she'd ever had.

Billy's mouth was still full when he jumped up and grabbed three books bound together with a leather belt off the table, slung them over his shoulder, and made a dash for the door.

"Hold it right there, young man," the sheriff said firmly. "You hardly touched your buttermilk."

"Aw, Eli," Billy moaned, and kicked the air above the floor before he lumbered back to the table. "The fellas are all awaitin' for me at the ol' bridge. Miss Prigg's gonna give us a tardy if'n we're late t' school agin.''

The sternness around the sheriff's mouth softened and he sighed. "All right. Go on," he grumbled.

Not waiting to be told twice, Billy tore outside.

Eli scraped his chair back, stood, and picked up the boy's buttermilk, then looked at Annie and shrugged. "I know I give in to him too easy," he said, as if he needed to explain. He moved to the cupboard, took out a bowl, and poured the milk inside. "It's just more trouble than it's worth to argue with him."

He waited for Annie to comment, but when she didn't, he walked to the back door, pushed open the screen, and set the bowl on the stoop. Turning around to face her, he braced one hand against the doorjamb and hooked the thumb of his other hand in the front pocket of his jeans. "Well, don't you have any advice you'd like to offer?" he asked with an arched brow. "Every other female in this county does."

Annie widened her eyes and tried to be discreet about swallowing the lump in her throat. She smoothed her gown over her knees and searched her brain for a reply. Hell, she didn't know anything about onery young 'uns. That was a fact. Still, it was a troublesome thought to be outdone by *every other female in the county.* She felt obliged to put in some kind of suggestion of her own.

With a deep breath, she sat up straight and

folded her hands on the table. "Well . . . I reckon the boy has been through a lot, losing his folks the way he did and all. Maybe he's not fully finished grievin' for 'em, and that's what makes him so disagreeable sometimes. Sometimes when a body's hurtin' real bad inside—you know, right here." Tilting her head, she rubbed the center of her chest. "Well . . . I kinda figure it makes 'em angry when they cain't do nothin' to stop their sufferin'. I reckon they aim all that hatefulness at who'sever's close by 'cuz . . . well, sheriff, maybe it just gets t' be too much to bear at times."

Annie frowned, contemplating all she'd said. She clasped her hands tightly together and stared at them. "Leastways, that's the way I felt when my ma died," she murmured. "I wasn't no bigger'n Billy."

She met Eli's steady gaze. He appeared to consider her words. "The hurt fades with the passin' days," she added. "Billy'll settle down soon."

The sheriff narrowed his eyes on her, then his lips curled slightly upward. "You're something special, aren't you, Annie," he stated rather than asked. His voice was so soft and low that it was barely audible.

But Annie heard him. Loud and clear, like a band in a town square on the Fourth of July. His words and the way he spoke them made something akin to noonday sunshine ooze through her, warming her from the inside out.

Eli stood there staring at her for a moment

longer. She *was* special. He was of a mind to believe that maybe they could have been happy together under different circumstances. If it weren't for Betsy and the promise he'd made at his parents' graveside—but there *was* Betsy and his obligation to his family. Nothing could change that.

He shifted his weight and cleared his throat. "I have to—" He pointed a thumb over his shoulder. "I have to get on into town. I'm expecting a wire from the sheriff in Tyler today." Pushing away from the doorframe, he walked toward her and stopped by her chair.

Annie slanted her head back, looked up into his face, and noted his concerned expression. "I'm not going to have to worry about you running off, am I?" he asked.

Annie blinked, then wrinkled her nose. "Why would I want t' go and do a fool thing like that for, sheriff?"

Eli raised one brow skeptically. "Do I have your word that the minute I leave, you won't hightail it out of here?"

She nodded, though she was baffled by his need for her to make such a gol-dern silly promise—especially when there was really no call for it. She was his wife, for crying out loud.

"Good," he said, then started down the hall.

Annie got up and trailed after him. "Sheriff . . . um, I saw my boots out on the stoop, but I didn't see my clothes." She watched him take his Stetson from the hat rack and set it on his head. "Can I have 'em back? My britches and stuff, I mean. I cain't very well mosey around in this here—"

"No." He set his mouth firmly, then turned and walked out the front door.

Annie followed, but stood her ground on the front porch while he mounted his horse. "But why not?" she hollered.

"Mainly because I buried those rags this morning," he said, reining his prancing stallion alongside the steps. "Besides, I don't figure you'll wander too far in your nightgown," he added, then smiled, tipped his hat, and galloped off.

For lack of anything else to do, Annie tugged on her boots and set out for the barn to check the sick mare. Eli sure had a fine place, she observed as she strolled along. Though there were a few things in need of fixing, she figured the view made up for the chipped paint, broken fences, and cluttered yard. Green rolling hills surrounded the spread. Huge shady elms were scattered in every direction Annie cared to look. The rest of the landscape was sprinkled with full-blooming redbud and dogwood trees.

Reaching the barn, she caught hold of one side of the wide door and pulled it open. It creaked loudly in the process, and she noted that one hinge was missing and the other was loose and rusty.

It was cool inside and smelled of fresh-cut hay. Annie stood for a long moment in the center of the big barn and watched dust particles flutter in the slanted sunlight shining through the cracks in the high roof. Oncet, when Frank was drunk and on a mean streak, she'd hidden in a barn in Dregg's Flat. She'd found kittens in the hayloft.

Smiling at the memory, she walked toward the stalls and passed a stack of boards, new fencing, and unopened paint cans. She reckoned Eli had so much sheriffing to do in town that he hadn't gotten around to mending things around the place.

The only occupied stall held a chestnut mare who snorted and backed up as Annie approached her.

"It's all right, girl," she said softly, climbing up on the railing that hemmed the horse in. "I ain't gonna hurt ya." The skittish mare eyed Annie with no small amount of skepticism. "The sheriff tells me ya been feelin' poorly," she commented conversationally, then cocked her head. "Ya don't look all that sick." The horse calmed as Annie spoke in a soothing tone and very carefully lowered herself into the stall. Moving in slow measures, she reached out and stroked the mare's nose. "There, there. Now that's a girl. Let ol' Annie look ya over and I'll see if I can fix whatever's ailin' ya."

All she could find wrong with the horse was a fairly good-sized scratch on her left front leg. She made a poultice from mud and some mint she found growing around the pump in the back yard, applied it to the wound, then made her way back to the house. She wandered from the kitchen into the parlor. A thin layer of dust covered everything, indicating the room hadn't been used in some time. But there was something special about this room, Annie decided as she admired the crocheted doilies on the pedestal tables. It looked as if a real fine lady had placed things just so.

There was a vase filled with colorful peacock feathers in one corner. A well-stocked bookshelf took up a whole wall. And scattered all about were photographs, to Annie's delight. Lots and lots of photographs in fancy little frames.

She spent the better part of the morning going from picture to picture, trying to guess which ones were of Eli. She kept returning, however, to one particular tintype of someone other than her husband. The young man in the photograph wore a Confederate uniform and favored Eli across the eyes. Annie was wondering about his kinship to the sheriff when she heard a knock at the front door.

Peering around the doorframe of the parlor, she saw Betsy's smiling face on the other side of the screen.

"Hello," Miss Bruecks called, then shifted the big basket she carried from one arm to the other and let herself in.

Annie stepped into the hall to block her way. "Eli ain't here," she said, none too friendly-like. She gave the woman's crisp, blue calico dress the once-over, then lifted her chin a notch. "He's off doin' some sheriffin' in town. Won't be back till late this evenin'."

Betsy's brightness flickered a tad, but her

smile remained intact. "I came to see *you*, Annie. I thought we might chat a little and get to know each other better."

Annie didn't want to chat. She was about to tell the woman so when Betsy's eyes widened on the silver-framed tintype of the Confederate soldier in Annie's hands. Her smile went flat and she paled a mite. She blinked, then looked from the photograph to Annie and back again. "May I see that, please?"

"Who might this Reb be?" Annie asked out of curiosity, passing her the picture.

Apparently lost in some memory, Betsy neglected to answer for a moment. "Hmm?" She focused on Annie, then attempted to smile. "Tom? Oh, he was Eli's brother."

"Was?"

"He was killed in the war," Betsy replied quickly as if the words hurt her.

Annie shoved her hands into her pockets. "He don't look old enough in that there picture to be a-fightin' no war."

"He was only seventeen when he died," Betsy commented, staring at the tintype again. Her lashes fluttered as if she had something in her eye, then she sidestepped Annie and walked into the parlor. She set the photograph on one of the end tables, trailing her fingers along the edge of the frame before she turned and smiled brightly once more.

"Well," she said, and moved toward Annie, "I have sassafras root for tea and hot apple muffins straight from the oven." She attempted to catch Annie's arm, but Annie shrugged out of her reach. Appearing not to mind, Betsy withdrew her hand and headed off in the direction of the kitchen. "And I've brought a few dresses I can't wear anymore," she called over her shoulder. "I thought maybe we could alter them to fit you."

Annie followed reluctantly. She paused in the doorway, getting up the gumption to tell Miss Bruecks that she didn't want no dresses, nor no sassafras tea, nor nothin'—

Her thoughts slowed as she caught a whiff of something wonderful when Betsy took a red gingham bundle from the basket and laid it on the table. She folded back the corners of the cloth, revealing the biggest golden-brown muffins that Annie had ever seen.

Against her will, Annie stepped forward. "I . . . well, I reckon it wouldn't hurt none to have me just one of them muffins," she said, then wet her lips. "I mean, seein' as you went to the trouble of bringin' 'em and all."

A single bite of Miss Bruecks's apple muffins was almost worth the agony of that long afternoon. Annie spent most of it standing on a chair in the middle of the kitchen while Miss Bruecks took up the dresses she'd badgered Annie into putting on. Annie had finally come to the conclusion that there just wasn't any arguing with the woman and figured the sooner Betsy got the dern dresses done, the sooner she'd go on home.

"There," Betsy said at last. She tied off and snipped the thread attached to Annie's hem. "I think that will do." She stood back and appraised her handiwork with a smile. "You look lovely, Annie," she said.

Annie climbed down off the chair, ignoring Miss Bruecks's offer of help. She wasn't quite sure what to make of Betsy. She had a powerful urge to tell her she was much obliged for the loan of the dresses, but refrained from doing so. "Do ya s'pose Eli will like this 'un?" she asked instead, running her hands along her tucked-in waist.

"Why, yes, I'm sure he will."

Annie met Betsy's gaze. She couldn't help envying the woman. Betsy was so cool and collected. It was no wonder Eli was sweet on her.

"Oh dear," Miss Bruecks said, glancing through the back screen door at the setting sun. "It's getting late. I need to get home and fix Paw's supper." She hurried down the hall, snatched her bonnet from the hat rack, and turned as Annie moved up behind her. She reached out as if to take Annie's hand, but suddenly changed her mind. "I had a real nice afternoon," she said, sincerity shining in her dark eyes. "I hope you did, too."

Annie didn't respond when Betsy said good-bye, but went to the front door and watched the woman's buggy make a dust trail down the drive.

She hadn't ever fancied herself having tea with a lady . . . hadn't ever had the occasion to spend much time in the company of a female. But today she'd done just that, and hadn't found the experience all that unpleasant.

And, dad-blast-it, though Annie tried with all her might to deny it at the moment, Betsy *was* a genuinely amiable person. She'd gone out of her way to be nice to Annie, when most folks would have crossed the street to avoid a half-breed outlaw like her. Annie couldn't help but admire her on that account.

Despite all that, as she watched her new neighbor's buggy melt into the horizon, her original conviction about Betsy Bruecks hardened. It wasn't going to be easy, but she planned on doing her damnedest to squelch whatever hold the woman had on Eli.

Chapter 9

The telegram from the sheriff in Tyler that Eli had been walking the floor waiting for finally arrived late in the afternoon. Scanning the message briefly, he frowned. It wasn't good news, but rather confirmed his suspicions. The Calhoun gang had taken to moving southward into Texas and had robbed the Katy Railroad somewhere between Rusk and Palestine. The conductor had been wounded, and one of the passengers killed. The sheriff in Tyler had lost the Calhouns' trail, but expected the gang to double back through the Bartlett Springs area and warned Eli to be on the lookout.

Eli tacked the telegram on the wall, then turned toward Hollis, who sat tipped back balancing on two legs of his chair with his feet crossed at the ankles and propped on the desk. Thumping the bottom of the deputy's boot, Eli roused Hollis from his nap.

The man awoke with a start, awkwardly righting his chair before he toppled backward. "Just restin' my eyes a bit," the old deputy said, then stifled a yawn. "Did the telegram from Tyler git here yet?"

"Hensly's boy just delivered it." Eli gestured toward the posted telegram as he strode over and took his hat from the peg on the wall. "We're going to have to get a posse together. Frank Calhoun and his gang made a wider sweep into Texas and will be circling back to hole up in the Territories soon. I plan to cut them off before they get there." He narrowed his eyes pensively. "Think you can handle rounding up some good men?"

The deputy sat a little straighter and tugged down his cowhide vest. "Well, a'course I can, sheriff."

"Good. Tell them we'll be moving out first thing in the morning. They'll need to be here early so I can deputize them." Eli put on his Stetson and started for the door. "I think I'll head on home. I have some things to settle there before I leave."

The closer Eli got to his ranch, the faster he pushed his horse. Apprehension had set in almost the moment he'd left town. Visions of Annie being long gone by the time he arrived home had crept into his thoughts. Clothes or no clothes, he couldn't imagine what would keep her there if she took a notion to run off. He must have temporarily taken leave of his senses that morning to actually trust the word of an outlaw.

With a deep sigh, he closed his eyes for just a second. Even if she *was* still at the ranch, what in the hell was he going to do with her while he was off tracking down her brother? He supposed he'd have to leave one of his men behind to watch her.

He cursed silently, proclaiming himself a dang fool for getting into this mess. But behind his lids he saw those sky-blue eyes looking up into his. Annie's eyes had completely undone him this morning. Within that short span of time when her gaze had held his, she could have more than likely made him believe anything. *Anything.*

Eli shifted in his saddle. She'd invaded his thoughts . . . not just last night when he'd peeked through the screen in awe and realized that she was indeed a woman. And not just this morning when she'd made her big-eyed, all-innocence promise to stay put. But *all damned day long.*

Grimacing, he tugged his hat lower on his forehead and pressed his boot heels into his mount's flanks, urging the steed onward. This *wasn't* attraction, he assured himself. It couldn't possibly be attraction. The whole notion of being physically attracted to the Calhoun Kid was absurd . . . utterly ridiculous.

Granted, underneath all the dirt smudges, scraggly hair, and baggy clothes, Annie had turned out to be a passable female.

Passable. Eli's keen sense of honesty balked. Once she'd been cleaned up, her looks were considerably more than merely passable. And he damned well knew it. He simply hadn't, until this moment, willingly acknowledged that fact.

All of a sudden, he wasn't in such a big

hurry to get home. He didn't much relish finding Annie gone when he got there. Pulling back on the reins, he slowed his horse's pace as he turned onto the long winding drive that led to the house.

Okay. So he'd admitted it. Annie was pretty. And though she lacked polish, she possessed a special, simple kind of charm all her own . . . a certain something that tugged him in her direction. It was all the fault of his cursed tender streak, he decided. It had somehow bypassed all the other Larson men, this uncontrollable urge Eli had to aid the less fortunate—strays, orphans, and the like. It was an unnatural trait, especially for a lawman, one he'd never quite been able to come to terms with. That was it. The stirrings he felt for Annie had to do with nothing more than his damned big heart.

Eli nudged his hat up and wiped the sweat from his forehead. On the other hand, it could be simpler than that. His response to Annie could be due to the fact that he hadn't had a woman in a couple of months. In which case, a sure cure would be an hour or two with one of the girls at Gracie's Palace. He wasn't a regular customer there, by any means. But a man had certain needs now and then, and since it was unspeakable to expect someone as virtuous as Betsy to tend to them, over the years he'd done what any man would, and made discreet visits to the Palace.

As he neared the house, he made a firm decision. Regardless of the reasons for his present turmoil, one way or another he was going to get the Calhoun Kid out of his system—and out of his life—as soon as possible.

The house looked quiet, empty, and almost lonely, Eli mused as he rode past it toward the barn. Annie had probably lit out the moment he'd left for town. But then, the house usually looked that way, at least until Billy came barging in around suppertime, long after school had been let out. Eli knew the boy dawdled on his way home. But only the good Lord knew what Billy did. Eli was generally too tired to ask. On the few occasions when he had inquired, Billy's wild stories nearly always resulted in the boy being sent to bed without supper.

Reaching the barn, Eli unsaddled Stonewall. He brushed his horse down, deciding he and the stallion could both use a little rest before he set out in search of Annie. By now, he was certain she'd left the vicinity. Otherwise, he figured she would have already been out there pestering him.

He absentmindedly observed the red dust his boots stirred up as he walked toward the house. He'd brew a pot of good strong coffee to revive himself. He needed to throw some grub together to take along. He'd have to wait for Billy, then take the boy to Betsy's for the night. He hated to inconvenience Betsy, with her paw ailing and all, but on such short notice he had no place else to leave the youngster.

Damn it all to hell and back. Why hadn't he just taken Annie with him that morning and stuck her in a cell for the day? What in

God's name had possessed him to trust the little—

The back screen door slamming brought Eli's head up. He stopped in mid-stride, half-way to the house. Annie stood on the stoop, tangling her fingers together at her waist. The pale yellow dress she wore complemented her honey coloring and outlined every swell and curve of her slender body. Her dark wavy hair billowed about her shoulders in the slight breeze. But what went straight to Eli's heart was the bright, shining smile in her eyes that floundered and turned uncertain as it reached her lips.

Annie attempted to read her husband's features. She shifted from one foot to the other. From Eli's blank expression, she couldn't decipher whether he liked the dress or not. He just stood there gawking like she was Barnum and Bailey's bearded lady.

She nibbled her bottom lip, wondering if she should have waited in the kitchen as she'd planned. When she'd heard Eli ride up, she'd been in a tizzy about where to be standing when he came in—just so he'd see her best side. After a frazzled few moments of deliberating, she had decided to settle her-self at the table and act as natural as she could. She had done her mightiest to sit there striking a pose. But, tarnation, the sheriff took so long in the barn that she got a crick in her neck.

Annie swallowed as Eli started toward her. She did so want him to be pleased about the dress. Her pulse commenced to thumping, and pounded even harder with each step closer he came.

When Eli strode onto the back stoop though, he barely glanced at her. ''Evening,'' he said with a curt nod, then reached around her, opened the screen door, and disappeared into the house.

Annie stood rooted momentarily as her heartbeat quaked, sputtered, then slowed to a limping pace. She took a deep cleansing breath, trying to hold down the ire that was rapidly rising within. Dad-blame-it all. It was downright rude of Eli to pass by without commenting on her dress. She might have robbed a few banks in her day, but she hadn't ever been out-and-out rude.

Pivoting on her heel, she jerked open the screen door and stepped into the kitchen. She hadn't stood on that gol-dern chair all afternoon and let Betsy poke her with pins for nothing.

As the door banged shut behind her, Eli turned from the stove and held up a cast-iron skillet. He opened his mouth, apparently about to say something, but Annie cut him off.

''Well?'' she said, running her hands along the seams of her bodice, ''ain't you got nothin' t' say about this here dress Miss Bruecks brung me, Eli Larson?''

Eli couldn't keep his gaze from traveling the length of her. He had a lot to say. He would have liked to tell her that when he'd seen her standing on the stoop he had thought she was the most beautiful woman he'd ever seen—except that he didn't use words like *beautiful*, hadn't in fact ever said anything comparable to Betsy in all their years of courtship. But Annie . . . Well, Annie made him think of the poetry he'd studied in school, all those sweet phrases and sonnets. She reminded him of morning sunshine in that yellow dress. But he couldn't tell her so because he didn't dare encourage this relationship to go any further. "I think you look real nice, Annie." He dropped his eyes to the hardwood floor. "Real . . . respectable."

Nice. Respectable. Maybe it wasn't exactly what Annie had been fishing for, but she was satisfied with his answer, Leastways, it was a start, she reckoned. Could be the trail to loving ought to start with respectability.

Eli cleared his throat and glanced sideways at the frying pan he held frozen in the air. "I don't suppose you know how to cook."

Annie grimaced. "Well, Sheriff, truth be told, I cain't say I'm much good at it. The last time I tried, Deadeye said he'd about as soon swallow a live horny toad as eat my cookin' agin."

Eli grimaced too, then turned back to the stove. "In that case, I'll just rustle us up something."

"I can help though, cain't I?" Annie moved up behind him.

Too close for comfort Eli thought as he skirted around her and fetched a bag of potatoes from the cupboard. "Can you cut these up for me?"

"Sure can." Her lips curved into a wide smile. "I'm real good with a knife."

Annie reckoned most folks wouldn't have thought too much about the simple task of fixing supper. Just the same, as she dumped the bowl of potatoes she'd diced in with the meat frying in the skillet, she experienced an immense amount of pleasure. She remained at Eli's side, noted how he lit the stove, and watched him stir the hash. Handing him the salt and pepper when he asked for it made her feel useful, more like a wife. For once in her life, she had a sense of truly belonging in a particular place. Here. Here with Eli was where she belonged. There'd be no more running. Nobody telling her she had to move on. This was home.

She glowed inside as she helped her husband set the table. Even the ugly face Billy made at her when he came in couldn't dampen her mood. The boy was just going to have to get used to having her around. She figured on setting things straight with him in due time. She held that thought uppermost in her mind all through their meal and ignored the youngster's sulky glances.

Annie was cleaning up the last of the dishes when Eli and Billy came in from doing their chores. She turned with a bright smile for both of them.

Eli returned the smile before he thought better of it. He was still worried about her getting the wrong idea about their marriage. But when Annie smiled, she smiled with her heart, and it was the hardest damned thing, he was quickly learning, not to smile right along with her.

He purposefully sobered his expression, and slid his gaze from his too-tempting wife to Billy. "Do you have lessons to do tonight, son?"

"No, sir." Billy's blond silky hair swayed from side to side as he shook his head. "Miss Prigg didn't give us none."

"*Any*. Miss Prigg didn't give you *any*," Eli corrected. "And if you're absolutely sure about that, I think you'd best get on to bed."

Eli was certain the youngster had been mincing the truth when Billy skedaddled down the hall to his room without an argument. He made the decision right then and there to pay Miss Prigg a visit soon. At the moment he had a more pressing problem to deal with.

As his thoughts returned to Annie, so did his gaze. She was sitting at the table watching him with candid adoration in those big blue eyes.

Dread pressed against his sternum, making his shoulders slump slightly. He had to tell her about his plans for the annulment. And he would . . . eventually. As soon as he got a reply to the letter he'd sent Aunt Lottie. As soon as plans for Annie's future were finalized. As soon as he could come up with a way of breaking the news to her gently.

But looking at her now, her eyes shining with an inner peace and her lips curved with contentment, he had to wonder if he was ever going to be able to find the right words. He'd come up with at least a hundred explanations during the course of the day. But at the moment, none of them seemed appropriate. It was going to be hard enough tonight to tell her he'd be leaving in the morning to track down her brother.

Eli shifted his weight, uncomfortable with the way the lamplight played on her serene features. She was happy here. The evidence of that was written all over her face. He'd once noticed she had that same uncanny ability all Indians had to disguise their innermost feelings. But happiness, it seemed, was one emotion Annie couldn't hide.

It suddenly occurred to him that maybe happiness was a new emotion for Annie, sort of like a new toy that a child couldn't stop playing with. That thought pressed his lips into a hard line. He didn't want to return her smile . . . didn't want his heart tugged in her direction.

"Annie, I'm riding out with a posse tomorrow. We're going after Frank."

Her face fell, and she stared past him. "I reckon that there is your duty."

"He and the gang robbed a train near Rusk. A passenger was killed. I aim to bring Frank in alive if I can. I won't shoot him unless he forces me."

Annie nodded, then twisted her hands in her lap. "You're m' husband, Eli." Her eyes met his intensely. "I got t' stand by ya, no matter what ya do. But Frank . . . well, he's blood. I don't reckon I'll be able t' keep from frettin' a little."

Eli clenched his jaw. Everything would be so much easier if she wasn't so damned agreeable all the time. He turned his back on her and walked to the stove, wanting to hide his mood more than he wanted the coffee he poured. "I plan on having someone watch you while I'm gone." He dropped a spoonful of sugar into his cup and stirred it, then faced her. "I'll tell them to allow you to go about your business as long as you don't try to cross the property lines."

Annie looked at him solemnly. "I ain't gonna cause no trouble."

You already have caused trouble, he thought but didn't say. Instead, he sipped the steaming brew, then nearly gagged on the sweetness because he didn't normally take sugar in his coffee. Annie had him doing all sorts of things he didn't normally do . . . thinking things he didn't normally think . . . feeling things he didn't normally feel.

"Sheriff, you gonna stay inside tonight?" Annie's soft suggestion shattered the short span of silence, making Eli flinch and almost spill his coffee. She lowered her lashes a degree and glanced to the side. "Ain't no reason for you to be sleepin' in the barn. I mean, that mare is just fine and—" She shrugged. "Well, seein' as we're married and all, and that there bed in my room is surely big enough for both of—"

"Annie." Eli's voice cracked with the effort it took for him to speak. His gaze traveled around the room, while he searched his brain for something to say. "Annie," he blurted out again, finally meeting her eyes, "I . . . I think what we ought to do this evening is start teaching you to read." He nodded, then smiled complacently. "That's what I think we ought to do. Would you like that?"

Annie's smile wavered. She furrowed her brows and narrowed her eyes. "Are you funnin' me, sheriff? 'Cuz if'n you are—"

"No, of course not." Eli slid into the chair adjacent hers. He started to take her hands, but thought better of it and curled his fingers into fists on the table. "Annie, I'm serious. I'd like to teach you to read and write . . . if you'll let me."

Her lips parted as she pressed back in her chair. She was quiet, pensive a moment, before a small, breathy laugh escaped her. "Honest?" She leaned forward with her eyes round and bright and searching his. "Oh, sheriff, you think you could? Really and truly?"

"Anyone can learn to read, Annie, if they're willing to work at it."

Her tentative smile broke loose. "I'd work real hard, I would. And I'm a quick learner." She rocked back in her chair and laughed again, this time with unbound pleasure. "Deadeye ain't gonna believe this," she whispered to the ceiling, then set all four legs of the chair on the floor and focused on Eli. "Can we start right now?"

Eli couldn't keep from catching her enthusiasm. His own grew as he opened his dusty books and began working with her. Much to his surprise, she was every teacher's dream. She'd been right about her knack for learning. She possessed a unique ability, he soon discovered, to memorize things instantly. By the end of the evening, she could recite the complete alphabet.

It was late then they closed the books and blew out the kitchen lamp. He bid her an awkward good-night at the door of her room, and moved on down the hall in the direction of the parlor. Silently praying that sleep would take him swiftly, he stretched out on the horsehair sofa. But the dainty piece of furniture wasn't made to accommodate his tall frame, and the horsehair pricked his back.

And he was as uncomfortable on the inside, too.

Tremulous feelings that he couldn't stop shook the very center of his being. He was glad Annie hadn't again brought up the subject of sleeping with her. He wasn't so sure, in his present mood, that he could've resisted her offer twice.

With a deep sigh, he rolled over onto his side and folded his arm beneath his head. He tried to picture Betsy's sweet smile, yet the usually soothing vision wouldn't come to mind. So he attempted to concentrate on what route the Calhoun gang might take on their way back to the Territories.

But all he could think about was Annie.

Annie's eyes. Annie's smile. Annie, standing on the stoop in that yellow dress, waiting for him. Annie, all alone in that big four-poster bed right down the hall . . .

Chapter 10

❦

Annie tightened her grip on the handle of
the bucket she carried. On her way to
the water pump, she gazed at the rider on
the hill. The deputy had never approached
her, but every time she left the house, there
he'd be, watching her from a distance.

She set her pail on the flat rock beneath the
spigot and cranked the handle furiously. It
gave her the willies to think the man knew
her every move. She wished Eli would come
home, not just so the deputy would leave,
but because she'd grown powerful lonesome
for her husband over the past two days.

Billy hadn't been fit company, either. The
boy had just sulked or pouted or made faces
at her whenever she'd tried to strike up a
conversation.

Annie brushed a stray hair from her eyes
and picked up her filled bucket. She braced
her free hand against her spine, straightened, and glared at the man on the hill once
more. Then she turned and headed for the
house.

Opening the screen door, she went inside
and poured her water into the large pot on

the stove. Billy had wrinkled his nose and shoved his plate away last night when she'd tried her hand at Eli's recipe for hash. She hadn't found the meal all that bad, except for the burned parts. This evening, she wasn't taking any chances, though. She didn't figure there was any way she could mess up boiled taters.

The kitchen, the whole house in fact, was too quiet. To keep her spirits up, she hummed while she peeled potatoes and plopped them into the pot.

She could have told Eli he was wasting his time looking for her brother. Frank was as slippery as a catfish. He could smell a lawman a mile away. Of course, Eli wouldn't have listened to her. She'd learned that her husband was the sort who had to come around to things by himself.

A faint disturbance from the direction of the road caught Annie's ear. She ceased her humming, listened harder, and heard distinct shouts.

Wiping her hands on her apron, she hurried out onto the front porch. Suddenly she heard what sounded like a child crying. When she shaded her eyes, she spied Billy's small form rising from the ridge in the dirt drive. He was wailing and running like a bat out of hell. Three larger, obviously older boys followed close on his heels.

Annie tore down the step and raced toward the four. As she neared, she saw that Billy's lip was bloody and one eye was red and just about swollen shut.

"Here now!" she yelled, catching Billy's arm when he started to dart past her. "What's all this here about?"

The three boys skidded to a stop and Billy tried to wriggle free of her grasp, but she held him fast.

"See there," the tallest boy said, eyeing Annie with contempt. "He's an Injun lover too."

"He's a big baby," one of the others called out.

"*Baby, baby, baby,*" they all chimed in.

"Billy ain't no baby," Annie proclaimed. Taking a step forward, she shoved Billy behind her. "And three agin' one is dirty fun. Y'all ought t' be ashamed a yourselves—pickin' on someone littler. Now you'd best git afore I tan the lot of ya."

The biggest boy folded his arms across his chest and lifted his chin. "You and who else, *squaw?*"

"Her and me, James Matthews," the deputy answered as he galloped up beside Annie and reined his horse. "I suggest you take the lady's advice and hightail it out of here. You're gonna be in enough trouble when I tell all your paws about this."

James's two friends exchanged quick glances, then skedaddled. Finding himself standing alone, James did the same.

Annie watched the boys disappear down the drive, then squinted at the man astride the horse. "Much obliged, deputy."

"Ma'am," he said, tipping his hat. "I'll

mosey along after those young 'uns and make sure they're on their way.''

As the deputy rode off, Annie looked down at Billy and grimaced. ''Come on,'' she said softly. ''Let's get you up to the house and put something cool on that there eye.'' She slipped her arm around his shoulder, but he shrugged from her touch.

''It's all yer fault.'' He sniffled and wiped his nose on his torn shirt sleeve. ''James and them was a-callin' Eli a Injun lover 'cuz he up and married you. And I said he wasn't!''

Annie's heart twisted. Stretching out her hands, she took a step toward him. ''I'm sorry, boy,'' she whispered. ''I'm sorry they hurt ya because a me.''

Billy backed away and broke into sobs. ''Me and Eli was just fine till you comed along,'' he shouted, then turned and ran to the barn.

Annie followed, and found him sitting in the corner of Stonewall's stall, his head buried in his arms, crying. Moving as carefully as she had when she'd first approached the skittish mare, she crept in and sat down on the straw next to the boy.

''Go away,'' he muttered into his folded arms.

''Afraid I cain't do that,'' Annie replied. ''You and me, we got t' have ourselves a little talk.''

Billy swiveled around, pressing his face into the sideboards of the stall. ''I don't wanna talk t' no dirty Injun.''

''I ain't all Injun, ya know. Why, my eyes

are as blue as yours." Annie focused on the blond strands of hair curling at the back of his neck. "Bein' part Injun ain't so bad. Injuns know lotsa things white men don't."

Billy peered at her over his shoulder. "Like what?"

"Well, like how t' catch a fish with their bare hands, and what berries make good medicine. I could show ya sometime."

Billy frowned, casting his damp lashes down. "I don't wancha t' show me nothin'," he grumbled. "All I want is fer ya t' get the heck outa here and leave me and Eli be."

Annie stared at the boy for a long moment, then stood. "I ain't leavin', Billy," she said calmly, brushing straw from her skirt. "I'm Eli's wife, and that there's a fact. So you'd just as well get used t' havin' me around. Now, we can either be civil-tongued to each other or we can be ugly. I'm gonna leave that up t' you." Without waiting for a reply, she left.

"Annie?" Billy hollered just as she started out of the barn.

She paused, pivoted, and placed a hand on her hip. "What?"

The boy peeked at her through the slats of the stall. "Ya wasn't really gonna whup James Matthews a while ago, was ya?"

"Ya dern tootin' I was. If'n they woulda tried t' lay hands on ya agin, I woulda whupped 'em all good." She waited a short spell for some response. When none came, she whirled around and started for the house. "I need t' see t' supper now, Billy," she called without breaking her stride. "Come on in when ya get ready for me t' tend that eye, ya hear?"

Billy lumbered into the kitchen like an old bear an hour or so later. He took a chair at the table, and Annie set a bowl of what had accidentally turned into potato soup in front of him. He winced as his spoon touched his bruised lip, but swallowed the contents, then took one bite after another.

Annie stood back and silently watched him. Wasn't no sense in pushing the boy, she figured. He'd come around as soon as he was ready. But when he'd finished his supper, she fetched him a dish towel she'd soaked in a pan of ice-cold water from the springhouse. "Here," she said, kneeling beside him and pressing the cool rag to his injured eye. "Let's see what we can do about gettin' that swellin' down."

Staring at his empty bowl, Billy reached up, snatched the wet cloth, and held it in place himself. "I ain't no baby," he mumbled.

"Well, a'course you ain't." Annie's hand hovered above the boy's head. She had the strongest urge to brush the straw-colored hair from his forehead. Instead, she settled into the chair across from him and folded her hands on the table.

"I coulda licked James Matthews if'n those other two hadn't sided with 'im," Billy said to his bowl.

Annie nodded. "Sure ya could've. Ain't fair, is it? When three gang up on one."

Billy shook his bowed head ever so slightly, and a teardrop hit the tabletop. "Ain't nothin' fair about nothin'," he muttered, then rubbed his nose.

"You talkin' 'bout what happened t' yer folks?"

Billy's small shoulders shook, and Annie clasped her hands tighter to keep from taking him into her arms. "I reckon I know how ya feel, boy."

"You don't neither!" Throwing the dish rag on the floor, Billy banged his fists on the table and looked up. His red-rimmed eyes were filled with hate. "Ain't nobody can know how I feel . . . *nobody!* How could ya? Huh? How could ya know?"

" 'Cuz my own ma died when I was just a bit younger than you," Annie said softly. "Injuns hurt too, Billy. When something like that there happens, they hurt just the same as whites."

Billy jumped up from the table. "I don't wanna talk t' ya no more!" he shouted, then ran down the hall and slammed his bedroom door.

Annie sat and stared at the flame of the kerosene lamp for the longest time. She listened to the youngster's muffled weeping. She'd been angry with the world after her ma had died, same as Billy was now. She wished she could stop his pain. But no matter how much she wanted to help the boy, she knew the only thing that would heal him was time. The best she could do, she figured, was be patient with him.

Late the next evening, Eli came home. Annie hadn't ever been so glad to see anyone in all her born days.

He was tired and dusty when he walked in the house, his chin stubbled with whiskers. Annie met him at the back door, but he swerved wordlessly around her and sank into a kitchen chair.

"Ya want some supper?" she asked with her heart beating in her throat. She wanted to tell him she'd missed him and welcome him proper, but his brooding mood made him seem so unapproachable.

"No. Just a hot bath and some coffee if you have a pot brewed." He laid his hat on the table, closed his eyes, and rubbed his temples.

Annie hurriedly poured him a cup, then sat down in the chair next to him. She could tell he was bone-weary. He didn't appear none too happy, either. "Ya didn't catch Frank, did ya," she stated rather than asked.

He opened his pale green eyes and shook his head slowly. "No. Once we chased them into the Territories, they just vanished. There were no tracks anywhere. We questioned a couple of farmers and a traveling preacher we came across. But no one we talked to had seen or heard anything."

Annie nodded. "I reckon that there is the way things are in the Territories, Eli. Honest folks don't want no trouble from outlaws, so they keep their mouth shut and do what they're told. One of them farmers was more'n likely hidin' Frank and the boys in his barn.''

Eli quirked a corner of his mouth. ''It does me a lot of good to know that now,'' he said sarcastically, then took a sip of coffee. ''Where's Billy?''

''He's in bed.''

''Already?''

Annie glanced to the side. ''He's been feelin' a mite poorly since yesterday.''

''Is he sick?'' Eli frowned and set down his cup. ''You think he needs to see a doctor?''

''The boy's not sick, Eli, but he's got himself a perty good shiner and a fat lip.''

Eli tilted his head, looked at the ceiling, and worked his jaw in a perturbed fashion. ''He's been fighting again.'' He sighed deeply. ''I can't let him get away with it this time. I don't know what I'm going to do, but I can't let him go on bullying—''

''It weren't Billy's fault, Eli. Three bigger boys chased him home.''

Her husband slanted his gaze to her. ''They followed him home?''

''Uh-huh. But that deputy ya left here run 'em off.''

Eli straightened in his chair. ''Is Billy all right?''

''I reckon his pride's hurt more than anything.'' Annie lowered her lashes and twisted her hands in her lap. ''I s'pose I ought t' tell ya . . . it was because a me that those young'uns jumped him. They was callin' you a Injun lover fer takin' me t' wife.''

"Lord," Eli murmured, massaging the nape of his neck. "It's not your fault, Annie. It's mine. I should have talked to the boy. I should have warned him the other children might tease him. I guess I've had a lot on my mind lately. But I should have—"

"Now, sheriff, don't you go blamin' yourself." Annie rose, moved behind his chair, and started rubbing his shoulders. "You're plumb tuckered. Need t' get ya some rest. Ain't no more t' talk about no how. What's done is done, and there ain't nothin' wrong with Billy that a little carin' won't mend in time."

Eli's tense muscles melted beneath her soothing touch. He was tired of chasing ghosts. It was as if the unassigned lands of Indian Territory had simply opened up and swallowed the outlaws when they'd ridden across the border. Annie was right about people sticking together in the Territories. The man who'd killed Eli's parents had disappeared in the area years ago, just as the Calhoun gang had this afternoon. Though all Eli had to go on was unofficial reports and sightings, he was certain his father's murderer was still hiding out somewhere in the unassigned lands. But he'd find him. Someday, some way, he would flush the man out into the open, and when he did, his search for justice would be over.

For the moment, all he wanted was a little tranquillity in his life. He longed for the peace his vengeful heart wouldn't let him have . . . longed for a solitary night of sweet dreams instead of nightmares.

Closing his eyes, he let Annie's fingers work their magic across his sore shoulders. He drifted as close to a restful state as he had come in years. He could get used to this, he mused in his exhaustion . . . having a woman to come home to.

"That's better, ain't it? I can feel ya loosening up a bit now." Annie's voice was soft and smooth and hypnotic as she stroked the tendons on the side of his neck. "I'm gonna heat up some water for a bath, and I'll scrub yer back. That'll be nice, won't it?"

A lazy smile creased Eli's lips. The idea of Annie scrubbing his back strongly appealed to him, but he liked the thought of her joining him in the tub even better. He laid his head back against her midriff and looked up into her blue eyes. She was his wife. He could hold her in his arms all night if he wanted. Maybe she could chase the nightmares away. He reached up and grazed her cheek with his knuckles, and she smiled.

All of a sudden, Betsy's face flashed before Eli's eyes. . . . Quickly dropping his hand, he leaned forward and shrugged from Annie's touch. God in heaven. How could he have forgotten about Betsy? About the annulment? For a few senseless moments, even his burning need for revenge had been overshadowed.

"Eli? What's—"

"Go to bed, Annie," he murmured, pushing out of his chair.

"But what about your bath?"

"I'll take one in the springhouse," he said, then picked up his hat and strode out the back door.

Chapter 11

For the next few days, Annie saw Eli's mood sway like a swing in a strong wind. Sometimes he would stomp into the other room without saying a word to her. Then there were times when he'd been downright pleasant. Billy had just been quiet and kept out of sight. Annie kind of figured she had a lot to learn about sharing a house with the two. For the time being, she decided it was best if she simply stayed as cheerful as possible and let the menfolk be themselves.

During Saturday night's lesson, just about a week after she had become a bride, she painstakingly printed her name onto the slate tablet Eli had given her. She'd never felt such pride as she had when she finished the task, looked up at her tutor, and saw approval gleaming in Eli's pale green eyes.

He raised a brow, and a smile tugged at one corner of his mouth. "Woman, have you been sneaking around behind my back and practicing?"

Annie sat a little straighter in her chair. "Ever since you showed me how it was done, well, I studied on it, and tried doin' it myself whilst you were gone. I wanted t' surprise you."

Picking up the slate, Eli examined her work more closely with a shake of his head. "This is amazing, Annie. I only wrote it down for you once." His gaze met hers, and his smile grew wider. "This is a wonderful surprise. If you keep learning at this rate, you're going to be able to read a whole dime novel in a couple of weeks. I'm very pleased, very proud of you."

Annie bit the inside of her lip to keep from bursting. *She could read already.* Leastways, she was sounding out three-letter words. Her appetite for knowledge had increased with every lesson. Eli had promised to teach her numbers soon, and she could hardly wait.

She looked at him, attempting to convey all the love and gratitude in her heart. His patience and praise had made learning almost easy. She didn't know how she could ever repay him for this precious gift of wisdom he offered.

"It was you who done it," she countered softly. "I couldn't have never learnt all I did without your help. I'm . . . well, I can't think of words that can rightly say how beholdin' I am to ya." She dropped her head to hide the fire in her cheeks, but peeked at him from beneath her brows. "You got a powerful knack for teachin', ya know. You coulda been a schoolmaster, if'n you wanted."

Eli stared at her for a long moment before his gaze clouded and he took on a faraway look. "Funny you should say that," he whispered, though Annie wasn't quite sure whether he was talking to her or to himself. "That's exactly what I always intended to be."

"You . . . *wanted* to be a teacher?"

Eli returned from whatever memory held him and focused his attention on Annie. "Yep. I went to school in Boston with the grand idea of becoming a schoolmaster. I even have a certificate." He paused, glanced around the room, then frowned. "At least, I think it's still around here. Probably tucked away in a drawer somewhere."

Annie leaned forward, bracing her forearms on the table. "You mean to tell me, you went to school an' everything, and got papers a sayin' that you're an honest-to-goodness teacher?"

"Yes, well, that was . . . it seems like a lifetime ago. Now, where were we?" He picked up one of the books and thumbed through it. "We were studying vowels last night."

"Eli?"

"Hmm?" He was concentrating on a particular page. "Okay. I think we left off right about—"

"If you went and did all that studyin' to be a teacher, then why ain't you one?"

"It's a long story."

Annie leaned back in her chair and folded her arms over her chest. "I ain't got no place else I got to be directly. Do you?"

"Annie, I really don't think—"

"Is there some reason you don't want to

talk about it?'' Cocking her head, she squinted one eye.

''I don't recall saying I didn't want to talk about it,'' Eli said indignantly. ''It's just that we need to go over these vowels again if we're going to get anything accomplished tonight.''

''Well, you didn't have to say it.'' Annie shrugged. ''Just appears to me you're actin' a bit strange about the whole thing.''

''I am *not* acting strange.''

'' 'Course, I don't mean to pry. It's your own business. I reckon we all got things to hide.''

Eli slammed the book closed, leaned forward, and narrowed his eyes. ''I don't have anything to hide.''

''No?'' She lifted a brow.

''No.''

''Oh. Well, in that case,'' she said, propping her elbow on the table and resting her chin in her hand, ''I'd be real curious to know why you're a dang lawman instead of a teacher like you oughta be.''

Eli started to reply, but the words stuck somewhere between his mouth and his brain. He didn't know how he'd let the woman lure him into this conversation. He was amazed at her cleverness. He felt somewhat like a rabbit with its foot caught in a trap.

Yet, as he watched the lamplight reflecting in her round, expectant eyes, he found he wanted to tell her about it. He hadn't dwelled on his longing to teach in years, had simply shelved the dream away when he'd done his duty by following in the footsteps of the Larson lawmen. He hadn't ever told anyone—not even Betsy—about how hard his decision to exchange his books for a badge had been.

No one in Bartlett Springs would have understood. They all compared him to his father and grandfather . . . and to Tom. They all looked up to him as if he were some kind of town hero.

God, if they only knew how loath he was to draw his gun, how sick he felt when he was forced to pull the trigger.

None of them could understand. But Annie—

Annie was different from anyone he'd ever met. She looked at matters from a totally different perspective, took life as it came. At the moment, she sat there waiting patiently, quietly, for him to explain, and somehow he knew he could tell her anything. Though she would most assuredly make a comment, he knew she wouldn't be judgmental.

Eli inhaled deeply and traced a knothole in the tabletop with his fingertip. "I come from a long line of lawmen, Annie. My father, his father, and his before him, they were all lawmen. My brother—"

"Tom?"

Eli shot her an inquisitive gaze.

"I saw his photograph in the parlor," she explained, before he could ask. "Miss Bruecks told me who he was."

"Tom." Eli stared at the flaming wick of the lamp as he repeated the name. A slight smile tightened the corners of his mouth.

"We were a threesome, Tom, Betsy, and I. It was really Tom who Betsy was sweet on when we were growing up. He was six years older than we were, and we tagged along after him. But he never seemed to mind."

He glanced at Annie, blinked, and let go of the bittersweet memories of his younger days. "Tom," he said quietly, "was supposed to be the next lawman in the family. He was cut from the right cloth, more suited for the job. But he . . . he was . . ."

"He was killed in the war. Miss Bruecks told me."

Eli nodded, glad he hadn't had to finish the sentence.

With a pensive frown, Annie rubbed her knuckles along her jawline. "But you don't take too much to bein' a sheriff, do ya? It appears to me you still got a powerful yearnin' to teach school."

Eli raised his eyes by degrees. As he met her piercing gaze, he had the uncanny sensation of being stripped naked. For a split second, he wondered if she was capable of seeing inside him, of knowing his innermost secrets.

He shook off the notion and lifted his chin a notch. "I did what I had to do."

Annie merely stared at him for a long, disconcerting moment. "You know what Deadeye says, sheriff?" Her voice came softly into the stillness of the dimly lit room and was barely audible above the hum of crickets outside. "He says life is too dern short to let things you really want pass you by."

"Oh, for God's sake, Annie." Eli closed his eyes and massaged the bridge of his nose. "Why do you go around quoting that old man as if he were some Supreme Being? Huh?" He slid his hand up his forehead and back through his hair, looking at her. "How could a worn-out outlaw possibly know anything about duty and honor and responsi—"

"Deadeye ain't no stranger to duty. He's been around longer than you and me put together, and he knows plenty about a lotsa things." Straightening her spine, she tilted her nose up. "I reckon he knowed enough about duty when he rode with Gen'rl Lee. And I s'pose a man would have to savvy just a little bit of honor if'n he lost an eye fightin' for the Stars and Bars."

Eli noted the rise and fall of her chest as she took a deep breath, then went on. "And I'll tell you what. He woulda never joined up with Quantrill's raiders and took to being an outlaw if he hadn't gone home from the war and found his wife and baby girl dead and buried, and his place burnt plumb to the ground. Why, I'd bet a brand new buggy if his family were alive today, he'd be just as upstandin' as—"

"Okay, Annie." Eli held up a hand, halting her mid-sentence. "You've made your point. I was wrong to say what I did and I'm sorry." He focused on the tiny flame flickering from the lamp, and absently turned up the wick. "And I'm sorry about Deadeye's family. But we all have choices of whether to go one way or the other in life—"

"Now, see there?" Annie leaned back in her chair and threw her hands up. "That's exactly what I was just tryin' t' explain to ya. You still got a choice here. If a schoolmaster is what ya want t' be, then that there is what ya ought t' be."

"I made my decision a long time ago." Eli gave her a melancholy smile, and wished he could view the world through her eyes.

She stared past him. He could see her mind at work, and quickly determined to change the subject before she came up with another argument. "We sure didn't get much of a lesson in tonight, did we?"

Annie remained thoughtful as Eli stood and stacked his books. "There'll be time for learnin' tomorrow," she murmured, still half distracted.

"I'm afraid not. Tomorrow's Sunday. I make it a strict rule not to conduct any reading, writing, or arithmetic lessons on the Lord's Day." Taking her hand, he helped her from the chair, then tugged her out of the kitchen and down the hall.

"Get a good night's rest," he said as they approached her bedroom door. He started to let go of her hand, but her small fingers tightened around his.

The simple gesture was powerfully suggestive. A knot formed in Eli's chest, hard and heavy. He was thankful that the shadows hid her face . . . and his. The moment stretched and suspended in mid-air. His heartbeat became erratic, his breathing labored, while he wrestled with the wisdom of making her his wife in more than name only.

Oddly, it was Annie who solved the quandary for him. She must have taken his prolonged silence as a refusal, for she sighed deeply into the darkness, then withdrew her hand.

Eli was stunned, not only by her action, but by his own reaction. Somewhere deep inside, he had wanted her to try harder. He was struck with a sudden urge to take her in his arms.

"It's all right, Eli," Annie whispered, stopping him just before he reached for her. "I reckon you just ain't ready yet. And maybe . . . well, maybe I ain't neither. I s'pose we need to get to know each other better. Then . . . then . . . Well, g'night, Eli." With that, she stepped into her room and closed her door.

Eli stood rooted to the floor, trying to comprehend what had just happened, but came to the swift conclusion that he would probably never figure Annie out.

Over the years, loneliness had often attacked him, yet never with the intensity that it was threatening to now. He had endured those lonely moments, accepted the voluntary isolation by telling himself that someday things would be different. Someday, after he'd brought the man who'd murdered his parents to justice, he'd hang up his gun belt and settle down with Betsy.

Eli closed his eyes, realizing that all his careful plans were going astray. Everything was wrong. This wasn't the time to fall in love. And Annie certainly wasn't the woman he had always pictured spending his life with.

Restless and aggravated by his thoughts, he walked down the hall and grabbed his Stetson from the hat rack. As he passed Annie's room on his way out, he rapped lightly on her door. "I'm going into town for a while," he said without waiting for a response. "There's a latch on the inside of this door. Use it."

Eli's headache grew tenfold as he stood with the congregation and mouthed the words to the opening hymn.

His visit to Gracie's Palace the night before had been in vain. After six shots of whiskey, he'd been too numb to appreciate the efforts of Gracie's best girl. Moreover, while the painted lady had wriggled on his lap, he couldn't make himself forget the woman who waited for him.

His face felt overly warm as he gazed sideways at Annie. Despite his guilty conscience and throbbing temples, he had to stifle a grin. Her hymnal, he noticed, was open to the wrong page. Nevertheless, her voice rose above the rest, almost overpowering the church organ. Though she hit every note perfectly, the words to the song were all her own.

At the end of "How Great Thou *Are*" the good people of Bartlett Springs seated themselves, and Reverend Perry took his place behind the podium.

Eli aimed to concentrate on the sermon, but his attention kept straying. To his left, Billy fidgeted more than usual and constantly rubbed the toes of his Sunday shoes together. Though the boy's squirming during church had never bothered him before, this morning Eli felt obliged to nudge the youngster frequently.

And Billy was only a mild distraction compared to Annie.

She was on the other side of him, the skirt of her slate-blue dress brushing disconcertingly against his knee. No matter how hard he strove to look straight ahead, his gaze kept wandering her way. With her mouth slightly parted and her eyes wide, she sat perched on the edge of the pew, listening intently to the lecture on the wages of sin.

Reverend Perry wrapped up his sermon by saying that it made no difference who you were or what you'd done, God was always willing to forgive. Upon that conclusion, Annie leaned back in her seat and sighed audibly, forcing Eli to cover his chuckle with a cough.

After the service, Eli attempted to usher Billy and Annie out of the church as quickly as possible. He intended to avoid the townsfolk who whispered, nodded, and threw inquisitive glances their way. Unfortunately, his hasty retreat was stalled by Reverend Perry.

The elderly minister stood sentry at the

door, greeting each member of his flock. He ruffled Billy's hair as the youngster bolted outside, then peered pointedly above the rim of his spectacles at Eli. "Well now, good morning, sheriff," he said with a placid smile. "I understand congratulations are in order."

At a loss for words, Eli nodded and made an effort to return the clergyman's smile.

Reverend Perry's gray eyes twinkled as they slid to Annie. "And this, of course, must be the new Mrs. Larson. Welcome to Bartlett Springs, my dear."

Annie gave him a shy smile, then ducked her head.

"Why, she's lovely, Eli." The reverend slapped him on the back. "You're a lucky man, my boy. A lucky man. I shall include the two of you in my evening prayers and ask the good Lord to bless you with a long, happy, and fruitful marriage."

Eli ran a finger around the inside of his starched collar. "That's . . . very kind of you. Well, uh . . . it was good talking to you, Reverend." He pumped the minister's hand, then grabbed Annie and hauled her down the steps.

Ida Phipps sniffed as they passed by. Snickers and giggles rippled through the cluster of women around her. "Mornin', sheriff," one of them cooed, just to drive the insult home.

Eli bobbed his head in polite greeting, but steered Annie clear of any other town gossips. Moving swiftly in the direction of the buckboard, he scanned the church grounds for Billy. He spotted the youngster not far from the wagon, where several boys knelt in a circle, playing marbles.

"Billy, let's go," he called as he helped Annie onto the buckboard seat.

Billy lumbered to his feet and kicked at the dust. "Aw, Eli. We ain't even finished this here game. You al'wys let me finish at least one game."

At the end of his patience, Eli started toward the boy, but someone caught his arm from behind.

"Elijah Larson," the husky female voice boomed over his shoulder, "you mean to tell me you're gonna run off without introducin' me to your wife?"

Eli turned slowly, facing the short, buxom woman and her brood.

She glowered and shifted the baby she held on her hip. Nearly a half dozen kids peered around her ample skirt, and the tall, lanky man at her side nodded a quiet good morning.

"Well? What's the matter with you, Eli? Did you leave your manners home in bed?" Without giving him a chance to reply, she looked up at Annie sitting on the buckboard. "I'm Jane Scallon," she announced, her round, rosy cheeks lifting as she smiled. "This here is my husband, Harold. And this here is Dinah." She reached behind her, pulled the oldest girl into view, then proceeded to line the children up in order of height, like a set of steps. Moving down the row, she placed a hand on each child's head. "Janie, Beau, John, Mark, and this littlest 'un here is Timmy." She started to snatch the baby's thumb from his mouth, but Timmy hid his face in her shoulder.

"Proud to make your acquaintance, ma'am." Annie smiled in turn at the children. "You certainly got yourself a fine family."

"Why, thank you, Miz Larson." Jane puffed her chest out like a strutting pigeon. "Don't s'pose it'll be long 'fore you and Eli'll be havin' babies of your own. Bein' newlyweds and all." She gave Annie a knowing wink. "Harold and I weren't married two months when—"

Eli cleared his throat. "Jane, Harold," he said with a slight inclination of his head. "It was good to see you, but we need to get on home." He tipped his hat, then strode over to where Billy had resumed his marble game.

Moments later, when he returned with Billy in tow, he found Jane whispering with his wife. All he could catch of the conversation was Annie's reply of, "I'll remember that." Frowning, he lifted the youngster onto the flatbed of the wagon.

After shaking Harold's hand, he climbed up on the seat and took the reins in hand. Eli tipped his Stetson one last time to Jane. "You all need to come for a visit sometime," he said, merely to be neighborly.

"Why, we'll just do that," Jane replied. She glanced to the side as if suddenly struck with an idea. "As a matter of fact, I'll be takin' some fried chicken out to Betsy's today. I hear her paw ain't doin' good a'tall. That's no doubt why she missed services this mornin'. But, say, I cooked up enough to feed the Union Army. There'll be plenty for all of us, so we'll just plan on droppin' by this afternoon.''

Chapter 12

The bright sun warmed Annie inside and out on the long ride home. It didn't matter that her husband sat beside her brooding, or moved his leg every time her knee jostled against his thigh. She was in a particularly fine mood, and as far as she was concerned, nothing was going to spoil it.

She dropped her gaze lovingly to Eli's hands. Bracing his forearms on his thighs, he held the reins loosely between his long fingers. On impulse, she reached out and laid her own hand over his.

He flinched at her touch, and presented her with a frown.

"Eli, I'm gonna just bust, if I don't tell someone how good I'm feelin'. That was my very first time."

He raised a brow. "Your very first time?"

"To attend a prayer meetin'," she explained. "I mean, I used to sit outside the church in Dregg's Flat and try to listen, but I was always afeared to go in. They woulda run me off for sure. I knowed they woulda. They wouldn't have wanted me in there standin' alongside 'em. All them other little

155

girls, well, they had their hair in curls and were a-wearin' fancy dresses. It just wouldn't have been right for me to go in.''

Eli pressed his lips into a hard line. ''Annie, the house of the Lord is always open to everyone.''

''I know that now.'' She withdrew her hand and entwined it with the other in her lap. Straightening her spine, she smiled all the brighter. ''I thought for sure I was headed for hell. You know, for all them bad things I done? But did you hear what Rev'ren Perry said today? He said, 'All will be forgiven if'n you're sorry'—which I am.''

Eli's features softened as he stared at her. She thought he might've even looked a little sad before he turned his attention on the road ahead. ''I'm glad you enjoyed attending services this morning,'' he remarked quietly.

''Oh, I did. Rev'ren Perry was so nice to me afterward. And did you hear? He said I was lovely.'' She lifted her chin, striking a pose, then giggled. ''Cain't never imagine anyone thinkin' *I* was lovely. And did you hear him say he was goin' to pray for you and me? That was real nice, don't you think?''

Annie couldn't tell whether Eli smiled or grimaced, but his eyes never wavered from the dirt road. ''Yeah. That was *real* nice of Reverend Perry,'' he mumbled.

Annie took a deep breath and glanced around. The sky appeared bluer than she could ever recall it being. She was downright certain the trees and grass were greener than they'd been this time last year. Everything was nigh on perfect.

"I liked them Scallons, too," she commented as she scanned the countryside. "They got the prettiest bunch a kids I ever seen. I'm lookin' forward to them visitin' t'day."

Eli grunted, or groaned, or something, but Annie paid him no mind. "You wouldn't never have guessed Harold was a hanging husband, would ya? Jane saved him from hangin' just like you did me."

Eli cocked his eyes her way. "Did Jane tell you that?"

Annie nodded. "She also offered a few other encouragin' words."

"Like what?"

"Well—" Annie smoothed her skirt, wondering whether she ought to impart this tidbit of information, since it had been given somewhat confidentially. "Well, Jane tends to think these sorts of marriages can work out just fine."

"Oh, she does, does she?"

"Uh-huh."

Eli set his gaze on something in the distance. "Annie, you didn't—" He glanced over his shoulder at Billy, then continued in a whisper. "You didn't tell her we weren't sleeping together, did you?"

"Well, a'course not." She tucked her chin and peered at him from beneath her brows. "That there's sorta personal, Eli."

Annie hadn't never held a baby before, or even contemplated doing so until late that afternoon when little Timmy became restless in his mother's arms.

"He's sleepy," Jane said by way of apologizing for the fussy tot. "My milk dried up last week." She set up a furious pace in the rocking chair that Eli had brought out onto the porch, then nodded toward the creek. "You reckon the menfolk'll bring the young 'uns in from fishin' soon?"

Seated on the bottom porch step, Annie sighed. "They ain't been gone that long. Liable to be a while, I s'pose."

The baby let out a wail that made Annie grit her teeth.

"He just ain't been hisself lately," Jane remarked, and hoisted Timmy into another position over her shoulder. "I'll swan, there ain't no pleasin' him. None of my others cried this much. This 'un just plumb tuckers me."

Annie's heart went out to the woman. Jane looked so tired and frustrated. After a moment's consideration, Annie stood, dusted the backside of her skirt, then pivoted and climbed the steps onto the shady porch.

As she neared Jane and the squalling youngster, a few misgivings over what she was about to suggest fluttered inside her stomach. "Maybe . . . well, maybe I can help." Glancing from mother to child, she shrugged. "Got me a way with calmin' critters. Cain't never tell, it might just work with babies."

Jane slowed her pace in the rocking chair,

appeared pensive, then hopeful, then her face fell. "That's right kind of you to offer. But Timmy here, he won't let nobody but me and Dinah tend to 'im."

"Can I leastways try?" Annie bit her bottom lip and held out her arms.

Jane ran her fingers through the fretful toddler's curly brown hair. "Guess it cain't hurt none," she said as she halted her rocking and came to her feet. "Don't reckon he can yowl any louder than he already is."

Timmy ceased his bawling almost the instant he was thrust into Annie's arms. With his sobs reduced to short sniveling breaths, he pressed his tiny fists against her chest and leaned back to get a better look at her. Teardrops clung to his thick, dark lashes and rolled down his chubby cheeks with every blink. He seemed to be as fascinated with Annie as she was with him.

"Well, Lord a mercy," Jane murmured. "I ain't never seen the likes."

The youngster was only temporarily distracted by his mother's voice. He merely glanced her way, then stuck his thumb in his mouth and returned his full attention to Annie.

A strange, wonderful warmth floated around Annie's heart. Of their own accord, her lips curved upward as she stared at the child. Timmy was so soft, and smelled so clean and new, like something that hadn't ever been touched by human hands. It came to Annie that holding babies was something extra special. It weren't no chore like she might've expected. Felt as natural as could be, it did.

She eased herself into the rocking chair Jane had just vacated, taking care not to make any sudden moves. "There now," she said in the same soothing tone she used on ornery critters. "Ain't this better? Lots more peaceable, don't you think?"

Timmy's only answer was a quivering of his cheeks as he sucked harder on his thumb. He sat straight and stiff in her lap, still showing signs of wariness.

Annie began rocking slowly, softly humming a sweet song she'd once heard. In a matter of minutes, the baby laid his head against her breast. He curled up and snuggled closer, and the wondrous warmth inside Annie commenced to become an ache. Her voice cracked and warbled, though she continued the tune while she observed what surely had to be God's most precious creation.

Timmy batted his blue eyes twice, then gave in to slumber. As his breathing evened out, Annie's humming dwindled, but she kept rocking at a tranquil pace. Unable to do otherwise, she focused on his small, pretty features. "This here is what an angel must look like," she whispered, more to herself than to Jane.

Jane smiled, and her ample bosom rose with a deep sigh. "Ain't nothing quite comparable to a sleepin' child." Her gaze lingered on her son a moment longer, then she grabbed a quilt out of the same big basket that had earlier held fried chicken. "Much obliged, Annie," she said as she spread out the patchwork quilt in a shady spot on the porch. "I still cain't believe you quieted that young 'un. He won't even go to his paw." Coming to stand before Annie, she extended her arms. "Here. I know he gets heavy. I'll just put him down on his pallet."

Annie's eyes widened on Jane, then dropped to the baby again. "He ain't heavy." She tightened her grip on Timmy slightly. "Would ya mind terribly if I just helt him for a spell?"

Sleep taunted Eli that night, yet remained just beyond his reach. The house was quiet. He was so exhausted that he wasn't even bothered by the fact that his feet dangled over the end of the prickly sofa. He should have passed out hours ago. His brain, however, had persisted along the path of reliving each moment of the day.

He cupped his hands behind his head and watched images form in the darkness above. He saw Annie at church . . . saw her rocking the baby on the porch. He heard Billy and the other children squealing when one of them caught a fish. And he experienced every tender emotion attached to each scene all over again.

He had dreaded the Scallons' visit. He hadn't expected to have such a good time. But today had reminded him of lazy Sunday afternoons in the past.

This house had once been filled with

laughter. When his folks had been alive, company was welcomed often. There had been lots of warm, sunny hours spent splashing in the creek. Lots of fried chicken. Lots of laughter.

Eli sighed, craving an end to his thoughts. He had enjoyed this afternoon far too much, he only now realized. The wrong woman had been sitting on his porch. The laughing children who had surrounded him belonged to someone else. Still, he was being beckoned by family life. He was getting too used to having Billy around . . . growing too fond of Annie.

He shifted his weight on the tiny sofa. He was placing them both in a dangerous position. His mother had been the object of revenge against his father, simply because she was the most precious thing in Sam Larson's life.

Fortunately he wouldn't have to worry over Billy much longer. The boy's uncle was due to arrive any day to fetch the youngster back to Santa Fe. And Aunt Lottie would surely reply to his letter concerning Annie soon. Given the way she was learning and bettering herself, and charming everyone who gave her half a chance, she was bound to have the elite of Boston eating out of her hand in no time.

Yet his heart ached at the thought of sending her away. She was settling in nicely in Bartlett Springs, and would no doubt put up a fuss when he told of his plans.

Eli pressed his lips into a tight line. What

he had to remember, he told himself, was that he was doing the best thing for Annie. At the same time, another voice deep inside whispered that he was going to miss her like hell when she was gone.

The click of a door latch caught Eli's attention. Lifting his head, he pricked his ears. Bare feet padding against the hardwood floor trailed off down the hall in the direction of the kitchen. At the distinct creak of the back screen door, he sat up, quickly tugged on his boots, and grabbed his shirt.

The crescent moon lent little light to the darkness, but Annie's long white gown shone brightly. Eli spotted her moving down the trail toward the barn as soon as he walked outside. Staying in the shadows, he followed her.

While he slinked from tree to tree, a knot formed in his stomach. He couldn't believe what a fool he'd been. She was leaving. What other reason could she have for traipsing around in the middle of the night? Unless . . . could she be secretly meeting with one of the Calhoun gang?

All his suspicions were foiled when Annie stopped short of the barn and climbed up on the rail of the corral. Eli ducked behind a bush. Completely perplexed, he watched as she tilted her face to the sky and pressed her hands to her breast in a prayerful fashion.

Suddenly Annie cocked her head over her shoulder and looked directly at him, though how she'd pinpointed him in the depths of the night shadows he'd never know. "Wanna come join me, sheriff?" she asked.

Eli straightened from his crouched position. He stood momentarily squelching the awkwardness he felt at being caught. Then it occurred to him that he had every right to keep up with the whereabouts of his wife. With a lift of his chin, he jerked his shirt on and walked toward her.

He stopped beside her, braced a boot on the bottom rail, and hooked his thumbs through his belt loops. "Just what in the hell are you doing out here?" he asked, more or less to justify his own sneaking around in the dark.

Perched on the top of the fence, Annie was just about even with Eli. Her smile began in her eyes and gradually reached her lips. "Wishin'," she replied.

"Wishing?"

"Uh-huh." She pointed to the sky. "See that there star? The one that's the very shiniest of all the others? That there is what ya call the North Star."

Eli glanced from the star to her and back again, then quirked a brow. "I see it."

"That there's the wishin' star, Eli."

He looked at Annie and found her gazing up at it as if all her hopes and dreams hung suspended from that single twinkle in the sky.

"The night my ma died, whilst they were a-gettin' ready to bury her, Deadeye took me off inta the woods. We sat down on a fallen tree. He talked and talked, but I never heard much of what he was saying. Not till he showed the North Star t' me.'' She looked from the sky to Eli. ''Know what he said?''

Eli's throat had tightened to the point that he could only shake his head.

Annie's lips curved slightly upward as she looked at the star again. ''He said if'n I ever wanted something, anything at all, I just had t' wish for it. He said that anytime the North Star was vis'ble, if'n I wished with all my heart, my wish'd come true.''

Eli closed his eyes and rubbed his temples. He wondered if Deadeye had ever once considered how his ludicrous notions would affect Annie's outlook in the years to come. Hadn't the crazy old outlaw had any idea that he was giving Annie unreasonable expectations?

As Eli opened his eyes and saw her staring off into space, he felt obliged to set her straight. ''Annie, you're a woman now. When Deadeye told you what he did—well, don't you see? He was merely trying to console a grieving child. I'm sure he never meant for you to actually believe you could wish on a star and magically get anything you wanted.''

With her face still tilted toward the sky, Annie blinked twice, then slowly turned her head his way. ''Deadeye ain't never had cause to lie to me. He knows 'bout such things as wishin' stars, he does. Now maybe that there star—'' She pointed at it again. ''Well, maybe it don't give out wishes to them that don't believe. But for us that do, well, I'm here to tell ya, it works just fine."

"Oh for crying out loud, Annie. Listen to me—"

"No, you listen." She twisted around to face him. "I been wishin' for a good while, and every single wish has come true." Annie ran her tongue over her upper lip, and lowered her lashes. "I didn't b'lieve it at first, not till I found you near dead in the woods. Ya see, I wished for you to get well, and you did. I didn't know what else to do. You were bad with the fever, and tendin' you was the most notable thing I'd ever done. I hadn't been much good for nothin' up till then. Deadeye was the onliest one that had anything t' do with me. None of the others never paid me no mind. Even Paw . . . well, Paw favored Frank. Me, I was just in the way, just a half-breed. Frank's ma was a Kansas City dance-hall gal."

Annie looked up and smiled. "I reckon what I'm tryin' t' say is that carin' for you was important t' me. Made me feel like I had some sorta worthy purpose. And I never forgot ya, Eli. Ever. I thought about ya all the time." She bent forward and looped her arms loosely around his neck. "I wished for this, Eli. You and me. I wished that someday . . . somehow you and me would get hitched. So ya see—" She dropped her gaze to his mouth, and her smile wavered. "I . . . I done forgot what I was fixin' t' say."

Eli swallowed, hard. The strong scent of honeysuckle went straight to his head. She was too close. Too sweet. The night was too warm. And he was too worn down to resist her any longer.

Maybe if he kissed her, just once, he could get her out of his system. After all, this was merely . . . attraction. Everything about Annie was wrong for him. Kissing her would no doubt prove just that.

Slowly, he edged his face forward, searching her eyes for any objection. Lowering her lids as he neared, she remained perfectly still, not moving or breathing.

Her lips parted slightly as he touched his mouth to hers. A sigh combined with a faint moan escaped her, then she leaned into the kiss and tightened her grip on his neck.

Eli's eyes widened. No woman he'd ever kissed had actually *sighed* in appreciation, nor returned his courting with as bold a demand for more. The reasons for his caution suddenly evaporated, and he clutched Annie's waist and lifted her from the rail. Enfolding her in his arms, he deepened the kiss as her soft, supple body slid down the length of his. A fire ignited inside him, way down below where his gun belt usually rode. His last dwindling thought was that a little bit of Annie wasn't nearly enough.

Chapter 13

Annie closed her eyes and clung to Eli with all her might. His mouth moved over hers thoroughly, possessively until her lips softened and parted with the pressure. Something warm and wonderful moved inside her, made her weak-kneed and light-headed.

Deadeye had patted her shoulder upon occasion, but nobody had ever squeezed her like this. She had no idea hugging and smooching could feel so good. She was of a firm mind that she and Eli were going to have to do this sort of thing a lot. An awful lot.

Eli eased his tongue into the sweetness of her mouth and felt her breasts press into him. Her heart beat fast and furiously against his chest, making the fire below his belt burn hotter, brighter.

Annie caught her breath as he scooped her into his arms and headed for the barn. He kept on kissing her while he booted the rickety door open. It was cool and dark inside, but Eli didn't pause. He seemed to know right where he was going.

He collapsed on a bed of sweet-smelling

hay, taking her with him. They lay side by side facing each other. Annie's brain stopped working as his hand spanned her breast. She strained toward him, and he groaned.

She couldn't fathom much after that, except next she knew, she was on her back with the bodice of her gown gaping open. His breath came warm against her skin, leaving each place his lips touched tingling as he moved to another spot. She tossed her head and stirred with the strange awakening of new feelings his caresses brought about.

Annie couldn't have said how or precisely when he settled over her. He was just there, his heart pounding hard against hers. She wrapped her arms tightly around him, willing the moment to never end. She wanted to become part of him, be with him every second of the day. She had to tell him . . . everything . . . needed to share all her secrets.

"Eli," she whispered, and ran her fingers through his hair. "You wanna know what I was wishin' for tonight?"

He murmured something about being more interested in her kisses than her wishes, then covered her smile with his mouth. He had her near senseless again before he dipped down to graze along the side of her neck.

"A baby," she said softly into the darkness. "I was wishin' for a baby."

Eli's lips froze on her throat while the rest of him went slack. "A what?"

"A young 'un. Yours and mine, Eli."

He scrambled to his knees and sat back on his heels. Annie couldn't see his features, but his silhouette stood out against the pale moonlight coming through the open barn door.

"Oh, God," he said and ran a hand through his tousled hair. "That's what I thought you said."

Annie's stomach twisted. She'd done something powerfully wrong. The closeness they had shared moments before was gone.

"Eli?" She reached out, needing to touch him, desperately grasping for whatever was left.

As her fingers brushed his arm, he caught her wrist. In one swift motion, he hauled her to her feet and practically dragged her from the barn.

They were halfway to the house before she found her tongue. Digging her heels into the dirt, she jerked free of his grasp. "Eli, what'd I do wrong?"

"We both did wrong," he snapped, turning around. His gaze flickered to her open bodice, then settled on something in the distance. "Fasten your gown, Annie."

As she fumbled with the task, her fingers went as numb as her heart. "Was . . . was it the baby? I figured you'd want one, same as me, seein' as how you took to them young 'uns t'day."

His eyes glinted as he brought them to hers. "There's not going to be a baby," he said, then pivoted and started for the house.

"But I done made the wish. I don't reckon there's nothing' we can do to stop it."

Eli halted at the base of the stoop, but

didn't look back. "There's not going to be a baby," he repeated in a tight, controlled tone.

Annie moved quietly up behind him. "You cain't know that for sure, sheriff."

He whirled around at the sound of her voice and took a stumbling step backward. "Yes, I can. Damn it to hell, Annie, it takes a lot more than wishing to beget babies. A man and woman have to . . . to . . ."

"Tangle," Annie supplied. "Deadeye said that'd have to happen." She furrowed her brow. "But ain't that just what we was a-doin' in the barn?"

Eli closed his eyes. "There's more to it. A lot more that I'm not in the mood to go into right—"

Annie clutched the front of his shirt and pulled herself in close. "Show me, Eli," she whispered.

"No!" Eli's eyes flew open. He caught her shoulders and held her an arm's length away.

"But why not?"

"Because it's just not right, that's why."

"But we're man and wife. Deadeye says it ain't no sin if'n you're married. Show me how it's done, Eli. Please? Just once? If'n ya don't like it, we don't have t' do it no—"

"Don't!" Eli's fingers dug into her forearms. "Don't say another word. Not another damned word. Do you hear?" He glared at her for a spell before he exhaled slowly and loosened his grip.

He dropped his head back and looked up, and Annie watched his throat work convulsively. "There's not going to be a baby," he said hoarsely to the night sky. "Not now, not ever. Do you understand? You're not going to be here that much longer."

She nearly toppled as he released her. He caught her elbow to steady her. In the brief moment that their gazes met, he seemed to want to say something else. Instead, he climbed the stoop and went inside.

Annie didn't know how she made it into the house. Eli had lit the lamp, and sat with his elbows propped on the table, head in hands. She stood by the screen door, uncertain if she ought to be there. Yet she had to ask the question that was screaming in her head. "Why?"

Eli looked at her, and instantly wished he'd died in a shoot-out. She was trying her hardest to maintain the impassive expression of her Indian forebearers, but the misery in her eyes couldn't be concealed. *I never forgot ya, Eli.* Her flattering confession hit him again, only this time it stuck in his gut. "Annie . . . come sit down." His voice cracked under the strain. "We have to talk about this."

She hesitantly came forward and seated herself. Folding her hands on the table, she stared at the golden, dancing wick.

Annie's silence was more disturbing than anything she could have said. He'd never seen her so quiet. He shifted in his chair, searching for the right words. But deep inside, he knew nothing could make this easy for either one of them.

"Annie . . . I didn't want to tell you until all the arrangements were made. I wanted to

settle everything first." His heart split down
the middle at the way she sat completely motionless, acting as if she were only half listening. It was as if she'd put up a wall around
herself to stave off the blow. He started to lay
a hand over her entwined fingers, but she
slid them just out of his reach.

"I have an aunt in Boston," he said, forg-
ing on with no small amount of difficulty.
"You'll like Aunt Lottie. And she'll like you.
After the . . . the annulment of our marriage—"

Annie met his gaze, and blinked. "I don't
know what that there word means, but I got
me a purty good idea. S'pose you make it
real clear for me, just so's I know we're a-
ridin' along the same cattle trail here."

Though Eli opened his mouth, nothing
came out. The knot in his chest had leaped
into his throat, making speech impossible.

Annie narrowed her eyes. "Means we ain't
gonna be married no more. Ain't that right?"
She paused not quite a second for his response. "Well, don't it?"

The only affirmation Eli could give her was
a quick, jerky nod.

Her gaze inched away from his and settled
on the dwindling blaze of the globed lamp
again. She took a long shuddering breath. "I
ain't never heard tell a no place called *Boston*, Eli. And I don't give a mule kick whether
your Aunt Lollie, or whatever the hell her
name is, likes me or not. What I asked ya was
why." Her eyes glistened in the soft glow of
the room. "I mean, I know I ain't no beauty

like Betsy. And I cain't cook a lick. But I'm a quick learner. You said so yourself. And I'm a-tryin' real hard to latch on to what it takes to be a wife. I could be a good one, if'n you'd let me."

Eli swallowed. He grabbed both of Annie's hands, curling his fingers tightly around hers until she ceased her struggle to withdraw them. "This has nothing to do with Betsy."

"Yes it does," she said, and tried to pull away from him again. "You're gonna up and marry her soon as you're rid a me."

"Annie, I can't be married to anyone right now. Not Betsy. Not you. Not anyone. Understand?"

She shook her head no, and Eli realized she couldn't possibly understand when he'd given her no explanation. He brushed his thumbs across her knuckles. "There's something I've vowed to do before I can get on with my life," he murmured. One glance at Annie told him this abbreviated version of an explanation wasn't going to satisfy her.

The memory of his parents' death had been embedded in the back of his mind. Though he'd never forgotten that horrible day, he'd been careful not to dwell on it. And the bad dreams still came in the middle of the night.

His hands constricted around Annie's as if he could somehow draw strength from her reserve. He cringed at the prospect of discussing what had happened. He feared facing the past head on, yet he could think of no other way to justify the shattering of Annie's dreams.

"There's . . . a man I have to see brought to justice. From all I've found out, Garrett Buckley's been running from the law a long time. He supposedly killed three men before the age of eighteen, but was acquitted because his father was an influential rancher who had ties to the governor. But that didn't stop my father from going after him when Garrett rode into this county and nearly horsewhipped a fourteen-year-old boy to death. My father saw to it that he was sentenced to a good long stretch of hard labor. I was only eight or nine at the time, and Paw had forbidden me to go to the trial. But as they dragged Garrett from the courthouse, I could hear him yelling from where I stood across the street that he'd see Sam Larson suffer pure hell before he was done."

Eli exhaled deeply, and met Annie's attentive eyes. "And he did," he whispered hoarsely. "A few years later, Garrett escaped from prison and took up with a band of Yankee deserters." He dropped his gaze to the flickering lamp, and the shouting . . . the gunfire . . . and his mother's screams tore through him anew.

Suddenly he found himself speaking in a calm, faraway voice. "It was shortly after we'd gotten the news about Tom. We were all still grieving. Paw usually kept a gun in the house, but he'd had them out in the barn cleaning them when word came about Tom. He forgot all about that chore and spent the next several days trying to console my mother. I'd taken to crawling under the front porch to hide while I cried. Tom and I, we were about as close as brothers could be, but I didn't figure Paw would understand about the tears."

Eli focused on his hands entwined with Annie's, and noticed they had somehow changed positions. She was doing the holding now. The tender gesture comforted him, enabled him to continue. "I was almost twelve years old, almost a man, and I had disappointed my father before. He never said as much, but I could see it in his eyes when I'd flinch as I'd aim for the whiskey bottle he'd placed on a fence post, or when I made some excuse not to go hunting with him and Tom. I wasn't like them. A gun just didn't feel right in my hand. But I should have done something. I should have done *something* to stop those murdering bastards when they showed up here."

"Oh Lord, Eli." Annie squeezed his fingers. "You saw 'em, didn't you? You saw 'em kill your ma and paw."

He shook his head slowly. "I didn't see it happen. I was under that damned porch again when the six of them rode in shooting and hollering. I heard my father run out, heard his footsteps on the boards overhead. I guess he was trying to get to the barn. I don't know. But they were on him before he ever got off the porch. There was a struggle and they dragged him back inside."

Eli slipped his hands from Annie's grasp, leaned back in his chair, and closed his eyes. Beads of sweat formed on his forehead. He was quivering inside. He'd gone too far to turn back. He had to finish it—for his own sake now, as well as Annie's.

"They were in the parlor. One of the men said he'd come to show Sheriff Sam Larson how sweet revenge could be. All the sounds blended together then. The men laughing. My . . . my mother . . . screaming. And my father . . . For the first time in my life, I heard my father beg . . . *plead* with them not to . . . not to . . ."

His voice trailed off, but his father's exact words came forcefully to mind. *Garrett, for the love of God, leave her be. It's me you want. Please, oh, God . . . don't hurt her.* Eli pressed his fingertips to his closed lids to stop the sting of tears. "I couldn't move. I . . . just lay there under the porch, like the sniveling little coward I'd always been, and covered my ears."

The drawn-out silence that followed amplified the sound of bugs hitting the screen door. Eli never heard Annie move behind him, but her hands fluttered against his shoulders, then slid around his chest as she bent and rested her cheek alongside his. "You were just a boy, Eli," she whispered.

"I was almost twelve years old." There was an angry edge to his voice that he hadn't intended, but couldn't restrain.

"That ain't much older than Billy is now. Wasn't nothin' you coulda done agin' six full-growed men."

"I should've run to the barn for a gun."

Annie straightened and started combing

her fingers through his hair in slow, serene strokes that made him drowsy. "Even if ya had," she consoled softly, "even if ya had gotten yourself a gun, Eli, ya mighta shot one or two of 'em, but the rest of that bunch woulda wrestled it away from ya, and they woulda kilt you, too."

Eli's throat swelled shut. In that instant, he wanted more than anything to turn into her arms. He wanted to carry her into the four-poster bed and make love to her until the break of day. He wanted her to lighten the burden of his obligation, to help him forget the past.

But he couldn't forget.

The way she was touching him was torturous. It had him torn between duty and desire. Afraid he would fall the wrong way, he forced himself from his chair, letting her fingers trail down his spine when he stepped out of reach. He walked to the screen door and braced a palm against the frame. "I won't let it happen again, Annie," he said without a backward glance. "I've tracked them all down, except Garrett. Every single one of those bastards but him is either dead or behind bars."

Eli looked out on the hazy silhouette of trees lining the rolling hills, and inhaled the cool night air. "I'll get Garrett Buckley, too. He can hide in the Territories. He can change his name as many times as he wants. But someday he'll make a mistake, and when he does, I'll be there." Eli felt his jaw tighten and start to ache. "The law says I have to bring him in for a fair trial, and my conscience would never let me do it any other way. But if he escapes justice again, I don't want anyone else hurt. Do you understand? I won't have anyone else hurt.''

''You got a right to how ya feel.'' Annie's tone was subdued. ''But it appears to me a wife ought to be at her husband's side durin' troubled times. I can ride and shoot better'n most menfolk, Eli. Real fast, I am, on both counts. Ya might just be needin' me.''

''Damn it, haven't you heard anything I've said?'' Eli swung around and found her moving toward him with outstretched arms. ''Hold it right there. Don't come any closer.'' He pointed a finger at her as if that would stop her. It must have been effective though, because her footsteps dragged to a halt, and she clasped her hands against her waist.

Eli realized his mistake instantly. His command had stopped her in front of the lamp. The low light penetrated her white cotton gown and outlined every curve, vividly reminding him of the first night he'd brought her home.

Desire burned through him again, and he squeezed his eyes shut. ''Annie, you've got to stop this. Stop talking that way. Stop . . . *touching* me. I don't know what it is about you that makes me want you like I do, but God help me—''

His last words had slipped into his mind uninvited, rolled right off his tongue, and scared the hell out of him. He'd never been one to say anything without thinking it through.

Suddenly he couldn't take enough air into his lungs. He bumped the screen door open with his shoulder and hip. Distress hurled him outside, and he damned near tumbled off the stoop.

Chapter 14

The huge four-poster grew bigger when Annie crawled into it that night. Eli was lonely, too. She'd seen it in his eyes when he'd told her about his parents. She reckoned he had been lonely for a long, long time. Seemed he'd kept folks at a distance since he was a boy.

She tucked the covers around her and hugged her pillow, making believe she was wrapping her arms around Eli again. But it wasn't the same.

She laid a hand across her forehead, wondering if she might be coming down with the fever. She was hot, then she was cold. One second she'd feel terrible, and in the next she'd get hit with a sprinkling of pure pleasure.

It was for certain she wouldn't get a wink of sleep. Fever or no fever, she had plenty of thinking to do.

The wishing star had given her Eli just as she'd asked. It hadn't occurred to her to haggle for a blissful marriage. She'd loved Eli for so long that she'd sort of figured happiness would naturally spring up betwixt them. As it was, she reckoned making this union agreeable was going to be left up to her.

She thought and thought about the way Eli had kissed her. She went over and over every move he'd made that evening, what he'd said and how he'd said it.

Along about dawn, it came to her that it didn't make much sense for a body to kiss someone if he didn't cotton to her. Eli must've had some kind of feelings for her. Maybe love was too strong a word to use just yet. Still, he'd sure enough felt something.

Annie rolled over and nestled her cheek into her pillow. She was of a mind to believe that what was stirring inside Eli was the very beginnings of love. That notion lifted her heart and made her smile.

"There is so gonna be a baby, Eli Larson," she whispered ever so softly, then closed her eyes. "Fact is, there's gonna be a whole passel of 'em."

As the week wore on, Annie went about the business of showing Eli how handy she was to keep around. While she might not know everything a wife ought to just yet, she could still be useful, she figured.

So she commenced fixing up the place. After she picked up the clutter in the yard, she rummaged through the supplies in the barn, finding what was needed to fix the loose board on the porch. She whacked her thumb a couple of times before she got the hang of hammering nails. But by the time she got around to mending the barn door, her aim had improved considerably.

Eli appeared not to notice, but she knew dang well he did. One day she stood just out of sight at the window and watched him run a hand over the new hinges on the barn door. She also noticed him stopping to glance about the yard. And he couldn't have missed the new paint on the front porch.

He didn't comment on the work she did though. In fact, he didn't say much of anything at all. He gave her her lessons each night as usual, but always made sure not to get too close.

It was a mite hard for Annie to stay cheerful while Eli shied from her company, and Billy generally shouldered past her with some snippy remark. But she'd made up her mind to keep her spirits high, and wouldn't give in to low feelings.

When Friday arrived, she got a notion to ride into town. She came up with the idea that taking Eli lunch might be a nice, wifely thing to do. So she filled a basket with potatoes left over from supper the night before. She put in two handfuls of blackberries she'd picked behind the springhouse and a big slice of the bread that Betsy had dropped by.

Harnessing the mare to the buckboard was no easy chore. It took her a while, but she finally figured it out.

She hummed church hymns as she bumped along the dusty road. Wishing Eli hadn't buried her hat, she used her hand to shade her eyes from the bright sun and admired the colorful patches of wildflowers dotting the hillsides.

She pulled into town and left the buckboard at the livery. But as she strode from the cool shadows of the stables, a few misgivings quivered inside her. Staring down the street toward the jail, she wondered what Eli would say when he saw her. He hadn't been all that friendly lately.

Taking a deep breath, she fortified herself with the memory of his kiss. Then she shifted the basket in the crook of her arm, lifted her skirt, and stepped onto the covered boardwalk.

As she neared the general store, Mary Farguson came out and started sweeping the walk. Slowing her pace, Annie glanced down and checked her boots for any clumps of dried mud.

"Why, Mrs. Larson." Mary smiled, set her broom aside, and wiped her hands on the white apron she wore. "It's good to see you out and about. My, don't you look pretty."

"How-do, Miz Farguson." Annie greeted her with a timid nod and smoothed a stray hair away from her face, thinking she should've spent a tad more time tidying herself. She might've tried putting her hair up instead of pulling it back with a ribbon at her nape.

"Whew, summer's gonna be a hot one this year, I'm afraid," Mary commented, and plucked at her bodice. "Hasn't yet reached the middle of May and it's already warmin' up something fierce."

"Yes'm, I reckon so." Annie felt a little strange attempting polite conversation. Most any other storekeeps would've shooed her off the walk with the broom. She wet her lips and searched her brain for some agreeable remark to add to the discussion. "Um . . . there's a few clouds a-gatherin' to the west there." She pointed them out, and Mrs. Farguson stooped over and squinted at the sky. "Might just get us some rain later on t'day."

"Well, I certainly hope so." Mary straightened, and tugged at her blouse again. "We sure could use a good downpour to cool things off." She gestured toward Annie's basket. "What's that you got there?"

Annie switched the lunch basket to her other arm. "I . . . I brung Eli some vittles."

"Well now, that's nice." Mary cocked her head and smiled. "Tell the sheriff howdy for me, will you?" She picked up her broom, then glanced to the side as if another thought had come to her. "And you tell him I said you need a bonnet with summer coming on and all. Your face is going to blister. You tell him we got some nice, sturdy straw ones in just last week."

Annie nodded, then headed on down the walk. There weren't many stirring about with the day being so warm. A few folks mumbled a greeting as she passed. Most just gawked, while one or two others turned up their noses and looked away. But none of 'em called her no name or nothin'.

It felt a mite peculiar being treated respectable-like. She reckoned the good citizens of Bartlett Springs were fond of her husband, and figured that was the reason they didn't run her out of town.

Upon reaching that conclusion, she felt her chest commence to swell. She was Mrs. Eli Larson. She lifted her chin a notch and met the eyes of passersby, even chanced a smile a time or two.

Annie was stepping fairly high by the time she reached the sheriff's office. She ignored the stomach flutters that started up again when she opened the door and walked inside.

Eli looked over his shoulder from where he stood tacking a wanted poster on the wall. Hollis aroused from his nap with a snort. As the deputy's eyes widened on Annie, he quickly removed his feet from the desk, sat up straight, and ran a hand over his balding head. "Uh, afternoon, ma'am," he said.

"Afternoon, Hollis." Annie slid her gaze from the deputy to her husband and softened her tone considerably. "Afternoon, Eli."

"Annie?" Eli frowned and strode toward her. "Is something wrong?"

"Nope." It didn't take any effort at all for Annie to give him her best smile. She always felt like smiling when she was around him. She thrust the basket into his hands. "I just brung you a bite to eat, that's all. Figured you might be hungry."

Eli quirked a brow, then lifted a corner of the gingham towel covering the food. He nodded his head slowly. As he met her gaze, he did something with his mouth that Annie figured was supposed to be a smile.

"That's . . . uh, real thoughtful of you, Annie. But I've already eaten. I mean, I always have the daily special across the street at Maybelle's. Isn't that right, Hollis?"

"Hmm? Oh, yes ma'am, that there's a fact." The deputy shook his head up and down. "The sheriff here don't come in t' town without samplin' Maybelle's apple pie."

Annie was sure the upturned corners of her mouth quivered. Hell, she didn't know the first thing about conjuring up apple pie.

Eli must've noticed how his words had affected her, for he lifted the basket a little higher and his features brightened. "But this looks awfully tasty," he said, then set the vittles on his desk. "I believe I'll have some later."

In the long stretch of silence that followed, Hollis propped an elbow on the desk. While he idly scratched his beard, he glanced back and forth between the two.

Finally, Eli cleared his throat. "Did you need anything else?"

Annie shifted her gaze from the potbelly stove to the hat rack, then to the wanted posters, and finally rested it on her husband again.

"Miz Farguson says howdy," she commented, desperately groping for a reason to linger. "She says to tell you that I need me a bonnet t' keep my face from blisterin', you know, with summer comin' on and all. But truth be told—" She spread her arms wide and shrugged. "I'd just as soon have my old hat back. I can dig it up myself, if'n you'd just tell me where you buried my things."

Eli closed his eyes a second and edged his tongue along his upper lip. "Mrs. Farguson is right. You *do* need a bonnet, and I'll see to it that you get one, but right now I'm kind of busy." He gestured toward a stack of papers on his desk. "I have some work to do that's probably going to take me the rest of the afternoon."

"Oh. Well. I s'pose I ought to mosey on home," Annie said, but made no move to leave.

Eli nodded. "I think that's a good idea."

Annie turned, put her hand on the door-knob, and gazed over her shoulder. "Will you be comin' home early this evening'?"

For a few fleeting moments something settled over Eli's features. A look. The same one that had been present just before he'd kissed her out by the corral. Then he blinked, and the look was gone. "No. I'll be late."

They exchanged polite farewells as if they were strangers.

Annie's footsteps weren't nearly so spry when she left. She barely had enough grit to move herself down the walk in the direction of the livery.

Deep in thought, she didn't pay much attention to people she passed, just glanced at them occasionally. As she moved by a tall, lanky cowboy leaning against one of the clap-board buildings, he pushed away from the wall and blocked her path. "Afternoon, Miz

Larson," he said, and touched the brim of his hat. "It is Miz *Larson* now, isn't it?"

Annie stared up at him, trying to place his face, but couldn't recall ever seeing him before. He had a hint of meanness about him— narrow slits for eyes and a wide jeering smile surrounded by a black stubbly beard. Annie peered down at the two Colt .45s he wore low on his hips, and felt a tiny prickling at the nape of her neck. Gunslingers carried two guns.

She started around him but he sidestepped in front of her and caught her arm. "Whoa there, little lady. What's your hurry?"

"Mister, I don't know who you are or how you know my name." Annie set her jaw and glared at him fiercely. "But you'd best be ta-kin' your hands offa me, if ya know what's good for ya."

His chuckle sounded low and gritty, and he tightened his grip as she tried to jerk away. "Frank said you might kick up a fuss, but he never said nothing about you being so pretty."

Annie froze at the mention of her half-brother's name. Her heart pumped hard, pounding in her ears. "You tell Frank . . . you tell him to leave me be, ya hear? You tell him I don't want nothin' more to do with him!"

The man's smile fell into a hard line. "Look, lady, I don't want no trouble. So you just keep it down." As he made an intense survey of the area, he lowered his voice. "I don't care about your family squabbles with your brother. Frank sent me to find out where the holdup money is, and I got a fair share ridin' on your answer.''

''I don't know where it is.'' Annie pried at the fingers cinching her arm. ''That's the gospel truth, mister. I took a topple offa Ol' Blue and the bank bag went flyin'. Ain't nobody been able to find it. Now, dang it, you let me go.''

The midday sun glinted in his narrowed eyes as he glared down at her. Annie got chills.

''I think maybe we ought to continue this discussion in the alleyway, Miz Larson.''

Eli stood staring at the door of the sheriff's office, and fought the urge to call Annie back the moment after she disappeared from view. He glanced at the picnic basket on his desk, and his chest started to ache.

He was feeling all this anxiety, he assured himself, because he hadn't wanted her to leave thinking he was ungrateful. He ran a hand through his hair, and quickly disregarded the small voices inside that insisted there were other reasons as well.

She was trying so hard to put her lawless ways behind her. She'd put forth a genuine effort to make a new start. He just didn't have it in him to discourage her now.

With a deep breath, he strode to the hat rack and grabbed his Stetson. ''I'll be back in a few minutes, Hollis,'' he said, then headed for the door with absolutely no idea how to soothe Annie's hurt feelings without getting himself in hot water.

As soon as he stepped onto the shaded boardwalk, a commotion up the street caught his attention. Cussing a blue streak, Annie was clinging to the hitching post next to the alley. A tall stranger clutched her waist, struggling to pull her free.

Heat crept up Eli's spine, into his head, as he started forward, then loped into a run down the walkway. He automatically went for his gun, had it drawn and pointed at the man before he reached the two of them.

"All right, cowboy, that's enough of that," he shouted. "Let the lady go!"

The pair stilled in the midst of their grappling and turned startled faces his way.

"You heard me." Eli made a dangerous gesture with his gun. "I said let her go."

"Easy, sheriff." The stranger released Annie slowly, and raised his hands in measured moves. "I got no quarrel with you."

With labored breath, Eli stepped up to him. He pushed the barrel of his gun under the man's chin and backed him against the clapboard building. "If you've got a quarrel with my wife, mister, you've got a quarrel with me." A red haze coated Eli's vision. He felt a tightening in his jaw and chest, and cocked his gun. "I'm going to give you exactly three seconds, cowboy, to explain why you were manhandling the lady. And mark my word, you'd better come up with a damned good excuse, because right now I'm relishing the thought of putting your cold, stiff, grey body in a storefront window.''

The man stood motionless against the wall with his hands raised high above his head. His gaze slid to Annie and back again. Despite the beaded sweat on his forehead and the throbbing at the base of his throat, he grinned. ''Annie and I are old friends, sheriff.''

''He's lyin'!'' Annie cried, grabbing Eli's sleeve from behind. ''I ain't never seen him before t'day.''

''You hush, Annie,'' Eli commanded without a backward glance. ''I'll talk to you later.'' He pulled away from her grasp and eyed the stranger suspiciously. ''Mister, being acquainted with my wife doesn't give you the right to accost her. You still haven't given me reason enough not to put a bullet in you.''

''I didn't mean no disrespect, sheriff,'' the cowboy drawled lazily. ''She didn't say she was married. I was just trying to get her to have a drink with me, that's all. Hell, as I recall, Annie used to like a little roughhousing.''

''That ain't true! Dern you, you tell the sheriff that ain't so, you lyin' sonova—''

''Annie!'' Eli silenced her with a sharper tone than he was accustomed to using. The stranger's cocksure grin grew wider, and Eli's trigger finger started to itch. He had a burning desire to do the man in for the things he'd said about his wife.

Yet the cowboy's insinuations made him wonder just who was telling the truth.

At the edge of his vision Eli caught sight of townsfolk gathering around. Murmurs rippled through the crowd.

"Land's sake," someone whispered. "Have ya ever seen Sheriff Larson so riled?"

Eli dropped his gaze to the barrel of his gun that pressed into the man's throat, and suddenly realized how close he'd come to pulling the trigger. He took a deep breath to clear his head, and very carefully eased the hammer into a safe position. "What's your name, mister?" he asked, keenly aware of those watching.

"Harden, sheriff. Wiley Harden."

"I've heard of you. You're a hired gun."

"On occasion. I wrangle some."

Eli stepped back, withdrawing his gun from under Harden's chin, but keeping it pointed at his chest. "We don't have any use for a hired gun in these parts, so I suggest you get on your horse and ride."

"Fine with me, sheriff." Wiley Harden relaxed. "I was just passin' through anyhow." He lowered his hands cautiously, and, holding them a fair distance from his holster, pushed away from the wall. "I'd just as soon be on my way." The onlookers parted as he moved toward an unfamiliar stallion tied to the hitching rail.

Eli holstered his gun, but trailed the wrangler to his horse. "Harden," he said as the man climbed into the saddle, "don't plan on doing any wrangling near Bartlett Springs, understand? If I see you around here again, I'll run you in for disturbing the peace, accosting the ladies, and anything else I can think of."

"I hear you, sheriff." Harden reached up and tugged the brim of his hat, then grinned. "You'll tell the missus good-bye for me, won't ya?"

Eli checked the urge to jerk the hired gun off his horse and beat the devil out of him. Instead, he caught the stallion's bridle and glared up at Harden until the man's smile wavered. "Mister," he said in a low, dead-calm voice, "if you *ever* so much as look at my wife again, you'll be grinning in your grave." Turning the horse toward the end of town, Eli let go of the harness. "Now get the hell out of here."

Harden spat into the dust, snickered, then slapped his stallion's backside and rode off.

Eli stood in the middle of the street and watched him disappear. Without bothering to alter his expression, he faced the townspeople gathered on the boardwalk. "You all go on about your business," he said, then focused on Annie and strode purposefully forward.

The few stragglers scattered as Eli approached, grabbed Annie by the arm, and steered her at a swift pace in the direction of the livery. He wasn't unmindful of the fact that she had to almost run to keep up with him. At this point, he simply didn't care.

"Eli, I—" she began.

"Not here," he said out of the side of his mouth, keeping his eyes straight ahead. "Not a word. We'll discuss this when I get home this evening. Lord knows we've given them enough to gossip about for one day."

Annie held her tongue, trying to match his stride until they entered the cool, shadowy interior of the livery. Then her footsteps dragged.

Eli guided her to the buckboard and swung her up onto the seat. "Go on home," he said. "I'll settle the bill with the stable boy."

"He was lyin', Eli." Annie's quiet, shaky remark stopped him as he started to walk away.

He turned around slowly. She sat with her head bent, twisting the sides of her skirt, and he silently cursed himself for being so affected by the sight of her.

Then pure fury stirred his insides. He moved forward and caught the side of the buckboard seat. "Damn it, Annie," he whispered, "I can't say what happened out there a while ago. All I know is that I almost killed a man in cold blood. He wasn't even going for his gun and I had him backed against the wall, ready to shoot. Do you understand? I may have lost my nerve a time or two while I was aiming a gun at some poor soul, but I've never lost my temper. Never. Today, I almost killed that man because I couldn't bear the sight of his hands on you."

"That sonovabitch was lyin'," Annie repeated, and lifted her gaze to Eli's.

Eli stared into her blue eyes for a long moment before he realized that, somehow, she'd conned him once more into confessing his innermost feelings.

Anger seized him all over again, and he pushed away from the wagon, wanting to strike out at the object of his confused emotions. "I'm not so sure anymore who's lying, Annie," he said. "Maybe *you* are. Maybe you've been lying to me all along. Now you go on home and stay there, you hear?" He whacked the mare's rear before Annie could reply, sending her on her way.

Chapter 15

A nnie held the reins slack between her fingers while the mare followed the road home out of habit.

Annie was aware that the sky had gone gray to suit her mood. She heard the thunder rumble, but was inside herself, and took no notice of the rain until it had soaked through her clothes and chilled her bones.

Lightning flashed, turning everything bright white. The mare whinnied and broke into a trot. Annie blinked as huge raindrops hit her lashes and streamed down her cheeks.

Her heart was a hard lump and had settled at the base of her throat. Eli had looked at her with pure venom blazing in his cool green eyes. She couldn't fathom what he had meant by accusing her of lying to him all along. It pained her sorely that he'd come up with the notion that she hadn't been truthful with him.

Annie shivered, though not from the damp cold.

She should have foreseen what had happened today. She should have known her half-brother would send someone to nose around. Frank had a greedy streak as wide and deep as the Cimarron River. The more money he stole, the more he yearned for. It had been plumb foolish for Annie not to figure he'd come after the bank bag.

And come he would. Annie reckoned it was just a matter of time before he showed up himself. And when he did . . . oh Lord, when he did, he'd be sure to muddle things up betwixt her and Eli—even more than they already were.

A dull ache commenced behind Annie's eyes. Seemed Frank had put a hex on near everything pleasurable she'd ever latched on to. One way or another, he'd always robbed her of whatever she'd held dear.

Through a blur of confusion and pelting rain, Annie saw the turnoff to Eli's place just ahead. On impulse, she tightened her grip on the reins and guided the mare past the dirt drive.

Fear spindled through her as she moved down the muddy road. Glancing sideways at the border of Eli's property, she surveyed the area for any signs out of the ordinary.

At this very moment, Frank could be hiding among the trees. He could be in the house. He knew where she was now. He knew she'd married the sheriff. And Frank wasn't one to stand idly by and be crossed. He would come after her. Sure as hell, he would.

Annie came to her senses suddenly. She didn't have the slightest idea where she was going. The rain was coming down in sheets, blinding her. With each flash of lightning and clap of thunder, the mare bolted. The horse was liable to break a leg if she didn't hole up somewhere soon.

Wiping her eyes, she squinted and could barely make out a small farmhouse just ahead. Maybe the owners would give her shelter in the barn until the weather cleared.

She pulled the wagon into a small shed beside the house. Then she hopped down off the buckboard seat and made a dash for the porch, figuring she ought to ask the farmer if he'd mind her staying there for a spell.

She rapped hard on the door to be heard above the thunder. Her fist stilled in mid-air as the curtain was drawn aside and Betsy's face appeared in the big oval window. Annie was about to turn tail and run when Miss Bruecks swung the screen door wide open.

"Gracious sakes alive," the woman cried, tugging Annie inside. "You're soaked to the bone."

Betsy hustled her into a warm, cozy kitchen filled with the cinnamony smell of baking. She settled Annie in a ladder-back chair by the wood stove, left the room momentarily, and returned with a quilt.

"Here," Betsy said, draping it over Annie's shoulders. "Get those wet things off this instant."

Annie felt like a fool, but obeyed. Beneath the cover of the quilt, she stripped off her clothes and handed them one by one into Betsy's waiting hands.

Miss Bruecks went about the business of

spreading each piece about the kitchen to dry, then turned and cocked her head. "Annie, what on earth are you doing out in this weather?"

Annie stared at Betsy. She wasn't quite sure herself why she'd done what she'd done, but she couldn't tell the woman that. So she blurted out the first answer she could think of. "I . . . come over to . . . to see if'n you might learn me t' cook apple pie."

"Apple pie?" Betsy furrowed her brows. "You rode over in a storm like this to ask me that?"

"It's a favorite of Eli's." Annie dropped her gaze from the woman's skeptical expression. Miss Bruecks clearly wasn't swallowing a word of this.

"Annie?" Betsy put her hands on her hips. "There's something else, isn't there? Something's wrong."

Annie clasped her hands together in her lap and studied them. "Yes'm. I reckon a whole lots has gone wrong t'day," she said, then frowned and tried to decipher why she'd felt so dang compelled to confide in a rival.

Thunder cracked overhead. Lightning lit up the kitchen, and the pitter-patter of rain on the roof accelerated into a downpour.

"Pull your chair up to the table," Betsy said softly. "I need to check on Paw. But I'll be right back and fix us some nice hot tea. Then we'll have ourselves a good long talk."

Miss Bruecks left the room, and Annie gazed at the ruffly blue gingham curtains on the window, wondering what the hell she was doing here. She was out of place in this sweet-smelling kitchen, and had no call to bother Miss Bruecks with her worries.

Annie was on her feet and headed toward the door when Betsy came back. Miss Bruecks raised a brow. "Annie, you can't possibly be thinking of leaving in this gully-washer."

Annie sunk her hands in the folds of her skirt, looked down, and noticed mud dripping off her boots onto the floor. "I'd best be gettin' on home. I . . . I done made a mess of your floor. Besides, I reckon you got plenty t' do."

"Nonsense." Betsy hooked an arm through hers and guided her to the table. "The floor will wash, and I haven't had company in a month of Sundays. Now you just sit yourself down and visit with me a spell," she said, maneuvering Annie into a chair.

Annie watched as she moved to the stove and put the kettle on. Betsy glanced over her shoulder while she reached into the cupboard and took down two cups and saucers. "I don't mind telling you, it gets a mite lonely way out here at times. Folks used to drop by often before Paw got sick, but—" She shrugged and brought the cups to the table, slid into the chair opposite Annie, and smiled that bright, beautiful smile of hers. "Well, I'm glad you've come, that's all."

Annie looked into her warm brown eyes and suddenly realized there was a woefulness hiding behind all of Betsy's brightness, though she couldn't imagine what the cause of it could be. Miss Bruecks was everything Annie wasn't. Beautiful. Poised. A good cook. Educated.

A muffled coughing came from somewhere in the house. Worry passed over Betsy's pretty features and she excused herself.

Annie rocked back in her chair and observed as Betsy tiptoed down the hall, then opened a door and peered into the room. Setting her chair back on all four legs, Annie recalled that Betsy's paw was bedridden. No doubt that was the cause of Miss Bruecks's woe.

"He's still sleeping," Betsy said when she reappeared in the kitchen. She poured them both tea, then took her seat again. "You know, Annie, it's good to have a friend to talk to when things don't go just right."

She left Annie no choice but to agree. One remark led to another, and somehow, before she knew it, Annie found herself telling Betsy precisely why she was so downhearted. Once she started talking, she couldn't stop. The words poured out of her mouth. She told Betsy everything . . . how Wiley Harden had lied and Eli had accused *her* of not telling the truth, even that she feared Frank would soon be coming after her.

Betsy reached across the table and patted her hand when she was done. "Menfolk are strange creatures, Annie," she said. "I'm apt to believe that they often act exactly the opposite of how they're actually feeling. I suspect Eli did just that today, knowing him as I do."

Annie glanced up at Betsy, expecting to catch a possessive look on her face. But all she saw were those steady brown eyes that still held something a little sad.

"You need to tell him about Frank as soon as he gets home this evening," Betsy went on. "And you be sure to tell him what that man Harden said to you. He'll understand, and he'll know what to do about Frank. Eli's a good man, Annie. He won't let anyone harm you."

Annie slipped her hand from Betsy's grasp. She toyed with the top button of her blouse as she avoided Miss Bruecks's gaze. "I . . . I oughtn't to have voiced all these complaints to you, not with the way things are betwixt you and Eli."

"The way things are?"

Annie shrugged. "I mean, well, I knowed you two were promised afore he married me."

"Oh . . . Annie." Betsy sighed, propped her elbow on the table, and cupped her chin. "I'm not sure I know how to put this. I guess I never really thought about it until you came along. You see, everybody in town just naturally assumed Eli and I would marry someday. Including me. But, you know what? He has never come right out and asked me. Even if you'd never come to town, I don't think we would have done it." She looked out the window, seemingly mesmerized by the steady rainfall. "There has always been something keeping us from walking down the aisle. His damnable duty to uphold the law. My paw falling prey to sickness. But not until Eli married you did I realize it wasn't really any of those reasons that kept us apart.'' Betsy met Annie's gaze and smiled serenely. ''Don't you see? I should have been jealous of you and I wasn't. Instead, I found myself hoping you would make Eli happy . . . give him all the love he deserves.''

Annie blinked, absorbing Betsy's confession. She'd often wondered why the woman had been so kind to her.

Betsy reached out and squeezed her hand. ''I do love Eli, Annie. But not in that special way I suspect a woman ought to love the man she plans to marry. I never have. It was always Tom I loved in a very special way. Maybe I just wanted Eli to take his place. But I just can't imagine lying beside Eli . . . or bearing his children. He's too good of a friend—more like a brother to me. But I've never been able to tell him so.''

Thoughts and questions whirled in Annie's head, though she couldn't verbalize any of them. She merely parted her lips and stared as if the woman had up and sprouted wings.

They sat in silence for several moments. Draining her teacup, Betsy looked out at the storm again and finally said, ''We needed this rain. But rainy days bring about a gloominess that tends to stir up all our troubles.'' Turning away from the window, she gave Annie that lovely smile that she alone could produce. "You know what I always do during troublesome times?" she asked.

When Annie shook her head no, Betsy stood and walked over to the cabinets. She opened the pantry, snatched a clean apron from a peg, and tossed it to Annie. "I always bake a batch of apple pies. Would you care to help while your clothes dry?"

It had quit raining by the time Annie left the Bruecks farm. A bright ray of early evening sunshine slanted between the few remaining clouds.

Annie inhaled the fresh, clean air and walked alongside the horse so the wagon wouldn't get stuck. Her boots sank into the mud as she steered the animal clear of puddles and ruts in the road. But she didn't much mind getting the hem of her dress dirty. Her spirits had lifted considerably.

Betsy had been right about tapering your troubles by fixing apple pies. Annie had found peeling and slicing apples to be a soothing task. She had enjoyed rolling out the crust. Meanwhile, Betsy had chattered about what she had planted in her garden this year, the upcoming barn dance, and such things. The two of them had talked and laughed and forgotten all their worries.

As Annie rounded a line of trees, she spied a huge arch of pink, green, and yellow streaking across the sky, hovering just above Eli's property. She hung her heart on that rainbow, taking it for a good omen. While she walked along, she watched the colors blend into the purple shades of dusk that were just beginning to darken the sky.

Annie turned into the drive, and something special wriggled inside her. She could hardly wait to give Eli her peace offering. She figured there was no way he could keep his dander up once he saw what she'd brought him.

She clicked her tongue and tugged the mare forward, but the sludge that had collected on the wagon wheels didn't allow them to move any faster. When Annie crested the ridge where the house came into view, she ceased her attempt to hurry.

Eli's tall figure stood outlined on the front porch. Annie didn't have to see his features to know he was in an uproar. She could tell he was in a right foul mood by his hands-on-hips stance.

He came down the steps, striding toward her like the devil himself, and met her halfway to the house.

"Where in the hell," he asked as he snatched the reins from her hand, "have you been?"

Annie gazed at him, and suddenly decided she didn't like his sour expression at all. She didn't much care for his tone, either. She set her chin at a haughty angle. "I been over t' Betsy's a-learnin' myself how t' cook."

While Eli stood there with his jaw dropped, she retrieved the pie she had wedged underneath the seat. As she climbed down, she waved the towel-covered pastry pan under his nose, then headed for the house.

"Annie!" she heard him call, but she refused to turn around. "Damn it, Annie, you come back here!"

His hollering faded farther into the distance with every step she took. When she reached the porch, she glanced over her shoulder and smiled, for it appeared Eli's curses were now directed at the mare as he struggled to guide the wagon toward the barn.

Billy was at the table, finishing his third piece of pie when Eli came in, slamming the screen door behind him. Annie busied herself, shying from her husband's scowl. She could feel Eli's glare pierce her spine while she puttered around the kitchen.

"Billy." Eli's voice reverberated with anger. "Go do your chores."

"Aw, Eli, I ain't done with my—"

"Now!"

Billy hopped up from his chair, gobbling the last bite. He dragged a cuff across his mouth, glancing from Annie to Eli, then frowned. "Um . . . Miss Annie?"

Annie faced the boy, careful not to let her gaze linger on Eli.

"Miss Annie," Billy repeated, then hedged toward the door. "Well . . . um, that there was—" He grimaced as if the words pained him. "That there was the best dang supper I ever had," he finished in a rush, then burst outside and took off running.

Annie placed a hand against her midsection. She'd been hoping Billy would come around. But she hadn't expected that a curt compliment from him could make her heart sway so.

She looked at Eli, but his dour expression put a quick end to the beginning of her smile. "You ready for your supper?" she asked, arching her brows.

"What I'm ready for is some honest answers."

"I can explain everything," Annie said, instinctively shrinking away from him when he advanced and took hold of her arm.

He ushered her to the table, pressed her into a chair, then seated himself across from her and lit the kerosene lamp. "Okay. Explain. Why don't you start with why you decided to trot over to Betsy's when I distinctly told you to come straight home." He leaned back, folded his arms over his chest, and gave her a grim smile. "Then we'll get around to the rest of it."

Annie dropped her head, rubbing her moist palms together in her lap. "Eli . . . I knowed I done wrong by not heedin' you like Mr. Farguson said I oughta when he up an' married us. I got a world of regrets over it, I do." She glanced at her husband, then wet her lips. "But the closer I got to home . . . well, I just got this terrible notion that Frank was here a-waitin' for me. And I was afeard, Eli. I was afeard he'd done come t' take me away."

"Annie—" Eli tightened his mouth in an agitated manner and glanced around the dimly lit room. "Where in the hell did you get such a notion?"

Annie took a deep, shuddering breath. "From that gunslinger, that's where."

"Wiley Harden?"

She nodded. "Frank sent him, Eli. He sent him t' find out where I hid the bank money."

Eli narrowed his eyes. He stared long and hard at her. She could see his mind at work, could tell what course it was taking. She started shaking her head slowly a fragment of a second before he spoke.

"So help me God, Annie. If you've known all this time where that money is—"

"Eli, I didn't . . . I don't—"

He jabbed his finger forward, cutting her sentence short. "You listen to me. And listen good. The folks in this town have taken you in. Most of the people who've treated you kindly had their life savings in that bank. So if you've ever truly wanted to do something decent, you tell me, right now, where you stashed that money."

Annie blinked back the sting of tears. She looked past her husband, out the screen door, and focused on the dark silhouette of rolling hills beyond. "I swear on the Good Book, Eli, if I knew, I'd tell ya."

Eli ran a hand over his face in apparent exasperation. "Damn it, Annie, that money couldn't have disappeared into thin air. Yet my men and I combed the area thoroughly and found nothing. Now, you *have* to know where it is, and all I'm asking—"

"But I don't," Annie whispered fiercely, meeting his gaze. "I swear to God above, I don't." She closed her eyes a moment, and steadied the trembling of her chin. "I know it sounds plumb crazy, but it's as if the bank bag *was* just spirited away somehow. I recollect holdin' it in my hand when I flew off Ol' Blue. When I come to, it was gone." She searched Eli's face for signs that he believed her, then sighed. "I'm gonna be honest with ya, 'cuz I know that's what ya want me t' be. I woulda hid it . . . If I coulda found the money and had the time, I woulda hid it. But fact is, my brain was just startin' to work agin when y'all rode up."

Eli lowered his head and massaged the bridge of his nose. "Why didn't you tell me about Harden this afternoon?" He looked at her from beneath his brows. "Why didn't you tell me Frank had posted him in town while I had Harden there and could've questioned him?"

"You said not to say anything, Eli . . . kept tellin' me t' hush and all."

Eli muttered a curse, then ran his hand up his forehead and back through his hair.

The creak of the door turned their attention to Billy as he shuffled into the kitchen. He stopped just inside, stuffed his hands into the pockets of his overalls, then stared at his shoes. "I done my chores, Eli," he mumbled, glancing at him, then at Annie. "And, uh . . . since y'all are havin' yourselves . . . um, a grown-up talk, I reckon I'll get on t' my room and do my lessons."

"Billy," Eli said, stalling the boy's hasty exit.

Billy turned to face him. "Yes, sir?"

"I wasn't angry with you a while ago, son. Annie and I . . . well, we needed to discuss some things, you understand?"

"Yes, sir, I reckon I do." Billy shifted his weight, then scratched his ear. "My ma and paw? They had these talks sometimes, and I had to go sit on the porch. When Paw came t' fetch me, he'd always ruffle my hair and tell me women was worth the trouble." The boy's eyes glistened in the lamplight with a distant image only he could see, then his lips curved slightly upward. "Well, g'night, Eli. Miss Annie."

"Good night, son," Eli said.

"Night, Billy," Annie echoed, and twisted in her chair to watch the boy disappear down the dark hall. She had the oddest inkling that Billy was siding with her for some reason. Puzzled over why the boy had suddenly decided to switch mules where she was concerned, she quirked one side of her mouth, then swiveled back around toward the table.

Eli stared at the empty doorway, apparently in deep thought.

"Is anything wrong, Eli?" Annie asked.

"Hmm? Oh . . . no. It's just . . . well, that's the first time Billy has mentioned his parents. I was beginning to worry about him."

Annie smiled. "Well, now see? I told you the boy would come around. You're good with young 'uns, you are. I reckon all it takes sometimes is somebody a-carin' for ya t' make ya come outside yourself. Leastways, that there is what I figure you done for Billy. Betsy was right about you, you know. She said you was a good man, and ya are. Got you a heart as big as Texas, you do. And you're smart. I reckon Betsy was right about you knowin' what to do about Frank, too.''

Eli blinked, then slid his gaze from the doorway and settled it on her. "What?''

"I said, Betsy was right about you knowing—''

"Never mind.'' He stopped her with a raised hand. "I heard you. You mean you told Betsy about Frank?''

Annie nodded.

"And Wiley Harden? Did you tell her about what happened in town today?''

His expression made Annie bite her bottom lip. "Well, you ain't never bided me not to talk to Betsy.''

"Oh Lord. You did.'' Eli ran a hand over his jaw. "Hell, you might as well have gone to the *Bartlett Springs Gazette* so they could print it in tomorrow's paper.''

Annie felt pressure against her chest. All at once, the kitchen didn't have enough air to breathe. "I done wrong agin, Eli,'' she said, glancing wildly about the room. "I'm sorry . . . I . . . I'm so sorry. I'm tryin' t' do right. I don't mean t' rile ya all the time. I want things t' be different. I want ya to—''

"Annie. *Annie.*'' Eli reached out and brushed his fingers along the side of her face. She stilled at his touch and leaned into his palm. "Shh . . . it's okay. You haven't done anything wrong," he said, making tranquillizing circles with his thumb against her cheek. "Everything you do . . . everything you say is so straightforward, so direct and uncomplicated. You're beautiful, Annie, inside and out. And you're wise. Don't you see? It's me. Understand? Not you. *Me.* I . . ."

His words trailed off, but the warmth of them lingered in Annie's ears. And where his voice left off, his eyes took over, sending messages that Annie was certain came from his heart.

"God, Annie," he whispered, and his throat moved convulsively. "I wish things could be different, too. I wish . . ."

As if suddenly startled from the depths of a dream, Eli widened his eyes. Then it looked to Annie as though a veil covered his gaze. An instant later he closed his lids.

Slipping his hand from Annie's cheek to the back of her neck, he pulled her forward and touched his forehead to hers.

Annie's pulse quickened. She remained motionless with her eyes closed, cherishing the moment of closeness, praying it would last forever and a day.

She didn't budge, not even when Eli's breath grazed her skin as he chuckled. When the chuckle progressed into laughter, she laughed, too, because she had no other choice.

"Oh, Annie," he said, giving her neck a squeeze. "It's not going to make one damned bit of difference whether you told Betsy or not. You know why?"

They parted, both straightening in their chairs, and Eli threw his arms wide. "Because Ida Phipps will surely have the story about Harden spread all over town by tomorrow morning. And the way she blows things out of proportion, I can just imagine—" He chuckled again and shook his head. "In her version, undoubtedly I will have pistol-whipped some poor, mild-mannered traveling salesman."

"Why, Eli, there ain't nothin' funny 'bout a body spreadin' untruths," Annie commented, but couldn't stop the corners of her mouth from twitching when he laughed all the harder.

"Oh, but there is. Everyone around here knows how Ida is. Nobody ever believes her."

Annie rolled her eyes and shook her head. She couldn't suppress a giggle or two, however, as she watched her husband's mirthful mood dwindle.

Silence hung heavy once Eli's glee had died down. To hurry the awkward stretch along, Annie pressed back in her chair and slapped her knees. Then she rose and went to the cupboard. "Well, how 'bout having our supper now?" she suggested, pivoting with the towel-covered pastry tin in hand.

Eli's face lost all traces of his former humor. "Oh, no. Thanks, but I'm not very hungry and I'd better—" He pointed a thumb over his shoulder. "I think I'll just go on out to the barn and turn in."

Annie arched a brow, walked to the table, and set the pan down in front of him. "You sure?"

Eli nodded. "I'm really tired and—" He stopped mid-sentence, sniffed the air, then lifted a corner of the towel. His eyes gleamed as he peered up at Annie and grinned. "Is this *apple* pie?"

Chapter 16

Eli and Billy were downright sociable company through the weekend. After whipping up two more pies on Saturday, Annie was pert-near sure she was making headway into their hearts.

And she was determined to stay on their good sides. After church on Sunday she took to the kitchen again.

It came to Annie, while she sat at the table paring apples, that she might have lit upon the secret to keepin' menfolk happy. She figured there had to be a certain amount of horse sense in conjuring up the idea of appealing to a man's stomach.

She had just trimmed the crust when she heard voices out front. A woman's tinkling laughter. Eli's deep chuckle.

Annie shoved the pans in the oven, then started down the hall, untying her apron. Her hands stilled on the task and she halted in mid-stride at the sight that greeted her through the screen door.

Eli stood on the porch, Betsy on the step just below him, smiling up into his face. They exchanged an easy flow of pleasantries. Annie's gaze dropped to their clasped hands. *I do love Eli.* Betsy's avowal came uninvited into Annie's head, and made her heart stumble.

"Oh, Eli, it hasn't been that long," Betsy said as she climbed onto the porch, nudging him aside in a frolicsome fashion. "Since you already have your dander up, I might as well tell you that it's really Annie I've come to see. Is she inside?"

Annie quickly took off her apron, and in a moment of indecision as to where to put it, hung it on the hat rack. Walking forward, she smoothed her hair, dusted her bodice, then stepped out onto the porch. "Afternoon, Miss Bruecks," she said and did her best to smile.

Betsy moved toward her, caught Annie's hands, and squeezed them. "Hello, Annie."

Despite her misgivings of only moments before, Annie couldn't keep from grinning at Miss Bruecks.

"Have you tried making a pie on your own yet?" Betsy asked.

"Try?" Eli injected. He pushed away from the porch beam he'd been leaning against. Joining the women, he laid a hand on Annie's shoulder. "This little lady could win the blue ribbon at the county fair for apple pie. Just don't tell Maybelle I said so."

Annie smiled shyly and ducked her head. "I accidentally put a dab more cinnamon in yesterday." She glanced at Betsy. "Eli said it was the best dern pie he'd ever had."

Betsy's eyes twinkled. "Well, if anyone

hereabouts knows a good apple pie it's Eli,'' she commented. ''He judges the apple pies at the county fair, you know.''

Annie looked up at him for confirmation, and he wiggled his eyebrows and nodded.

''If you have some slack time next week, Annie,'' Betsy remarked, ''I thought I might teach you how to make buttermilk biscuits.''

Annie slid her gaze to her husband. ''You fond of biscuits, Eli?'' she asked.

''I have a particular fondness for biscuits and gravy.'' His lopsided smile warmed Annie, making her almost forget Betsy's presence until the woman cleared her throat.

''Well . . . I can't stay,'' Betsy said, clutching her hands at her waist. ''I just stopped by to see if you'd like to ride into town with me tomorrow, Annie. I need some things from the general store, and Jane sits with Paw for me every other Monday so I can go in for supplies.''

Annie cringed at the memory of her last trip into town. ''I'm much obliged, Miss Bruecks, but I reckon I shouldn't oughta—''

''Please, Annie? I'd like the company.'' At Annie's lack of response, Betsy added, ''Besides, I thought we could pick out some cloth to make you a dress or two. I could help you stitch them up.''

Annie grimaced. ''It's . . . awfully kind a you to offer, but . . . well, I don't reckon I need no more dresses. These you brung me'll do just fine.''

''Oh, but, Annie . . . well, you were so thin when I fitted those dresses.'' Betsy pursed her lips, appearing uncertain as to how to proceed. She turned to Eli and gestured awkwardly toward Annie's top half. "Eli, you can see Annie's . . . well, filled out in a few places, can't you?"

Eli's gaze settled on Annie's bust, then skittered away. His face turned the color of a beet. Then he wobbled his head in a strange movement that Annie supposed meant that he agreed. "I think that's a matter that you two women should discuss. I promised to meet Billy at the creek." He started off the porch, but stopped at the bottom of the steps. He stood there a moment with his back to them, then reached up and scratched behind his ear. "Get yourself a sun bonnet, too, Annie," he said and glanced briefly over his shoulder. "A real nice one, you hear? Tell Mrs. Farguson to put anything else you need on my account."

A little bell above the door tinkled as Betsy and Annie stepped through the door of Farguson's General Store.

"Morning, ladies," John Farguson called from behind the long counter that spanned one whole wall. "Is there something in particular that I can help you with today?"

Betsy smiled a greeting, stepped up to the counter, and pulled a folded paper from the inside of her cuff. "I have a list as usual, but you needn't hurry, John. Mrs. Larson and I plan on browsing awhile."

"Well then, you two just browse all you want." John held Betsy's list at arm's length.

He tucked his chin down, adjusted his spectacles, and peered at it. "Mary's just over to the post office. She'll be back directly if y'all need any help with dry goods."

"Thank you," Betsy said, then motioned Annie to follow her as she headed for the back of the store.

Annie trailed behind, taking in the various merchandise. She wove around an upturned pickle barrel with a checkerboard on top that she hadn't noticed on her wedding day. Then again, she reckoned she'd only had eyes for Eli that day.

She joined Betsy in the rear where a table displayed an assortment of fabric.

"Oh, look, Annie, this would be perfect for you," Betsy said, draping a generous measure of red gingham over her arm.

Annie was about to agree when her gaze was drawn to a shiny piece of cloth the color of wild violets. Her palm tingled as she ran her hand over the bolt of smooth purple satin. "I'm real partial to this 'un here, I am."

Betsy caught a corner of the deep lilac fabric between her thumb and forefinger. "Hmm . . . it *is* lovely. But it's a bit impractical, don't you think?"

"I reckon so," Annie murmured, then sighed. "Don't s'pose I'd have nowheres to wear it anyhow."

"Oh fiddlesticks," came Mrs. Farguson's voice from behind them. "It'd make a right nice dress to wear to the dance they're holding out at the McDaniels' place."

Mary sidled next to Annie and picked up

the bolt of satin. "Etta Fae Jackson wore a pink silk one last year," she commented, as she unwound a stream of the purple cloth, then held a section up to Annie's chin. "Just look at that, Betsy. The color suits Mrs. Larson."

Betsy cocked her head. "It does bring out the blue in her eyes."

"And I could let you have it for a fair price. One of the girls over at Gracie's Palace ordered it special from St. Louie. By the time the bolt arrived though, the gal had up and taken off with a drifter." Mary rolled her eyes and shook her head. "Ordered a yard of ribbon to match, too."

Betsy smiled at Annie. "I suppose we'll just have to take it off your hands then. Of course, you'll be sure to include the ribbon in the price, won't you?"

"Well—" Mary appeared to consider the matter a moment. "I believe I could do that."

"Good," Betsy said. "Then we'll take the red gingham, too. And a few yards of this serviceable blue here."

Annie touched Betsy's arm. "But Miss Bruecks, I don't need but one dress. The purple will do just fine."

"Annie, you can't wear satin to church or while you're baking pies." Betsy turned to Mrs. Farguson before Annie could reply. "And Mary, we'd like to see those new bonnets you got in."

Annie chose a simple straw bonnet instead of the fancier hats that Betsy insisted she try on. Some of Betsy's favorites had feathers and frills that seemed out of place on Annie's head. Sorta like a blue-blooded huntin' hound sittin' atop a crow's nest, Annie thought when she put one on.

Annie was overwhelmed by the time they rounded up all their purchases and set them on the counter for Mr. Farguson to tally. While Betsy took care of the accounts, Annie stood and stared at a big white notice tacked to the wall, sporting bold, black letters. She silently sounded out two of the printed words: *land run*. But her mind was too preoccupied with thoughts of purple satin to do much more.

She barely heard the bell above the door jingle. She glanced over her shoulder briefly to see Ida Phipps enter. Mrs. Phipps strutted halfway into the room, then stopped and narrowed her eyes at Annie. "Land sakes, John," she said, pulling a handkerchief from her ample bodice and pressing it to her nose. "Someone must have left the door open and let trash off the street blow in. There's a simply awful stench in here. Would you mind taking my order right away?"

John dropped his brows and repositioned his wire-rimmed spectacles. "Now see here, Ida. You've got no call to come in here and—"

"It's all right, Mr. Farguson," Annie cut in. "I can wait outside."

Betsy's fingers clamped around Annie's arm. "You'll do no such thing," Miss Bruecks whispered fiercely, then pointed at

Ida with her chin and raised her voice. "*She* can wait. We were here first."

Mary moved to stand by her husband and folded her arms across her chest. "That is a fact," she remarked.

"Well!" Miss Phipps glared at everyone at the counter. "I never!" she declared, then whirled, marched to the rear of the store, and commenced rummaging through the dry goods.

"You never learned to keep your mouth shut, Ida, that's what," Mary muttered under her breath while she went back to bundling Annie's fabric.

Annie's cheeks stung as she gathered up her purchases. She said her farewells to the Fargusons, intending to make a quick getaway, but Betsy caught her sleeve at the door.

Turning to face Ida Phipps, Miss Bruecks curved her lips sweetly. "Good day, Ida," She called out in a honey-filled tone.

Miss Phipps made a show of ignoring her.

"I plan on stopping by Reverend Perry's later on, Ida," Betsy persisted. "Would you like me to give him your regards? No? Well, I'll be sure to mention what a kind and neighborly soul you were today."

When Ida whipped around with her cheeks and chest bulging, Betsy tugged Annie through the door.

Outside on the walk, Betsy burst into a fit of giggles. "Oh . . . my . . . Annie, did you . . . see her face? She looked like . . . like a bullfrog. Didn't she?"

Annie half smiled, but couldn't quite see

what Betsy found so funny. "I didn't mean to cause no trouble, Miss Bruecks. I probably had no right a-goin' in there in the first place."

Betsy's laughter ceased abruptly, though a smile lingered on her lips. "You have the right to go anywhere you take a notion to go," she said, then looped her arm through Annie's and started walking them in the direction of the rig. "You didn't stir up any trouble. Ida Phipps did. That old persimmon has been making folks hereabouts miserable with her uppity ways and gossip for too long. It's past time someone told her off."

Annie thought of Delbert, and wondered how much misery Ida had dealt her own flesh and blood. "I met Miz Phipps's son once," she commented. "He came t' visit me in jail. Seemed like a real nice fella, he did."

Betsy appeared pensive a moment. Her eyes sparkled in the midday sun. "Delbert . . . Delbert is the most kindhearted man you'd ever chance to meet. It's such a shame . . . well, it's a crying shame, that's all, that his mamma keeps him tied to her apron strings the way she does." Betsy cast her lashes down and shrugged. "I pity Ida's poor husband, too. She's got him so henpecked, he hardly leaves the boardinghouse."

Betsy glanced at Annie, then rolled her eyes heavenward. "Will you just listen to me? Here I am gossiping myself. Why, I'm no better than Ida Phipps."

Annie smiled and lifted one shoulder. "Aw, now, Miss Bruecks, don't go bein' so hard on yourself. I ain't much of a judge on such things, but after what I seen today, I'd say you could take pride in bein' a lots less uppity than Miss Phipps.''

They were both laughing when they reached the buggy.

"Mrs. Larson," Betsy said as she climbed into the rig and settled beside Annie, "there's something you and I need to get straight.''

Annie felt her features flatten. "What's that, Miss Bruecks?''

"Stop calling me *Miss Bruecks*." Betsy flicked the reins, setting the horse and buggy in motion. "You call me Betsy, the same as everyone else, you hear?''

Two days later, Annie stood in her kitchen, attempting for the third time that week to make a decent batch of biscuits.

She couldn't fathom how she'd caught on to making pies when the biscuits she'd made at Betsy's the day before had turned out so rock-hard that the dogs wouldn't even eat them.

The small of Annie's back ached as she straightened and stared at the conglomeration of flour and buttermilk that almost hid the tabletop from view. She'd put in too much flour, then too much buttermilk, then too much flour, and so on. The dough had grown to such a sizable proportion that Annie had had to stretch her upper half over the huge lump to knead it.

Annie sighed, and ran a hand down her bodice, making a trail in the white powder that covered the front of her dress. Despite her frustration and weariness, she set her mouth in a grim line and started tussling with the dough again.

From the corner of her eye, she saw a movement just outside the screen door. At first, she figured she had only imagined someone watching her. Then the light that filtered through the door flicked once more.

Something akin to spider legs skittered along her spine. She stilled in her task and peered through the screen, a mite harder than she had before.

As her gaze traced the doorframe, she caught sight of a thatch of blond hair. She exhaled the breath she'd been holding. "I see you there peepin' at me, Billy," she said loud enough for him to hear, then resumed her kneading. "You might as well come on in and do your gawkin' inside."

The screen door creaked open. Billy stepped into the kitchen, puckering his lower lip. "I wasn't gawkin'," he claimed in a sulky tone.

"Oh? Then s'pose you just tell me what it was you were a-doin'."

Billy shrugged, leaned against the door-jamb, then folded his arms over his chest.

Annie thought it was mighty peculiar for the boy to be hanging around the kitchen this time of day. She couldn't help but wonder what he was up to. "What're you doin' home from school so early for?" she asked. "You're generally out rompin' with your friends till close to supper."

"Don't reckon I felt much like playin' t'day."

Annie nodded. "I s'pose it *is* lots more fun t' stand there and watch me make a fool a myself fixin' biscuits." She grinned and gave him a wink. "Yep. I can see by your face that you're a-havin' yourself a high time. Ain't that right?"

The corner of Billy's mouth quirked up. He moved behind one of the chairs and ran a finger across the top. "They was talkin' about the Calhoun Kid at school t'day. You know what they said about you?"

"Nope," Annie replied, her voice straining as she rolled out the dough. "And I ain't sure I wanna know. Whatever it was, I'm for certain it wasn't good."

Billy gripped the sides of the chair, craning his head forward. "They said you was the fastest draw in the Territories. Is that true, Annie?"

Annie looked into the youngster's wide, shining eyes. There was something special about this moment that she wanted to always remember.

He shifted his weight impatiently. "Well? Is it so?"

Annie lifted a brow. "Does ten pounds of flour make a big biscuit?" she asked, then reached out and tweaked his nose, leaving a glob of dough behind.

Billy chuckled and wiped his shirt sleeve across his face. Then he took on a more serious expression. "Would ya teach me how it's done . . . teach me how t' shoot?"

"Cain't see how I can do that, Billy. Eli won't let me have a gun."

Billy's shoulders slumped and his face fell. "Aw, shucks," he muttered, then kicked the floor and turned to leave.

"I'll tell you what," Annie said as an idea struck her. "You help me finish up these biscuits, and I'll learn ya how to quick-draw."

Billy squinted at her over his shoulder. "But you ain't got no gun. You just said so."

"Don't need no gun t' learn how to draw." She dropped her hands to her sides, then whipped them from pretend holsters and pointed at him. "Fingers'll do just fine."

Chapter 17

Eli rode up to the house that evening with a heavy heart. No matter how hard he tried not to dwell on Annie, she popped into his thoughts at the most inconvenient moments. She was beginning to mean more to him than he wanted her to, beginning to interfere with his life. He could think of no other reason why he wasn't out looking for the Calhouns, or following up on the leads he'd received recently concerning Garrett Buckley. Annie was definitely getting in the way of his plans.

Even today, while Widow McGuinty had complained about Henry Jennings being inebriated and serenading her beneath her window in the middle of the night, Eli had only half listened. Instead, his mind had wandered back to the night he'd kissed Annie by the corral, remembering how soft and sweet her lips had been. The fact that he'd had to ask Mrs. McGuinty to repeat herself several times had caused the widow great agitation.

To make matters worse, Hollis, of all people, had noticed Eli's absentmindedness. The deputy had tiptoed around all afternoon, eyeing him suspiciously. When Eli had started to leave the office for the day, Hollis had stalled him at the door. With a sympathetic look, the old deputy had laid a hand on Eli's shoulder and suggested he stop by Doc Biddle's on his way home.

Eli climbed from his saddle and flipped the reins of his horse around the hitching post. He had to do something about Annie, but he wasn't sure exactly what. Whenever he was around her, he seemed to forget the things that were most important to him. He hoped Aunt Lottie would send word soon.

He started up the steps of the front porch, but the sound of laughter coming from the back yard broke his stride. He pricked an ear, identifying Annie and Billy's voices, though he couldn't quite believe the two of them were actually carrying on a conversation. Least of all, a good-natured one.

Eli hopped over the porch railing onto the ground, then rounded the house. As he neared the back yard, he saw Annie and Billy in the shade of the big elm. They were playing some sort of game, but he wasn't sure exactly what.

Curiosity got the best of him. Folding his arms, he leaned a shoulder against the corner of the house, and narrowed his eyes on the two.

"That was real good, Billy," Annie was saying. "But you got to loosen up your legs a little more. See? Like this."

Billy mimicked her bent-knee stance. "Is this loose enough?" he asked.

"Uh-huh. Now see that there whiskey bottle I set on the stump by the springhouse?"

Billy shaded his eyes. "I see it. But why in tarnation did ya tote it way out yonder for? I ain't never gonna hit it that far away."

Annie straightened and put her hands on her hips. "You couldn't have hit it no how, Billy. We ain't got no bullets." She crouched back into her former position. "Now, squint your eyes into teensy little slits. Close your mind and sight to everything but that there bottle, like it's the onliest thing in the whole world." Annie let a moment of total silence pass, then asked, "You got your mind closed to everything but that whiskey bottle, Billy?"

"Yes'm . . . I reckon so."

"Okay. Now hold your hands just a hair away from your holsters."

"But I ain't got no holster."

"We're makin' believe we got 'em, Billy," Annie said out of the side of her mouth. "You holdin' your hands just slightly away from your holsters, are ya?"

"Uh-huh."

"All right, then flex your fingers good. But you take care not to touch your holster whilst you're a-flexin', you hear? The man you're facin' down might just think you're goin' for your gun and draw on you first."

Eli pushed away from the house, disapproving of the course this game was taking. "Billy," he hollered as he strode forward.

"It's time to do your chores and get washed up for supper."

"Aw, Eli," Billy moaned. "Annie was showin' me how t' quick-draw."

Eli nodded and slid his gaze to Annie. "I'm real glad you and Miss Annie are getting along, son. But I need to talk to her, so you run around front and take my horse to the barn." He gestured in that direction. "Go on now."

Billy cocked his head and squinted one eye at Annie. "Can we do some more make-believe shootin' tomorrow?"

Annie smiled and ruffled the boy's hair. "I reckon so. But only if ya do like Eli says and fetch his horse t' the barn."

Billy grinned, then took off galloping toward the hitching post.

Annie twisted the midsection of her dress as she faced Eli. "Did I do wrong by teachin' the boy how t' handle a gun, Eli? Is that why you're a-frownin' so?"

One corner of Eli's mouth quirked upward. He had planned on telling her just that, but her obvious distress made him want to put it another way. Laying an arm across her shoulder, he steered her down the path that led to the back door. "I suppose Billy will learn to use a gun, sooner or later, whether you teach him or someone else does. These are lawless days we're living in. I know that better than most." He took a deep breath and glanced at the orange hue tinting the evening sky. "I guess I can't help but hope that by the time Billy grows up, a man won't have to carry a gun."

Eli guided Annie onto the stoop, then opened the screen door for her. Apparently knee-deep in her own thoughts, she walked into the house ahead of him.

He wrinkled his nose when he stepped inside the kitchen. "Annie? Do you smell something—"

"Cursed hell," Annie blurted out. Her hands flew to her cheeks. "My biscuits are burnin'."

Annie stood before the looking-glass in her room. She didn't generally fuss so with her hair, but today was special. There was going to be a big doings after church at Cochran's pond. Betsy had told her that every year at the church social all the ladies donned their very finest.

Since none of her new clothes were done yet, Annie had put on her yellow dress. Something in the way Eli looked at her whenever she wore the yellow one gave her the idea that it was his favorite. She couldn't wait to see his face when her purple dress was finished.

"Annie?" Eli called through her closed bedroom door. He knocked twice. "We're going to be late for services if you don't hurry."

"I'll be right there," Annie replied. "Tell Billy to load the pies in the wagon, and that he's t' mind that they don't tump over whilst we ride t' town." She cast a last look in the mirror. She tucked a curl behind her ear, then pinched her cheeks the way Betsy had showed her.

"Annie!"

"I'm comin'!" she hollered back, grabbing her bonnet and fixing it on her head.

Eli was on the sofa next to Billy, tapping his hat against his knee when Annie entered the parlor. "Well, I'm ready," she announced.

"Good," Eli said, and stepped forward to take her elbow. "You look real nice. Now, we need to—"

"Aw, Eli, she cain't go like that."

Annie and Eli both looked at Billy.

The boy's frown deepened. "She ain't gotta chance of winnin' the best bonnet contest wearin' *that*." He pointed to Annie's plain straw bonnet. "Joey Cox's ma is gonna be wearin' one with a big pink feather. He done said so."

"Oh for cryin' out loud, Billy." Eli rolled his eyes. We don't have time—"

"Wait," Annie said, then dashed to her room and snatched her purple ribbon off the dresser. She returned to the parlor and dangled the strand of satin in front of Billy. "Will this do?"

Billy twisted his mouth to one side. "I reckon it'll fancy your bonnet up some, all right. But it ain't gonna beat out no pink feather."

"I don't believe this," Eli muttered beneath his breath, then grabbed Annie's wrist and hauled her outside. At the bottom of the step, he paused, stooped down, and snapped off several stems of the daffodils growing alongside the porch. "Here," he said, shoving the cluster of yellow flowers into Annie's hand. "You can weave those into your hatband on the way." He turned his gaze on Billy, who stood on the porch watching him with a wide grin. "Now, can we go to church?"

Billy tucked his thumbs through his suspenders, rocked on his heels, then nodded.

Annie arranged her pies on the plank board stretched between two sawhorses that the menfolk had set up next to the pond.

"Hurry, Annie!" Billy hollered, appearing from nowhere. He caught her sleeve and tugged. "They're fixin' t' judge the bonnets!"

Annie eyed him askance. "Billy, did you stick your finger in this here pie on the way t' church?"

"Yes'm, I did, but it weren't on purpose."

"Well, I s'pose you'll have t' have the piece with the hole in it."

"Fine by me." He glanced over his shoulder, then grabbed her hand and pulled her toward the crowd. "Come on, Annie. They're a gettin' ready t' start."

Annie reluctantly allowed herself to be dragged along. "Billy, I ain't gonna win. You saw Ida Phipps's hat. Hers has a bird's nest and what-not, and a hunnerd diff'rent colors of flowers and bows."

"Yep," Billy said, quickening his pace.

"And it's the ugliest dang hat I ever did see. Looks like th' monster in my scary dreams."

Annie covered her mouth to hide her smile. She reckoned the boy oughtn't to speak of his elders that way—even if it was Ida Phipps. She was aiming to tell Billy that he shouldn't show such disrespect. But before she could say a word, he pushed her into a long line of women, then skedaddled off to join Eli and the other onlookers.

The whole congregation had agreed the Sunday before that Reverend Perry should be the judge of the best bonnet contest. He would be impartial, everybody had said.

Annie was fond of the kindly old reverend. Still, as he passed by, inspecting each bonnet with a keen eye, she shivered inside. He walked back and forth several times before he made his decision.

Annie couldn't move when she heard her name called out. Then she felt herself in motion, and glanced down to find Billy at her side, pressing her forward.

Second place. She'd won second place. Mrs. Cox had come in first with her pink feather. Ida Phipps had placed third.

Annie stared at the red ribbon Reverend Perry laid in her open palm, while folks clapped and gathered round. They all offered congratulations; some even patted her back.

All but Ida Phipps. Miz Phipps tilted her nose in the air, said she "hadn't never," then sashayed off, telling anybody who'd listen that she was going home.

Eli came forward as the few remaining

church members dwindled off to attend the next event. When he reached Annie, he threw his arm across her shoulders and gave her a squeeze. "You and your yellow daffodils," he said with a broad grin.

Annie looked up into his sparkling green eyes, and everything dimmed around his face. Tiny little stars commenced dancing throughout her line of vision. "Eli . . . I feel dizzy. I ain't never won nothin' before. Can we . . . could you . . ."

Eli frowned and caught her waist, bracing her against him. "Maybe we should go home," he suggested.

"No. Please, I'd like t' stay. I reckon I'm just a mite flustered, that's all." Annie glanced at her red ribbon again. "I won second place, Eli, did ya hear?"

"I heard." His mouth twisted into a smile. "Would you like to go for a walk?"

Annie nodded, and Eli offered his arm. He ushered her toward the pond, away from the others. Without speaking, they strolled along the water's edge, past tall reedy cattails.

Annie glanced at her husband from time to time. He appeared to be thinking, and she wished she could see inside his head. She had a yearning to know if there was truly a place for her in his heart. She'd begun to wonder lately, since his mood tended to flip-flop faster than a fish on dry land. He had spells when his words got tender, his voice went hoarse, and there was a certain something shining in his eyes. Then quicker than a body could bat a lash, he'd get all irritable and storm off. She couldn't figure whether he was wantin' her to stay now, or go to that there Boston place.

As they meandered into the woods on the far side of the pond, Annie got an itch to find out where she stood with him. "Eli, are you fond of me?" she asked.

He slowed his pace. "What?"

Annie stepped in front of him and grasped his forearms, stopping him in the midst of several tall elms. She took a deep breath and peered up into his face. "Are you fond of me?"

Eli blinked twice. "Well . . . of course I am."

"How fond?"

"As fond as I'll ever be of anyone, I suppose." He dragged his gaze from hers. "I think we ought to get back to the rest of the congregation. I'd like a piece of your pie before it's all gone."

"Wait." Annie tightened her grip on his arms. "Would ya do something for me first? Would ya . . . kiss me? Just once, that's all. I mean, I won second place, Eli, and I sure could use me a kiss. I won't ask ya no mo—"

Eli's mouth covered hers. He caught her waist, pulling her close. She stood on her toes and clutched his neck. He kissed her hard, sliding one hand up and down her spine, while the other dipped and cupped her backside. Then, oh Lord, he commenced to move against her, making slow circles with his hips. And a fire started, deep down, in the very center of Annie.

Just as things were getting good, all of a sudden, Eli stilled his lips on hers. He gave her one last squeeze, muttered something into her mouth, then set her back on her heels.

Annie kept her eyes closed. She stood there a moment in a gradual sway, her arms too limp to do anything but hang in the folds of her skirt.

"There," Eli snapped. "Is that what you wanted?"

Annie opened her eyes and saw anger flash across his features.

"Are you satisfied now?" he asked, spreading his arms wide.

Annie chanced a smile. "Yes, I am, thank you. That there was a fine kiss, Eli. A *fine* kiss. Now, let's go see if'n there's any pie left."

Hooking her arm through his, she began walking him in the direction they'd come from. He was quiet as they made their way back to the picnic, but Annie noted that his temper ebbed with every step he took.

Throughout the day, Eli stayed by Annie's side while they mingled with other church members. Together, they cheered Billy on in the feed-sack race and feasted on apple pie and fried chicken.

Although Eli never did say much and reddened every time he looked at her, Annie spied a certain contentment in his face and ready smile. It came to her that he had been more confused than angry earlier in the woods. The thought of him being rattled after kissing her made her smile all afternoon.

Annie held on to that smile all the way home. The ride was wearying, but she was happy. She felt as if her heart was riding on a butterfly. Eli was fond of her. He had said so. The way he had kissed had said so.

Chapter 18

◦⟁◦

Summer had come early, but Annie didn't mind the extra heat in the kitchen. She put a pot of chicken and dumplings on the stove, then left it to simmer while she waited in the shade of the front porch for Eli.

She posted herself in the rocking chair. Setting her sight on the dirt drive, she wiped moisture from her forehead with the back of her hand. Eli hadn't said anything more about sending her away to Boston, and she wasn't about to bring up the matter.

Things were just fine the way they were. Maybe Eli had finally figured that out for himself. He sure smiled and laughed lots more these days. He had even started complimenting her cooking.

Annie's mouth curved and she rocked her chair at an easy pace. She reckoned she'd come a far cry from her lawless ways since she'd chanced to meet Eli again. Although studying to be a lady had been a tiresome chore, all her hard work was commencing to pay off.

If she wasn't quite a real lady yet, she was dang near. She could read, and write, and cook, and she was learning to embroider. She had been invited into the Women's Circle and had helped plan church events.

Townsfolk weren't merely mannerly these days, they were downright friendly when she met them on the street. Well, all but Ida Phipps. The woman still pointed her nose in the air whenever Annie passed by. Annie couldn't hold a grudge though. After all, forgiveness was divine. Besides, word was that Ida was kin to Aloysius Bartlett, the founder of Bartlett Springs, so Annie supposed Miz Phipps had cause to be a bit proud.

The approach of a rider fetched Annie from her thoughts. She rose, and leaving the rocking chair in motion, braced a hand against the column that supported the tin porch awning.

Eli crested the ridge and galloped toward her. And her heart pounded so that it almost drowned out the sound of his stallion's hoofbeats.

His gaze held hers steady as he dismounted and tied his horse. Then the dogs surrounded him, demanding attention. After petting them in turn, he climbed the steps, a lazy smile lifting one corner of his mouth. "Evening, ma'am." He doffed his hat, then twirled it on a finger. "I heard in town that a man might be able to get a square meal here if he's real nice to the lady of the house."

Annie raised a brow, and placed a hand on her hip. "Well, I don't know about that, mister. My husband's liable to be home any minute. He might not cotton to me feeding his supper to some stranger.''

Placing an arm around her, Eli turned her toward the door. ''I'll bet he wouldn't mind just this once.''

Annie caught his waist and squeezed while she guided him forward.

Eli looked down into her sparkling blue eyes and an indescribable warmth filled him to the brim. He had spent each day of the past week in anticipation of reaching the rise in the road where the house came into view. Annie had taken to waiting on the porch for him every evening. And he had relished the sight of her there.

In these first few minutes when she welcomed him home, when she smiled at him the way she was smiling now, he'd discovered that he could leave the day's worries behind. He could forget about his badge, his duty, and all that stood between them. He could forget everything but Annie's smile . . . and how soft her lips had been when he'd kissed her.

Over the past week he'd decided to put his obligations aside for the short while Annie stayed with him. Garrett Buckley, or someone else like him, would always be there. Annie wouldn't. Eli had made up his mind not to deny himself the pleasure of her company, at least not to discourage any hand-holding or hugs. He figured he was headed for a heartache, regardless.

He had promised himself that when he heard from Aunt Lottie, he would do what he had to do. He would let go of Annie. But until then, he saw no reason that the two of them should waste whatever happiness they could give each other. There had been so few times in the past several years when he'd allowed himself simply to enjoy life.

"Mmm-mmm. Something smells awful good," he said as they stepped into the house and started down the hall.

Annie hugged him around the middle again, then gave him a wink. "Chicken an' dumplins'."

"Boy howdy." Eli hung his Stetson on the hat rack as they passed, then ran his tongue across his upper lip. "I do have a fondness for chicken and dumplings."

"Seems t' me, sheriff, you have a fondness for most anything that don't jump up and run offa your plate."

Eli chuckled, nodding in agreement. Her mellow laughter joined his, and he brushed a thumb over her shoulder.

It was odd that at times like this, he felt so comfortable with his arm around her. Especially when at other times, such strong cravings surged through him that he couldn't trust himself to be in the same room with her.

He was getting better, however, at saving those particular cravings until late at night when he bedded down in the barn. He would lie on the straw, stare at the stars through the cracks in the roof, and think of Annie in unrestricted terms. He would allow his mind to wander freely as he drifted off to sleep. Sweet, unbridled dreams would flow, and he'd awaken every morning drenched in sweat. An aching deep inside would follow in the moment he opened his eyes, turned his head, and realized that Annie had never actually been there beside him.

"You want some coffee?" Annie asked when they reached the kitchen.

"Hmm? Oh sure, I could use a cup." Eli dropped his hand from her shoulder and seated himself at the table.

She poured his coffee, set the steaming mug before him, then slid into the chair adjacent to him. "Did you have a hard day, Eli? Appears you're troubled by something."

"Just another problem I didn't need," Eli replied, disarmed once more by her perceptiveness about his feelings. "I got a telegram from Billy's uncle in Santa Fe today."

Annie's face fell. She straightened in her chair and pressed a hand to her heart. "I reckon that means . . . the boy won't be with us much longer."

"That's not exactly the case." Eli took a sip of coffee, then stared into his cup. "The man's telegram informed me of his recent marriage to a widow with five children. He and his new wife have decided that they can't possibly provide for another youngster."

A slow, serene smile settled on Annie's lips. "Well, then, Billy will just stay here with us."

"He'll have to for the time being." Eli rocked back on two legs of his chair and combed his fingers through his hair. "Annie, I rode halfway across the county today, look-

ing for a decent family that would take the
boy in. Tales of Billy's pranks had already
reached most of them. All the other folks I
talked to were doing well to feed their own.''

''But you told 'em about the upset Billy's
suffered, didn't you? And that he's calming
down?'' Annie frowned and set her jaw in
an irritated fashion. ''Why, Billy's just lively,
that's all. Ain't a thing wrong with a boy
bein' spirited.''

''That may be true, but people hereabouts
don't go begging for trouble.'' Setting his
chair back on all four legs, Eli took another
swig of coffee, then sighed. ''How am I going
to tell Billy, Annie? How can I explain to him
that his uncle doesn't want him . . . that nobody does?''

''*I* want him,'' she said softly. ''The boy
has done fenced off a special part of my heart.
I love him, Eli, just as sure as I'd love my
very own. I want to care for him. We could
keep him, you and I. We could—''

''Don't start this, Annie.'' Eli scraped back
his chair, walked to the screen door, and
scanned the back yard. ''I know you love
him. I care a great deal for the boy myself.
But we've already discussed the reasons that
we can't keep Billy.''

''Eli, listen to me. We can—''

''No! I can't listen to you.'' Eli spun around
and made an awkward gesture with his hand
that even he didn't understand. ''Every time
I listen to you, the next thing I know, you
have me half believing that life is like those
happily-ever-after storybooks you read at

night. And it *isn't*, Annie. You and I both know that. Life isn't like a fairy tale." He ran a hand through his hair, and searched Annie's face for a trace of any emotion, but there was none that he could see. "Annie, look, we have today," he said in a tempered tone. "Today, tomorrow, maybe another week or two. I don't want to spend the rest of our time together fighting. Understand? I don't want to fight with you."

Annie stared at him, her expression bland, her thoughts unreadable.

Eli waited, expecting her to protest or start quoting Deadeye Pete any moment. Instead, she merely looked at him with those big blue eyes and kept her opinion to herself for once. And her silence worried him more than anything she could have said.

Annie cleared the table of the supper dishes, grateful for Billy's nonstop chatter. The boy kept her mind off things.

She picked up Eli's plate, and her gaze touched his briefly. They had exchanged the same kind of glances all evening. Their eyes would meet, then skitter off in opposite directions. Annie didn't know what to make of it. No more than she knew what to make of his harping on her before supper. Dang him. He had gone and mixed up her mind again.

She couldn't imagine his sending her away . . . not now. Something special had cropped up between them in the past few days. Something special glowed in Eli's eyes whenever he looked at her, flowed from his fingertips when he touched her face or brushed her hair aside. Annie knew with all her heart that Eli felt that same certain something, too. For that very reason she was baffled by all his talk about the time they had left together. He wouldn't send her away. Not now.

Annie smiled to herself as she stacked plates in the dishpan. As far as she was concerned, she and Eli had their whole life ahead of them. Seemed Eli just hadn't opened his eyes to that fact yet. She reckoned he might try for a spell longer to ignore the matter, but sooner or later, he was going to have to look into his own heart.

She picked up a bucket and turned to find Eli staring at her. He quickly averted his attention to Billy's animated fish story, though it appeared to Annie that he was only half listening.

"I'm going out back to fetch some water," she said, wedging her words between Billy's.

Eli barely acknowledged the statement, and Billy continued his jabbering.

Annie pushed the screen door open and walked outside. The night air was cool and filled with the scent of honeysuckle. Bright stars speckled the black, moonless sky, but offered little light to the darkness.

Swinging the pail at her side, she made her way to the pump. She set the bucket on the flat rock beneath the spigot, then cranked the long handle up and down until water gushed forth.

Eli couldn't send her to Boston, she assured herself again. When it came right down to it, she had an inkling he wouldn't be able to follow through with his original plan. They had gone and gotten familiar with each other. They had shared endearing moments. Love was too close, maybe just around the bend. And Annie wasn't about to let Eli back away now. She aimed to wade through the troubled water that surrounded him. She could make life good for him. She knew dang well she could. She could—

A whistled birdcall sliced through the still night, jarring Annie's thoughts. Fear tightened her chest as she straightened and pricked her ears.

Above the hum of crickets, the well-known signal came again.

"Frank," Annie murmured under her breath. She pressed a hand against her stomach and looked toward the house. Through the screen door, she could see Eli and Billy sitting at the table in the soft glow of lamplight.

She froze in indecision. She wanted to tear out for the house or call for help. But she knew Frank wouldn't be too particular about where he aimed his gun if someone got in the way.

The summoning whistle sounded once more, and Annie scanned the thick line of trees that edged the pasture. Maybe she could reason with her half-brother. She had to try. Frank plainly wasn't going to leave her be until she explained about the bank money.

Oh Lord, she prayed as she took a step in

the direction of the pasture, *just this once let him listen to me*. She moved slowly, cautiously toward the line of trees, and halted a stone's throw away.

"Frank, I'm here," she whispered. "Frank? I want to talk to you. Frank?"

Annie sensed someone nearby, but all she heard was the breeze rustling through the leaves overhead. "Frank, I know you're there. You got to listen to me. I don't know where the money is. I swear I don't. I—"

Annie's words broke off when she was seized from behind. A coarse hand covered her mouth, and she was dragged into the shadows of the trees.

It wasn't Frank who clutched her so tightly against him. The whiskers that grazed her neck and the long stringy hair that brushed her collarbone hinted at the man's identity. But she knew exactly who he was when her fingers traced the hand that covered her mouth and she felt the narrow ruby ring he wore on his pinky. Nausea rose to the base of her throat.

"Hello, Annie," Buck murmured into her ear. "My, my. You've grown up, haven't you?" His grip slackened around her waist, then he started to stroke the front of her bodice.

Thrusting her elbow backward into his stomach, Annie sank her teeth into his palm. When he turned her loose with a string of curses, she wasted no time in putting a fair space between them.

Even as dark as it was, she saw his eyes

glitter. She had witnessed the grim smile on his face dozens of times, and had never failed to shudder at the sight. She hugged herself to keep from doing so now.

Buck massaged his wounded palm with the thumb of his other hand. He chuckled unexpectedly. "You're just the same, Annie. You haven't changed a bit, girl."

"Oh yes I have. I changed a lots, I have." She lifted her chin a notch. "I'm a lady now."

"A lady?" Buck laughed aloud, tossing his head in a manner that made his long hair drape over one shoulder.

Annie glanced toward the house, worried that Eli might have heard him.

"You're forgetting who you're talking to, girl. This is good old Buck, remember? Hell, I was outside the shed playing cards with your daddy the night that squaw birthed you." He stepped forward and ran a finger along her jawline. "I know what you are, Annie Calhoun."

"Good old Buck, my foot." She slapped his hand away. "You ain't got a good bone in your body, mister. And you don't know nothin' about me. You and Frank and the rest of them used to walk by me like I wasn't even there."

Buck chuckled again, then reached up and scratched the underside of his chin. "I suppose you're right about that." Annie felt the heat of his gaze rove over her body. "I sorely regret not getting to know you better. Hell, girl, if I had known what you were hiding underneath those baggy rags you wore, I mighta married you myself.''

Annie refused to respond to such a crazy notion. "Look, Buck," she said, "I ain't got much time here. My husband is bound to come looking for me and—"

"Let him come. I've sorta got a hankering to meet the sheriff." The outlaw's grin widened. "I ran across his paw a time or two. The old man didn't seem so tough. But I'd kinda like to see for myself if this young whelp is as good with a gun as they say he is.''

Terror struck the very center of Annie's heart. "You leave my husband be, Buck, you hear? He ain't got nothin' to do with all of this. Nothin'. You understand?''

"Annie?" Eli called into the darkness. His voice was followed by the slamming of the screen door. "Annie? Where are you?''

"I'll be right there," Annie yelled, then turned to Buck and lowered her voice. "Tell Frank I said not to send nobody snoopin' around here no more. You tell him that I ain't got no idea where the money is. If he wants it so bad, you tell him to look in the woods that leads to the pass. That's where I lost the bank bag.''

Annie headed for the house, but Buck grabbed her wrist. He jerked her against his chest, and lowering his face to hers, looked menacingly into her eyes. "I don't like being lied to, girl. I can hurt you, Annie. Real bad.''
As if to prove his point, he tightened his grip, twisting her arm until she bit her lip to keep

from crying out. "Your lily-livered brother didn't send me. He thought it was too risky to be seen around town after Wiley Harden told us about his run-in with your husband. You see, I just took it upon myself to pay you a visit. And I didn't come calling for nothing, girl."

Eli shouted her name again. Annie instinctively turned her head in the direction of his voice. With rising panic, she realized that he was moving toward the pasture.

Buck caught her jaw and angled her face right in front of his own. He must have read her fear and seen her concern for her husband, for he smiled slowly. "Talk to me, Annie," he whispered, then drew his gun and ran the barrel alongside her cheek. "If you don't want to be a widow within the next few minutes, you'd best tell me exactly what I want to hear."

A cold chill settled over Annie. She closed her eyes and set her wits to work. "I . . . I hid it," she blurted out, saying the first thing that came to mind. "I hid the money in the woods." She opened her eyes and stared up at Buck with every ounce of conviction she possessed. "But I can't tell you where. I'll have to show you. Eli will be going to Tyler for a few days week after next. I can get away without him ever knowin' I was gone. I'll meet you . . . you and Frank, at the Four Corners Saloon."

Annie peered from the cover of the trees and saw Eli's tall dark form standing a short distance away. He cupped his mouth and yelled her name at the top of his lungs.

Buck released her wrist, but in one swift motion entwined his hands in her hair, and pressed his lips to her ear. ''You'd better be there,'' he said in a barely audible tone, his breath coming hot against her skin. ''Because if you're not, I'll be back. And if I have to come here again, I won't leave the house or the barn standing. You got me, girl? I'll burn this place to the ground.''

Chapter 19

Buck hurled Annie away from him, and she stumbled from the thicket of trees.

Seeing the movement, Eli started toward her. "Annie? Is that you?"

"Yes," she uttered, but her voice lost pitch and cracked. Clearing her throat, she tried again. "It's me, Eli."

She glanced over her shoulder, then moved forward with her feet feeling as if they belonged to someone else. She picked up her pace steadily and as she neared her husband, broke into a run.

She nearly collided with Eli and clutched his waist as hard as she could. His arms closed around her tightly, so tightly that she couldn't breathe, but she didn't care. Her heart pounded harder and harder until her temples throbbed.

"Annie . . . are you all right?" Eli rubbed his jaw across the top of her head. "What is it? What's happened? Tell me."

Annie held her tongue. She didn't favor keeping the truth from Eli. If she told him about Buck though, he'd more than likely try to go after the outlaw. And everybody knew

Buck didn't harbor any fondness for lawmen. Good old Buck didn't have no qualms about shooting a man in the back, either.

Annie inhaled deeply and forced herself from the comfort of Eli's embrace. Straightening her bodice, she cast her lashes downward. "I . . . A coyote . . . I ran across a coyote. He threw a spook into me, that's all."

"A coyote?" Eli looked past her. "I ought to go get my rifle and check the pasture."

"No, the critter's long gone. I'm sure of it." Annie followed the direction of his gaze, then hooked her arm through his and turned him toward the house. "I chucked a few rocks at him . . . chased him off. Can we go on in now? It's getting a mite chilly."

Eli furrowed his brow, and Annie averted her eyes from his.

"Are you sure you're all right?" he asked. "You're not coming down with something, are you? You look pale."

"I'm fine. Just had me a little scare." Annie tugged him forward, but he didn't budge.

"Annie, what were you doing all the way out here anyway?"

"What was I doin'?" She glanced to the side. "Uh . . . I was . . . takin' care of a personal call of nature."

Eli stared blankly for a moment, then said, "Oh." He cleared his throat and started toward the house. "Didn't you hear me calling you?" he asked as they walked along. "Why didn't you answer?"

"I did." Annie ducked her head. "I reckon maybe I shoulda hollered louder."

While they crossed the distance between the pasture and back yard, the chirping of crickets intensified. Annie steered Eli to the pump and retrieved her pail of water before they headed up the path to the house.

When they reached the stoop, she glanced at the line of trees where Buck had been hiding. She couldn't stop the shiver that shimmied down her spine. She'd done a passel of lying tonight. She figured the good Lord might forgive her, but Buck and her brother sure as hell wouldn't. She had downright calf-roped herself by telling Buck she knew where the money was. She was going to have to do a heap of thinking to wiggle out of this one.

Eli held the screen door open for her, but instead of going inside, Annie simply stared at him. A knot formed in her chest, hard and heavy. She wanted to grab him again and hold on tight. She couldn't bear the thought of Buck hurting him because of her. Unless she could come up with a heaven-sent miracle in the next week or so, it appeared she might have no choice but to ride out of his life.

"Annie, is something troubling you?"

"Hmm? Oh . . . no. Well, I was just wonderin'—" She bit her bottom lip and folded her hands against her waistband. "Eli, have you ever thought of leavin' here? Maybe startin' all over somewheres else?"

Annie was fretful for the better part of the following week. She jumped at every little noise. She yelled at Billy more often than she should have.

Eli hadn't fancied her idea of lighting out for new territory. He had gone on and on about his responsibility to the town. He had ended their debate with the comment that other than the few years he'd spent in Boston, Bartlett Springs had been the only home he'd ever known.

By the end of the week, Annie's hopes that she could change his mind about starting fresh someplace else had fallen by the wayside. Every time she brought up the subject, Eli had made some excuse to go to the barn.

Come Saturday night, she was in a powerful dilemma over how to settle her differences with Buck and Frank. She had attempted to carry on as if nothing was amiss, but worry had made simple tasks a chore. Even the prospect of the upcoming dance at the McDaniels' farm hadn't lightened her mood.

She fumbled with the ribbon she tied in her hair, then grimaced in the mirror at the lopsided bow. Jerking the strand of purple satin loose, she tried for the third time to get it right.

Everything had to be perfect tonight. Eli had been looking forward to the dance. He was pacing the hall at the moment. She could hear him treading back and forth, waiting for her to finish dressing. He had already rapped on her door twice.

"Annie," Eli called out once again. "Are

you almost done? Billy's been sitting in the wagon for a half hour.''

''Coming.'' Annie made a quick survey of her efforts in the looking-glass. She ran her hands down the smooth purple bodice. She smiled despite her troubles, and decided the smile added the final touch she'd needed. She was proud of the dress. She had stitched it all by herself and it fit just right. The neckline dipped modestly. The puffed sleeves displayed only a decent amount of bare shoulders and made her waist appear smaller.

''Annie! They'll be playing the last waltz before we get there if you don't hurry.''

Annie opened her bedroom door and almost ran into Eli. He stood frozen, his fist raised in preparation to knock. His gaze traveled down the length of her, then returned to her face. He opened his mouth, closed it, then opened it again.

''Annie . . . Lord. You're beautiful.'' A wide grin creased his lips.

Leaning forward, Annie straightened his string tie. She slid her hand across his crisp white shirt and brushed a piece of lint from his dark lapel. ''You look mighty handsome yourself, sheriff. Mighty handsome.''

Eli's face colored a bit as he offered her his arm. ''I suppose we'll have to go show off that dress.''

Annie curled her fingers around the crook of his elbow and they walked down the hall.

''I don't know,'' Eli remarked when they reached the front door. His expression so bered. "I'm not sure taking you to the dance is such a good idea."

Annie's mood wilted. She blinked twice, then stared at her husband. "Why?" she asked in a weak voice, not certain that she truly wanted to hear his answer.

"I'm probably going to have a miserable time."

Annie furrowed her brow.

A smile twitched at the corners of Eli's mouth and he ushered her out onto the porch. "Yep. I figure I'll be spending the entire evening fighting for the chance to dance with my wife. Maybe I should bring along a big stick to fend off all the young swains."

Fiddle music floated on the air, and reached Annie's ears a quarter of a mile from the McDaniels' farm.

Eli guided the buckboard past the McDaniels' two-story clapboard house, past the chicken coops behind, and into the barnyard. While the wagon was still rolling, Billy hopped off the back and took off running toward the brightly lit barn. The sounds of laughter and revelry came from within. Eli reined the horses alongside dozens of other rigs. He climbed down from his seat, then turned to give Annie a hand.

Annie stood and smoothed her skirt. She glanced at the barn, then focused on her husband's outstretched arms. "Eli, there's something I got to tell you. I cain't . . . *can't* dance a lick. I ain't . . . I mean, I *haven't* . . . never been to no dance before."

Laughing softly, Eli caught her waist and swung her to the ground. "Annie, half of the people in there can't dance. They just think they can." He gave her a quick kiss on the nose, then steered her in the direction of the merrymaking.

"But Eli, I don't even have the first notion how it's done."

"Don't worry. It's easy. All you do is move with the music. See?" He swayed them from side to side as they approached the open barn door. "Come on, I'll show you."

Just outside, at the corner of the barn, a group of men stirred in the shadows.

"Evenin' sheriff," Henry Jennings said in a voice louder than necessary. He glanced sideways, then elbowed the man standing next to him who swiftly tucked a jug behind his back. "How-do, Miz Larson, ma'am." The rest of the group echoed his greeting.

Eli smiled and tipped his hat. "You boys having a good time?" When they all agreed that they were, he added, "You gents stay out of trouble now, you hear?"

Eli turned his smile on his wife and winked. Then to her surprise, he raised her arms, fixing them in a dance position, and waltzed her through the door.

Three and a half lively songs later, Annie gave up counting her steps. She let Eli and the fiddle music whirl her around the room. Dancing made her feel all giddy inside, and she couldn't keep from laughing.

She caught sight of Betsy swirling across the floor with Delbert Phipps. Annie waved to her friend, but Betsy was looking at Delbert and apparently didn't notice.

When the next song ended, Eli suggested they mosey over and have some apple cider.

Jane Scallon and Mary Farguson were helping serve. Eli talked Mary into giving him an extra large piece of spice cake by promising her a dance. Annie chatted with Jane while she dipped cider. They were discussing little Timmy when Betsy sidled next to Annie with Delbert in tow. Her tall, lanky escort merely nodded politely.

"I'm so glad you didn't let me talk you out of that purple satin," Betsy said with a smile. "You look absolutely stunning."

Mary cleared her throat as she passed Delbert a piece of cake. "If you'll recall, *I* told you the color suited her."

"And you were right." Betsy turned to Eli and tugged his sleeve. "What do you think, sheriff? Isn't Annie the prettiest one here tonight?"

"Yes, she is." Eli gazed at Annie in a special way that made her toes curl. He stared at her for a long moment as if he'd forgotten the others were present. Then seemingly embarrassed, he refocused his attention on Betsy. "You saved me a dance, didn't you, Bets?"

"Well, I *have* promised the next few to Delbert, but maybe—" She cocked her head toward the tall redhead beside her. "Maybe he wouldn't mind giving up just this one."

"N-no, not at all." Delbert shook his head, then nodded. "I . . . m-mean . . . I d-d-don't mind . . . if you dance with the sh-sheriff. I'll j-just—"

"Dance with me," Annie supplied. She grabbed Delbert's arm and hauled him out on the dance floor just as the fiddler struck up a new tune.

She shifted her feet in time to the music, and Delbert followed suit, never missing a step. Annie would've had to be blind though, not to notice that his gaze followed Betsy about the room. Betsy eyed Delbert, too.

Annie returned Eli's smile from across the way. He wasn't paying much attention to his dance partner, either. He craned his neck and tried to peer around other couples who sashayed between them and blocked Annie from his view. It tickled her that he was being so watchful.

When the song was over, they headed straight for each other, but Billy waylaid Annie. The boy grabbed her hands and commenced to dancing a jig. She raised an eyebrow and looked at Eli, but saw that little Janie Scallon had stalled him in a similar manner. With a shrug of his shoulders, he mouthed, "Next dance," then followed Janie's lead across the floor.

In the ensuing two hours, Annie's feet began to hurt. She had danced with John Farguson, Hollis, Charlie, Jim, and Billy. Billy, at least a dozen times. It seemed every time she and Eli got close enough to almost touch, someone would ask one or the other to dance.

When the fiddler announced the last tune

of the evening though, neither Annie nor Eli accepted an offer from anyone else. Annie's heart fluttered as her husband made his way toward her and took her in his arms. They glided together in a sweet, lazy waltz. Eli pulled her close, and Annie laid her head against his chest.

Light appeared to close them off in a circle. As far as Annie was concerned, Eli was the only other person in the room. Her heart overflowed with love.

"Well, can I? Huh? Can I?"

Annie opened her eyes and found Billy pulling on her skirt. She pushed away from Eli, gradually becoming aware that the music had stopped and the townsfolk were leaving.

Eli glanced from the youngster to Annie. Then he scanned the room, obviously flustered that he had continued dancing with his wife long after the fiddler had packed up his fiddle.

"Well? Can I, or not?" Billy asked again, wrinkling his nose in aggravation.

Eli turned his attention to the boy. "Can you *what?*"

Billy sighed heavily. "Can I sleep over to the Scallons' tonight? Beau, John, and Mark asked me, and their ma said it was all right."

Eli combed his fingers through his hair. "Don't you think Mrs. Scallon has enough youngsters of her own to tend to?"

"One more won't make that much difference," Jane commented as she walked up behind Billy and laid a hand on his shoulder.

"Let the boy stay with us, sheriff. We'd be real glad to have him."

"Ya see, Eli? Miz Scallon wants me t' come."

Eli glanced at Annie for her approval. She nodded, unable to see any harm in Billy accompanying the Scallons home.

Eli gave his permission reluctantly and made Billy promise to behave himself. The boy gave his word, then dashed out the door.

After saying their farewells to Jane and the few stragglers who lingered outside the barn, Annie and Eli made their way to the wagon.

Annie grew sleepy on the tiresome ride home. The dark rolling countryside was peaceful. Bright stars dotted the sky. She longed to lay her head on Eli's shoulder, but he had dang near scooted off the wagon seat to avoid brushing against her.

She had an inkling Billy's absence had brought on the awkwardness and strained silence. Eli was no doubt weighing the situation, just as she was. This would be the first night they had spent completely alone together. She reckoned he had a right to be a tad nervous.

Annie recalled how he'd held her on the dance floor, and smiled. They'd had such a wonderful time. Frank and Buck hadn't entered her mind. Leastways, not until now.

She shifted on the hard plank board seat and glanced at her husband's profile. He was in a sober, brooding mood. The thought that she might have to leave him soon surfaced without warning. Her heart constricted as she looked up and focused on the North Star. If she could only have one more wish . . .

"Well, here we are," Eli said, jostling her from her reverie. He stopped the wagon by the front porch, hopped off the seat, then assisted Annie to the ground. His hands rested on her waist, and she let her fingers dally on his arms.

"Can I help you unharness the horses?" she asked, peering up at him.

"No, thanks. I can manage. You go on in and get some rest. You're bound to be tired after all the dancing you did this evening." He pressed his lips to her forehead for a long, lingering moment, then stepped away from her. "Good night, Annie," he whispered. With that he climbed back onto the wagon and took up the reins.

"Eli?" Annie hugged herself. "Are . . . are ya dead set on sleepin' in the barn tonight?"

Eli angled his head toward her slowly. The wide brim of his hat shadowed his eyes, but Annie couldn't miss the grim line of his mouth. He took a deep breath that made his chest rise and fall. "Damn it, Annie." His voice was hoarse and barely audible. "Don't make this any harder than it already is."

He faced forward, flicked the reins, clicked his tongue, and sent the horses hurtling toward the barn.

Annie watched him disappear into the darkness. She sank onto the top step, propped her elbows on her knees, and cupped her chin. Her gaze automatically riveted on the brightest star in the sky, and she sighed.

Then the oddest thing happened. The North Star commenced to twinkling as if it were trying to send her a message. She twisted her mouth to one side and made a hard study of the blinking light.

All of a sudden, Annie kind of figured maybe she knew what the star wanted her to do. She stood, squared her shoulders, and smoothed her satin skirt. Sometimes, she reckoned, a body needed to give certain wishes a little push to make them come true.

Chapter 20

～⌒のC⌒～

Eli brushed down the horses and put them in their stalls while his mind wandered back to the last waltz. For that short span of time he had belonged to Annie . . . and she had belonged to him. Once again, he'd lost sight of all that had happened to him before she had entered his life. He'd lost himself. All that he stood for, his purpose, everything he believed in, seemed insignificant whenever he held Annie in his arms.

He closed the stall door and ran a hand through his hair. He was becoming more and more unsure of himself these days. He doubted decisions he'd made in the past, couldn't trust the gut instincts that he'd always depended on.

He'd known for quite some time that Annie had stolen his heart. He realized now that she'd also robbed him of his soul, just as surely as she had robbed the First National Bank of Bartlett Springs.

Eli looked through the open barn door at the dark silhouette of the house. A picture of Annie asleep in the big four-poster came instantly to mind . . . her long, wavy hair swirling over the pillow . . .

With a silent curse, he pushed the vision from his thoughts.

Jerking his shirt off, he walked over and blew out the lantern that hung on a nail by the harnesses. Bone-weary, but not the least bit sleepy, he laid down on his straw pallet. He cupped his hands behind his neck and stared at the sparse moonlight that seeped through the crack in the roof. By habit, the beginning of his recurring dream about Annie popped into his head.

He closed his eyes, willed the dream away, and replaced it with the vow he'd made at his father's graveside. He drifted backward in time, watched the dirt shoveled onto his parents' caskets. He let the pain return with the full force of that day. The fire of revenge burned inside him, crushed his chest until he labored for breath.

"Eli?"

He opened his eyes, thinking he'd only imagined Annie's voice. Then he turned his head and saw her shadowy form in the doorway.

She took a step forward. "Eli?"

"Go back to the house, Annie."

"I cai—I can't." She twisted her hands at her waist. "I ain't gonna be here much longer. I mean . . . well, you said so yourself."

Eli rolled to a sitting position and ran his hands over his face. "Annie . . . for God's sake, go back to the house."

"Only if you'll come with me."

"Damn it to hell!" Eli came to his feet and in one swift motion knocked the harnesses off the wall. He started toward her, then stopped and clenched his fists at his sides.

Annie stood her ground. "Please?" she said in a feeble voice.

"You know I can't do that. And you know why. I've explained about the annulment."

"I won't tell nobody. I swear I won't." She advanced as if she approached a skittish horse. "I'll stand up and deny anything ever happened if that's what you want."

Eli weighed the wisdom of staying where he was, yet he couldn't find the strength to retreat.

Annie reached out and took his hand. "Come on up to the house with me, Eli, and we'll talk this all out."

He let her lead him from the barn, followed her along the path, knowing he was doomed. He knew damned good and well there would be little talk once they reached the house.

And he was right. Without a word, she tugged him through the dark kitchen, down the hall, straight into her room.

At the foot of the bed, she squeezed his hand. "I don't know what comes next," she said softly. "You'll have to show me, but first . . . well, you reckon you could dance with me again?"

Eli took her in his arms and held her close. While they waltzed around the moonlit room, she hummed the last tune the fiddler had played. He was consumed with her sweet voice . . . with the honeysuckle scent of her hair. The thin, smooth satin of her bodice rubbed his bare chest with each graceful move she made. He tightened against the seams of his Levi's, ached with the anticipation of what would follow their midnight dance. Annie dominated all thoughts of family honor. Duty and obligation lost meaning as he trailed a hand down the back of her dress and unfastened the tiny buttons one by one.

Annie pressed her cheek to Eli's furry chest. In her ear, his heart beat with the same fitful thumping of her own. Whatever happened from here on out, this one night would always be hers. No one, not even Frank, could take the memory from her. No one could stop her from loving Eli.

An overpowering warmth made her throat swell, made the melody she hummed die away. Eli's footsteps slowed and so did hers, until they stood by the edge of the bed, slightly rocking together in a gentle sway.

With innocence and eagerness, Annie gazed up at him. "Give me something special to remember you by," she whispered.

Moonlight slanted through the window, casting shadows of the lace curtain across his face. His throat convulsed, and he took a small step backward and caught her shoulders. His finger trembled against her skin as he slid her sleeves down her arms.

Unaware that he'd somehow magically unfastened her, she was a little surprised when her dress fell around her ankles. But she stood undaunted and unashamed, while he slowly slipped her chemise over her head, then looked his fill.

Annie focused on the rapid rise and fall of his chest. She reached out and placed her hands over his heart and felt it pumping against her palms. A fire sparked somewhere deep inside her, flamed higher, burned hotter as she traced the narrow path of dark crisp hair that grew down the middle of his torso.

Eli sucked in his breath when her fingertips grazed his waistband. She undid his britches with slow measured strokes, relying on an instinct she didn't know she had. His reaction to her touch made her tingle with surges as powerful as lightning bolts, and told her she was doing the right thing.

Suddenly, he grabbed her wrist. "Sweet Jesus," he murmured. "This is going to be all over with before it starts if you're not careful."

He stepped away from her and quickly shed his pants, then pulled her into his arms and kissed her in a way that he'd never kissed her before. His mouth was hot and demanding, and his tongue sought hers with a desperate urgency.

Annie molded herself to him, reveling in the feel of his warm skin against hers. Her head swirled. She savored the closeness . . . savored everything about him: the taste of apple cider on his lips, the fresh smell of hay that clung to him, the possessive claim of his hands on her body.

Without breaking the kiss, Eli eased her

onto the bed, aligning himself over her. His weight pressed her deep into the soft feather mattress. She was like whiskey, tempting, intoxicating. He knew he was moving too fast. He wanted to slow down, wanted to stretch this time into eternity. But she moved wildly and willingly beneath him. And he couldn't control his need for her any more than he could stop the frenzied beating of his heart.

Annie's fingers dug into his shoulders. "Please, Eli," she whispered breathlessly against his lips. "I want . . . Show me, Eli. Show me what it is I want so badly."

All thoughts of dallying any further vanished from Eli's mind. Unable to hold back another moment, he parted her thighs with his knee. Raining kisses over her face and throat, he entered her.

She made no sound, but tightened her grip on his shoulders and fell utterly still. Raising himself on his elbows, he looked into her wide bright eyes.

By slow degrees, her mouth curved into a smile. "My. Oh . . . *my.* I reckon I never figured on . . ." She closed her lids, and a blush settled on her cheeks. "I never in my wildest dreams woulda guessed *that* was how it was done." Opening her eyes, she glanced to the side, then wiggled. She slid her gaze to his and stared at him in amazement. "Oh, Eli. I think I like this." She moved her hips against his once more and giggled. "I do. I like this a lots. A whole, whole—"

Eli covered her mouth with his. At first he

moved gently within her, but Annie set a more pressing pace. Her fingers played along the contour of his hips, driving him into madness . . . driving him home.

Annie floated higher and higher, like a hawk soaring in the sky. She hadn't ever imagined such a level of pleasure existed. It truly was wondrous. In the same sweet moment that her husband wilted against her, a rush of sunshine oozed through her . . . a pumping, a pounding that made her gasp.

She gripped Eli's arms so tightly that he braced his hands on either side of her head and looked down at her.

"Oh, my lord, Eli. I think I'm dyin' . . ."

He smiled at her with such tenderness that her heart fluttered, then brushed a damp strand of hair from her cheek. "You're not dying, Annie. You've just become a woman, that's all."

Annie frowned skeptically. "Honest?"

"Honest."

"Does it happen every time?"

Eli smiled and rolled onto his side, keeping her cradled in his arms. "If it's done right it does," he replied.

Closing his eyes, Eli rubbed his jaw against the top of her head. He'd never felt so full and complete, so at peace with himself. Annie had asked less of him than any woman he'd ever known and given more than he'd ever believed possible. How in God's name, he wondered, would he ever be able to give her up?

Annie snuggled against him and ran her

fingers through his chest hair. Something warm and soft glowed inside her, making her drowsy. After spending her whole life searching for a place to call her own, she felt as if she'd finally come home. "I do feel different, Eli," she murmured. "Like maybe I done something right for a change. Will we have a baby now? Eli?"

She looked up at him, and his head lolled to the side. His eyes were closed, his features relaxed. She noticed then that his chest moved beneath her palm in a deep, even rhythm. "I love you, sheriff," she whispered, then nestled her cheek against his shoulder.

From somewhere in the distance came the call of a whippoorwill. A slight breeze fluttered the lace curtains, and Annie gazed out the window. The North Star blinked. She smiled, and winked back.

Annie squinted at the brightness flowing into the bedroom. Rocking on the brink of consciousness, she rolled over and reached for Eli, but all she felt was an empty space and a cold pillow.

She sat up in bed, rubbed her eyes, and glanced out the window. Stretching her arms over her head, she observed the sun hovering above the horizon. The bright, beautiful sun . . . *high above the horizon?*

Oh Lord. She'd overslept. This was Sunday. She was going to be late for church if she dillydallied much longer. Throwing the covers back, she scooted off the four-poster and hurriedly poured her wash water from the pitcher into the bowl on the dresser.

She dressed quickly, then, figuring Eli had to be out hitching the horses, made her way to the barn.

But the horses were still in their stalls and Eli was nowhere in sight. Annie stood in the center of the barn, all sorts of imaginings filling her head. Her worst nightmare kept surfacing.

Buck. Dear God. What if Buck had come back? What if he'd found out she'd lied . . . and come back . . . and met up with Eli and—

Unable to finish the thought, she swirled and ran to the barn door. "Eli!" she screamed at the top of her lungs. Moving into the yard, she scanned the area for any signs of a struggle. Everything looked almost too peaceful.

Fear pricked the tiny hairs on the back of her neck. Her heart pounded harder and harder as she searched for some small trace of her husband. Shouting his name, she checked the house again, then the corral, the hayloft, and the springhouse.

She racked her brain for any place else she might look. Near panic, she thought of the creek. It made sense that he wouldn't have heard her calling over the rush of water.

The inside of her mouth grew dry as she raced down the path. He had to be there, she told herself, yet worry that he wouldn't be kept arising within her. She ran faster, weaving through the trees. She paid no mind to the mulberry bushes snagging her dress and scratching her legs.

Annie was close to tears when she broke through the brush and saw Eli in the distance skipping rocks across the water.

In an attempt to catch her breath, she fell to her knees and braced a hand against her aching side. Then, without rhyme or reason, she started to laugh and couldn't stop.

Eli turned at the sound of her laughter. His brow furrowed with concern as he strode swiftly toward her. "Annie?" Catching her elbows, he lifted her to her feet. "Annie, what happened? Annie? Jesus, look at your dress. What—"

"It's all right, Eli," she said, stifling her mirth. "Everything's all right." She threw her arms around his middle and squeezed. "I just got scared, that's all. Lord, I thought they'd come gunning for you."

"You thought *who* had come gunning for me?"

Annie froze, realizing she'd gone and said something she shouldn't have again. Turning him loose, she straightened her dress and brushed a stray hair from her face.

"Annie?"

She shrugged, then stared at the scuffed toe of his boot. "I don't know. One of them outlaws you're always after, I guess." She glanced up to see how he was taking this. "I . . . I couldn't find you this morning. I was afeard maybe somebody had—" She pressed her lips into a tight line.

Eli tucked a finger under her chin, raised her face to his, and smiled. "I don't think you have to worry about anything like that.

I had some thinking to do, that's all." His smile faded, and his green eyes paled. He stared at her for a long moment, then slipped an arm around her and turned her toward the house. "Come on. Let's go fix some breakfast."

Annie caught hold of his waist and walked down the path with him. "Aren't we going to church today?"

Eli narrowed his gaze on something in the distance. "I didn't think we should." He blinked, then looked at her. "I mean . . . well, I think we need to talk, Annie."

"About what?"

"A lot of things. But they can wait until after breakfast."

Annie sliced potatoes into a pan of salt pork while Eli stirred the concoction. She enjoyed working by his side. She closed her mind to everything but the present moment.

She poured them each a cup of coffee, and Eli filled their plates. While they ate breakfast they chatted about the nice weather, Billy, church goings-on—about everything, and nothing at all.

Annie knew Eli was headed toward a more sober conversation, though, when he lay down his fork and frowned at his plate. "About last night, I—" He looked up, placed a hand over hers, then closed his eyes. "I don't know how else to say this . . . except to just say it. I went down to the creek this morning, hoping the time alone would help me find the words to make it easier, but—"

"Just tell me, Eli. Nothing could be as bad as what I'm conjuring in my head right now."

His hand tightened on hers, but he still wouldn't meet her eyes. "What happened last night isn't going to change anything. I'm still going after Garrett Buckley . . . and you're still going to Boston."

Annie tugged her hand from his and entwined it with her other in her lap. Last night and this morning she'd been pretending that things would always be as they were. But deep in her heart, she'd known for several days that she had no choice but to leave. Boston might not be a bad place to go. She'd considered it. Frank would never think to look for her there. But she would never go to Boston without Eli. She'd never leave him at the mercy of Frank and Buck. At the same time, she knew it was hopeless to think she could ever convince him to give up his search for his parents' murderer.

Eli reached out and touched her sleeve. "Annie . . . I know this is hard for you to understand." His voice was tight and broken. "Hell . . . it's killing me. You've got to believe that." When she didn't respond, he dropped his hand. Leaning back in his chair, he cleared his throat. "I got a wire from Aunt Lottie last week. She'd been abroad and had just returned and opened my letter. She said she would be happy for you to come stay with her. I'm sure she'll take Billy in, too. She said she could use the company and would be looking for—"

"I don't want to talk about this, Eli." Annie shook her head slowly. "I don't want to talk about Boston. I don't want to talk about leaving." She focused on his clear green eyes and did her best to ignore the pain in her chest. "We got a precious few days left together, Eli. Let's play like we never had this conversation. Let's make believe I'm going to be with you forever—at least till I have to go."

Eli's eyes brightened. He swallowed hard, then nodded.

Annie struggled with a mishmash of emotions. Anger rose above all the others. She had set her sights too high in the first place. She should've remembered who and what she was. She'd been a dang fool to fall in love with the man sitting across from her. She shouldn't have hung her hopes on a star.

Fighting for control of her feelings, she willed her expression to go blank. "I'm going to change the subject now and . . . and talk about something else." She glanced at her hands clasped tightly in her lap. "Are you still going to Tyler next week?" she asked.

He appeared puzzled. "Thursday. Why?"

Annie stood and started clearing the table. "I just got some things I need to tend to before then." She turned away from him and carried the plates to the dishpan.

Eli scraped his chair back and came up behind her. He slipped his arms around her waist and set his chin on her shoulder. "Annie . . . would you like to go on a picnic today?"

She melted against him. Suddenly, it didn't matter that she'd been a fool. Nothing mattered but Eli. She might spend the rest of her life giving the devil his due, but for the next few days, she aimed to love Eli Larson to her heart's content. "I'd like that a lot," she replied. "An awful lot."

Chapter 21

〰〰〰

It was a beautiful day for a picnic. Annie packed a lunch basket while Eli hitched up the buckboard. They drove away from town, and after a good spell turned off the road onto an overgrown path that led to a secluded, shady spot beside a stream.

"What do you think?" Eli asked as he helped her down from the wagon seat.

Annie glanced around the wooded grove and smiled. "Can't say I've ever seen a prettier place."

"I used to swim here when I was a boy." Eli wiggled his brows and started unbuttoning his shirt. "Buck-naked," he added, peeling the garment back over his broad shoulders.

Behind her husband's smile, Annie saw the devil grin. "Buck-naked, huh?"

"Yep." He sat down on the bank, tugged off his boots, tossed them aside, then stood. As he cocked his head, his grin grew broader. "You *are* going to join me, aren't you?"

Annie shifted her gaze to the stream. The water was so clear that the smooth pebbles on the bottom were visible, making it difficult to tell how deep it was. "Eli . . . I never learned to swim," she said, and looked back at him in time to witness him squirming out of his tight jeans.

She'd seen him in the hazy glow of moonlight the night before, but the sight of him bare as the day he was born in broad daylight overwhelmed her. Feeling her cheeks turn red, she cast her lashes down.

His big feet moved into the line of her vision as he stepped toward her and tilted her face to meet his gaze. "Come on," he coaxed. "I'll teach you. The water here isn't over your head. It will only hit you about neck-high in the middle of the stream. Of course, if you're chicken—"

"I ain't chicken." Annie lifted her chin, disengaging it from his touch.

"No?" Eli shrugged, turned, and hobbled across the rocky bank to the water, then waded in. "Then what are you waiting for?" he asked without a backward glance.

He shivered as the icy water crept up his body. To take the edge off the chill, he dove under and swam the short distance to the other side of the stream. Emerging, he combed wet strands of hair from his face, but his hands stilled on the top of his head when he spied Annie undressing on the shore.

She moved in slow measures, removed each article of clothing and carefully hung them on the bush beside her, occasionally glancing in his direction.

Eli's desire rose to an incredible proportion, despite the frigid temperature of the spring-fed stream. Ripples flowed behind him as he strode forward to meet her.

Annie stepped into the stream and caught her breath when the cold water swirled around her ankles. She would have retreated if Eli hadn't caught her hands.

"Come on in," he said. "It feels good once you get used to it."

She resisted the gentle tug he gave her. "Eli, it's freezin'."

Ignoring her struggles, he pulled her into the water and wrapped his arms tightly around her. "I'll warm you up," he whispered against her lips. "Kiss me, Annie."

Annie pressed her mouth to his, matching his hungry intensity, meeting each sweet thrust of his tongue. She slid her hands up through the crisp damp curls covering his chest, over his shoulders, then grasped the nape of his neck.

He returned her kiss with a violent tenderness. His fingers splayed down her spine. Beneath the surface of the water, he cupped her hips, lifting her, positioning her, fitting her against his body.

Heat coursed through her. Her heart ached with a wild fierceness that made her tremble. She locked her legs around his waist and moved with him until both of them shuddered with a pulsating pleasure that seemed to go on forever.

There were no swimming lessons that lazy afternoon. But Annie didn't mind. She snuggled with her husband as they lay sunning themselves in a grassy spot on the shore.

Quietly, peacefully, they watched puffy white clouds drift across the blue sky. And she made believe that the whole of heaven belonged to her and Eli, that *everything* for the moment belonged to them . . . including time.

Annie moved through the next couple of days in a blissful, besotted state. She and Eli made love every chance they got—in the morning after Billy left for school, and in the afternoon before he came home. Annie snuck out to the barn in the middle of the night. They made love in the hayloft, in the big four-poster. They were slow and easy about it sometimes, at others fast and furious.

Upon the rare occasions when Annie allowed a thought to form in her head, she figured she was attempting to squeeze a lifetime into a few days. For the most part, she tried not to think at all. She didn't want to remember that come Thursday, soon after Eli left for Tyler, she'd be long gone and riding hard for the Territories.

By mid-afternoon on Wednesday though, it got to be a real chore for Annie to push thoughts of leaving from her mind. She busied herself making an apple pie. But for once, peeling apples didn't lighten her burden any. She was more downhearted than ever when she finally put the pie in the oven.

She sank into a chair at the table and stared out the back screen door. She breathed deeply, hoping the aroma of cinnamon and spice that filled the kitchen would lift her spirits. She wanted to be cheerful when Eli got home.

The sound of hoofbeats rousted her. She stood and quickly shed her apron. Smoothing her hair, she hurried down the hall toward the front door. She pasted a smile on her face before she stepped out on the porch.

Her smile grew broader all by itself when Eli crested the ridge. She moved forward and waved.

Pressure mounted in her chest as he climbed off his horse, walked up the steps, and took her in his arms.

Annie clung to him with all her might, kissed him with all the pain she was experiencing. She was certain he was hurting, too. She could almost taste the anguish on his lips.

In that moment, she knew that she would never be strong enough to ride away—knew that she could never give him up. There had to be a way for them to stay together. There just *had* to be something she could say or do to make things right for them.

Eli's lips left her mouth and brushed across her cheek to her ear. "Is that apple pie I smell?"

A chuckle caught in Annie's throat, and she nodded.

"Well, let's go see if it's done," he said, guiding her into the house. "I'm starving."

Annie patted his lean stomach as they moved down the hall in the direction of the kitchen. "Eli, you are always starving. I'm amazed your belly isn't as big as Hollis's is."

* * *

Suppertime was as pleasant as could be. Billy chattered about the last day of school, told all about the uproar they'd had that morning when Miss Prigg had opened her pencil box and found a horny toad inside. Eli and Annie had tried to keep straight faces, but had ended up looking at each other and bursting into laughter. Had anyone chanced to peek through the kitchen window then, Annie figured he would've seen a family as ordinary as any in Bartlett Springs.

Billy finished off his second piece of pie, hopped up from the table, and dragged his cuff across his mouth. "I already done m' chores, Eli, and I promised Joey I'd go fishin' with 'im. Can I go now?"

Eli smiled and ruffled Billy's hair, letting his hand linger on top of the boy's head. "I suppose it will be all right. There's plenty of daylight left since the days have grown longer. Just be sure to be back before dark, you hear?"

"Yes, sir, I will," the youngster said, then dashed out the screen door.

Annie began clearing the table. She had patiently waited to talk to Eli until Billy was out of earshot. But now that the boy was gone, she couldn't form her thoughts into words. She had to make Eli understand that they belonged together. She planned to tell him everything— about Frank and Buck, how they were hounding her for the money. Maybe her husband could think of some way to stop her half-brother. Eli was a sheriff, after all. Maybe he could put Frank and Buck behind bars where they couldn't ever hurt no one again.

Annie set the plates in the dishpan, closed her eyes, and took a deep breath. She was just going to have to speak her heart and trust that whatever came out of her mouth would be convincing enough. Prepared to do her best, she whirled around and said Eli's name at the very same time that he said hers.

"Sorry, Annie." Eli's lips curved in a little smile. "What were you going to say?"

"You go first." Annie walked to the table and sat down. She was almost afraid to hope that he'd come to the same conclusion she had: that neither of them would be able to go on living without the other. "What I have to say can wait."

Eli lowered his head, then reached out and took her hand in his. He brushed his thumb back and forth over her knuckles. "Annie . . ." His voice was tight and strained, and the long, lean fingers he curled around hers quivered slightly. "I purchased two tickets to Boston today. One for you, one for Billy. The train leaves Friday. I . . . I thought it might be easier on all of us if you left while I was in Tyler."

A numbness overcame Annie. She wanted to scream or throw something, but all she could do was stare at her husband.

Eli's eyes were tinged with red when they met hers. "Annie, please. Don't look at me like that. It will only be for a little while. I promise. Then I'll come to Boston to fetch

you and Billy home. And we can be a family
. . . just like you wanted. After I take Garrett
Buckley in—"

"And what if Garrett Buckley puts *you* in
your grave?" Rising from her chair, Annie
jerked her hand from his, and started pacing
the kitchen. "Huh? Tell me that, Eli. What's
going to happen to Billy and me then?"

Eli stood and caught her shoulders, holding her still when she tried to struggle free.
"Annie, you don't have anything to worry
about. I'll get Garrett before he gets me. You
have my word on that." He pulled her close.
When his arms folded around her, she
couldn't keep from hugging him, too. "And
I'll come for you when it's all over," he whispered against her temple. "I swear I will."

Tears welled in Annie's eyes, though she
held them at bay as she gazed up at him.
"Eli, we have to get away from here," she
blurted out, aware that she sounded frantic,
but unable to temper her tone. "We can go
someplace where nobody knows us. And you
can teach school and I'll have babies and—"

"Stop it." Eli held her away from him.
"Annie, you know I can't do that. You know
why I have to go after Garrett."

Annie glanced wildly about the room,
searching for some means to save Eli from his
compulsion to claim revenge.

Somewhere in the back of her mind, she
latched on to the only thing she thought
might possibly stop him. "Vengeance is
mine, saith the Lord," she said, and jabbed

a finger in the air just like Reverend Perry. "Judge ye not, lest ye be judged."

"All right, now that's enough of that, Annie." Eli took a step backward and held up his hands as if to ward her off. "You are not going to change my—"

"Forgive, and ye shall be forgiven!"

"Damn it, Annie." Eli pressed his lips together and shook his finger at her. "Don't you go quoting Bible verses to me. It's not going to work. Do you hear? It's not going to—"

"Sheriff!" Hollis yelled from the front porch, pounding his heavy fist on the door. "Sheriff, you better come quick!"

Eli strode swiftly down the hall, and Annie trailed after him.

"Hollis, what in the hell is the matter with you?" Eli asked as he swung the screen door open. "You don't have to knock the door down."

"Sorry, sheriff, but something awful's happened. Just awful." He puffed his cheeks in and out and waved his hands. "You gotta come quick."

Frowning, Eli laid a hand on his deputy's shoulder. "Now, just calm down and tell me what's happened."

"Little Janie Scallon and her brother—" Hollis scratched his ear. "Don't rightly know which one it was. I always get them Scallon boys mixed up. John? No. Well, maybe it was Mark. Or it coulda been—"

"Okay, okay. It was one of the boys." Eli nodded. "Go on."

"Well, they was out pickin' mulberries behind ol' man Jenkins's place." The deputy got excited all over again, and started bouncing his weight from one foot to the other. "And you ain't never gonna believe what they found."

"What the hell did they find, Hollis?" Eli asked impatiently.

"A locket."

"A locket?"

Hollis bobbed his head. "Janie Scallon swore it was the same as one Elmer Dobbs's daughter used to wear—you remember little Emily?"

Eli put his hands on his hips and stared blankly at the man. "So? All that means is that Emily lost her locket in the woods."

"Afraid there's a sight more to it than that, sheriff. Ya see, when Janie and her brother saw the locket on the ground they tried to pick it up, but it seemed the chain was caught on a root or something. When they started digging it up, they found it was attached to—" The deputy glanced at Annie, then whispered, "A dead body."

"Was it Emily?"

"Cain't rightly tell. Wasn't much left but bones."

Eli turned, reached around Annie, and grabbed his Stetson from the hat rack. Looking down at her, he laid a hand alongside her cheek. "We'll finish our talk when I get back," he said softly. "I have a lot more I want to say. I need you to understand, Annie. I need—" He pressed his lips into a tight smile, then gave her a quick kiss. "I'll be home after a while."

Annie stepped out onto the porch and watched Hollis and her husband ride off. The memory of Zeb Jenkins sneering at her through jail cell bars came to mind. The crotchety old codger hadn't been the most agreeable man she had ever met, but Annie couldn't believe him actually capable of—

She wrapped her arms around her middle and shivered. Sometimes young 'uns' imaginings got the best of them. Maybe all they'd found was some animal carcass. Leastways, she dearly hoped that was the case.

Pushing the gruesome train of thought aside, she turned and walked into the house. By the time she reached the kitchen, she was preoccupied with the notion that she and Eli hadn't settled a thing.

She sat idly with her elbows on the table, her chin resting on clasped hands, and stared out the back screen door. She watched the sun set, feeling as if the big orange ball pulled her heart down right along with it.

Annie couldn't have said how long she remained seated in the darkening kitchen. With a deep sigh, she finally rose and lit the lamp. It wasn't until she was replacing the glass chimney that she realized Billy wasn't home yet.

A wave of worry floated over her before she recollected that Billy was almost always late. Knowing how the boy dallied should've eased her concern, but it didn't.

She went outside, cupped her hands

around her mouth, and hollered his name. Of course, he wouldn't be able to hear her if he was still at the creek. Squaring her shoulders, she marched down the steps and headed in that direction. She swung her arms as she moved down the pitch-black path and grew more ill-tempered by the moment. She was of mind to box Billy's ears for upsetting her so.

Halfway to the creek, she bumped into him on the trail, and instead of boxing his ears, she hugged him. Once her relief was spent though, she gave him a good shake, then caught his arm and steered him toward the house.

"Dad-burn you, Billy. You like to've scared the livin' daylights out of me," she said, dragging him forward. "Didn't Eli tell you to be home before dark? Well, didn't he?"

"Yes'm." The boy sniffled. "I'm sorry, Annie. It wasn't you I was mad at. It was Eli."

Annie stopped in her tracks and looked at him. A streak of moonlight slanted across his upturned face. Tears pooled in his eyes. "You mean to tell me you stayed out on purpose? Just to spite Eli?"

He nodded, the motion making teardrops spill down his cheeks. "I . . . I figured if I stayed gone, he might take back what he said. I thought maybe he'd feel real bad."

Annie felt a twinge of pity for the weeping child, but kept her expression stern. "Billy, you know it was wrong of you to do somethin' like that."

"Yes'm. But I heard 'im, Annie." Sobs shook his small shoulders. "I forgot the worms I'd dug by the back door and when I came back t' get 'em, I heard Eli say he was sending you and me away."

"Oh, Billy." Annie dropped to her knees and held him tight.

"I . . . don't . . . want to go away," he said between short rasps.

"I don't either." Annie laid her cheek alongside his and combed her fingers through his cornsilk hair. "Shh now," she whispered, and rocked him from side to side. "It'll be all right, Billy-boy. Don't you worry none, you hear?"

"You w-won't let him . . . send us away, will you, Annie?"

She swallowed hard and squeezed him, then pulled him to his feet. "I can't make no promises for Eli." Smiling, she reached out and gently brushed damp blond strands from his face. "But I swear here and now that whatever happens, wherever we go, I'll be with you. You'd like that, now wouldn't you?"

Billy returned her smile and hugged her around the waist. "And you won't never leave me, will ya, Annie?"

"Not ever." She chucked his chin, and ignored the tiny urge to wonder if she'd just made another promise that she might not be able to keep. "Why don't we get on to the house and have us a big piece of apple pie. Hmm?"

Billy wiped his nose on his shirt sleeve and nodded in agreement.

Annie guided the conversation back to the horny toad in Miss Prigg's pencil box and had the youngster laughing by the time they reached the house.

"Then she got real mad and her eyes popped out like this."

Annie chuckled at the face Billy made. Catching his neck in the crook of her arm, she playfully wrestled him through the door and into the kitchen. "And I s'pose you didn't have nothing to do with putting that horned toad in her pencil box."

Billy laughed, wriggling in her grasp. "No. It wasn't me. It was Joey, I tell ya. But Miss Prigg thought it was me. Made me stand in the corner all mornin', and I didn't have t' do no work."

"Why, you little scoundrel, you," she chided, then commenced tickling the boy.

She ended her game abruptly when a sudden sense of dread overcame her. Something wasn't as it should be in the kitchen. The pie she'd left on the table was gone. One of the chairs wasn't in its place. She tightened her arms around Billy, stilling his frolicsome movements as she searched the shadows of the room.

"Hello, Annie," came a voice that sent chills up her spine and drew her gaze to a form sitting in the far dark corner of the room.

Buck stood, deliberately knocking over the chair he straddled. He sauntered into the dim glow of lamplight, grinning like a fox about to raid a henhouse. "Aw now, what's the matter, girlie? Ain't you glad to see me?" He took a step forward, and Annie skittered backward, hauling Billy with her. "No? Well, maybe you'll be a sight more civil toward your brother."

Frank emerged from the shadowy hall, empty pie tin in hand. Annie stared at her tall, lanky brother. All the gals seemed to be taken with the reddish-blond curl that fell across his forehead. But Annie hadn't ever understood what they saw in him.

"When the hell did you learn t' cook like this?" he asked, wiping crumbs from his mouth.

"Annie, who's—" Billy began.

"Hush, boy," she commanded, shoving the youngster behind her. She shifted her gaze warily from one man to the other. "Whata y'all want?"

Buck raked his knuckles along the underside of his stubbled chin. "Well now, I can think of plenty of things I want from you, Annie." He ambled toward her, and her heart raced. "First off, though, I want the robbery money."

Annie glanced at the door and eased in that direction. The pie pan flew across the room, barely missing her, even though she ducked. By the time she got her bearings, Frank's tall frame blocked the exit.

She backed Billy against the cupboard, shielding him behind her in the folds of her skirt. Buck moved in on her. A slow grin lifted one side of the outlaw's face. "You thought you could pull one over on ol' Buck, now didn't you, girl? But I know all about you and your lawman-husband's plans. You didn't hide the money. You and the sheriff've had it all along."

Annie widened her eyes. She started to deny his ravings, but he grabbed her jaw in a painful grip.

"Don't even think about lyin' to me again," he said with a black scowl. "I had someone watching the stagecoach and train depots. Heard tell your husband bought two tickets to Boston. You and him were going to skip town with the money, weren't you?" He sneered. "Didn't think ol' Buck would get wind of it, did you?" He tightened his fingers on her jaw until she winced. "I want the money, Annie, and I want it now."

"I . . . I don't have it. I swear, Buck. It's in the woods. I'll show you where, I will. You let the boy go and I'll take you to it. I swear."

"The boy? You mean that sniveling little worm hiding behind you?" Buck reached around her and snatched Billy by the ear.

The youngster's cry sliced through Annie, and she tore into Buck. She fought him with every ounce of her might while he attempted to wrench Billy away from her. She managed to hold Buck off until he backhanded her across the face.

The world went gray and tiny sparks obstructed her vision. In one terrifying moment, her fingers numbed and she lost her grasp on Billy. She reached for the boy even as she sank to her knees. But he was gone.

"You leave her be!" Billy yelled between sobs, bringing her back to her senses. With her ears still ringing from the blow, she focused in the direction of his voice.

Her half-brother had the struggling boy in a stranglehold. "Don't hurt him, Frank," she pleaded. "Don't—"

Buck clutched a handful of her hair and dragged her to her feet. Pressing her against the pantry door, he caught her by the throat. "You'd better start worrying about your own pretty neck, girlie. Now, I've searched this house over and the money's not here. Where is it?"

"I told you. I hid it in the woods. I can take you to it. I can show—"

"You telling me the truth, girl?" His hand constricted around her windpipe. That sick grin curved his lips again. "Ol' Buck's got ways of finding out whether you're storying or not."

Annie felt life leaving her body. She clawed frantically at his fingers. Just as she approached the edge of unconsciousness, his grip slackened, allowing her to gasp for breath.

"So the money's hidden in the woods, is it?" Buck asked.

Unable to take in enough air to speak, she nodded.

"Well, we'll just see, won't we?" He slid his hand from her throat down the front of her dress.

"Come on, Buck," Frank interrupted. "We ain't got time for none of that. The sheriff's liable to be back any minute."

"I s'pose you're right." Buck took hold of Annie's arm and jerked her away from the pantry. "There's no reason we can't finish this discussion back at the hideout anyway." He headed for the door, but stopped by the table, his gaze settling on the flickering coal-oil lamp. "Hold up a minute, Frank. There's something I been wanting to do ever since I first set eyes on this place." Shoving Annie into Frank's arms, he picked up the lamp and examined it, an ugly gleam flitting across his eyes.

"Buck . . . *no*," Annie whispered as his intention became clear. "For the love of God, Buck, please don't—"

"For the love of God?" The outlaw threw his head back and laughed. "Honey, I ain't never done nothin' for the love of God. I've done plenty of things just for the devil of it, but never for the love of God."

His grin growing wider, he met her gaze. He seemed to take great pleasure in her reaction as he lifted the lamp and hurled it against the kitchen wall.

Chapter 22

Weary from questioning Zeb Jenkins, Eli paced his horse at a slow trot along the dark road home. His mind wandered over the evening's events, and nausea rose to his throat once again.

The old man had finally broken down and admitted killing his three young wives. In a rage the likes of which Eli had never witnessed, Zeb had then proceeded to justify his acts by claiming the girls had all been disobedient.

Eli shifted in his saddle. He tried to block the vision of the decayed bodies. He and Hollis had found the other two girls in shallow graves exactly where Zeb had confessed they would be. They had gathered the remains and taken them to the churchyard for proper burials. The families would have to be notified in the morning.

Eli filled his lungs with the cool night air, hoping to calm his stomach. His father wouldn't have had this reaction, he told himself. Sam Larson had always been able to deal with his emotions. Eli closed his eyes, and wished he were more like his father . . .

wished he could still the queasiness . . . wished he could simply leave the past behind and teach school.

Tugging his hat lower on his forehead, he pondered the senselessness of it all. He'd heard it said that sometimes good came out of tragedy, though he had to wonder what good could come from the murder of Emily Dobbs and her predecessors.

The thought that Annie could have been Zeb's next victim had plagued him throughout the evening, and left him cold and empty. If he'd ever had any regrets about speaking up for the Calhoun Kid's hand, he certainly had none now. If good for nothing else, tonight's events had made him understand his feelings for his wife. Annie had filled a hollow space inside him. She had offered him everything a man could possibly want. Yet he had been willing to cast her aside.

And for what? To take a bullet in the back? Or gun down the man who'd killed his parents? To take pleasure in watching the murderer die? To lower himself to Garrett Buckley's level?

It had occurred to him when they'd unearthed the bodies, that life was unpredictable. No one knew when his time to die would come. He had realized then that every moment on this earth was precious and should be spent with special care. Now as he rode the shadowy trail home, he knew that what he wanted most in the world was to spend every moment with Annie. She made him whole. She gave him a reason for living—one much worthier than the need for vengeance he had harbored for most of his life.

He couldn't, *wouldn't* give her up. Not even if keeping her at his side meant surrendering his dream of watching Garrett Buckley dangle at the end of a rope. For once, he intended to follow his heart's desire. He didn't know how he'd manage to quiet his conscience, but he would find a way. Annie would help him. Together, they would battle the demons within him.

Restfulness settled over Eli. More at peace with himself than he'd been in years, he pressed his heels into his mount's flanks, nudging the horse into a full canter. He couldn't wait to see Annie's face when he told her that she could have all the babies she wanted.

His peace of mind ended abruptly when he rounded the line of trees that edged his property.

The sky glowed orange on the dark horizon. Smoke stung his nostrils. Eli's heart thundered as he rode hell bent for leather toward the house.

He went numb when he crested the ridge. The house was nothing more than a huge blaze. His horse reared and whinnied as they neared the fire, and Eli hit the ground running.

Shielding his face from the heat, he frantically tried to find a point of entry. But the roof had already collapsed and tongues of flame licked out at him, forcing him back.

"Annie! Billy!" he yelled over and over again while he circled the burning structure, the dogs yowling at his heels.

In the few terrifying moments when the charred frame toppled in on itself, hopelessness brought Eli to his knees. He shook uncontrollably. The only thought that surfaced was that Annie was gone . . . *Billy and Annie were gone . . .*

Suddenly everything in him screamed it wasn't true. *God in heaven, she couldn't be gone.* She wouldn't leave him this way.

Struggling to stand, he glanced about. He dragged his hand over his scorched face, barely aware of the sting, and his gaze came to rest on the barn.

He started in that direction, his footsteps wooden at first, then he broke into a run. Hope that he'd find Annie and Billy there grew steadily. Fear that he wouldn't stopped him at the open barn door. He took a deep breath, said a silent prayer, then entered.

Wan light sifted through the cracks in the roof, turning the interior a soft hazy lavender. "Annie? Billy?' Eli called toward the hayloft. "Annie? Are you there?"

The pulse in his throat quickened. He scanned the barn, searching for any sign of his wife and the boy. Maybe they were asleep. Maybe they were hurt. Maybe—

The open stall door where he'd kept the mare caught his attention. He moved forward, found it empty, and immediately looked at the tack wall. The extra saddle was missing.

Relief flooded over him. Annie must have gone for help, or taken the boy to Betsy's. Wherever she was now, at least she hadn't been in the house when the fire started.

Eli glanced over his shoulder at what had once been his house. A pile of dying embers was all that remained of it. *His and Annie's home.* He supposed that relief should be the only emotion coursing through him at the moment, but he felt sad, too. The house had been full of memories—old ones of his family before their tragic deaths, and newer ones of Annie and Billy. They all sliced at his heart.

He closed his eyes and massaged his throbbing temples. He was exhausted, he told himself. He wasn't thinking clearly. He unbuckled his gun belt and hung it on a nail on the wall. Then he leaned back against one of the poles that supported the loft and slid down until he met the straw-covered floor. Joining his fingers loosely between his knees, he studied the soot and singed hair on the back of his hands.

Since he hadn't passed Annie on his way back from town, she and Billy had to be at Betsy's place. He just needed a few minutes' rest, then he would find his horse and ride over to Betsy's. Annie would be there waiting, and would make everything right again.

A bright stream of sunlight pierced Eli's closed lids. He blinked, then bolted upright with recollection of a horrible nightmare. But one look toward the house told him that the fire had been no dream.

He rose and started to brush the straw from his jeans, but the first swipe against the coarse denim made his hands spasm with pain. Staring at his red, blistered palms, he tried to recall exactly what had happened. He couldn't remember anything between seeing the house aflame from the ridge and finding the stall open and the mare—

Annie. In his befuddled state, he'd merely assumed she'd taken the mare and ridden to safety.

Striding to the barn door, he looked out and saw the sun hovering high above the horizon. *Lord, how long had he slept?* It was nigh on noon . . . If Annie and Billy had been at Betsy's, wouldn't they have come home by now?

He focused on the charred ruins of the house. The same possibility that he'd so ardently rejected last night came to mind.

He couldn't move. He couldn't bear the thought of finding proof in the ashes that Annie or Billy was dead.

He would've rather believed that Annie had made a fool of him . . . that she'd been waiting all along for the opportunity to take off for the Territories . . . that he'd never truly known her.

An indescribable pressure pushed against his sternum. He had to find her. If she had survived the fire, he had to know where she was.

With a deep, steadying breath, he started forward, determined to examine the charred rubble, but a bright splash of yellow on the ground caught his eye.

As he stooped and picked up the cuff of Annie's yellow dress, he saw two words apparently scratched by the toe of a boot in the dirt: *Frank. Money*.

In the time it took Eli to straighten, he had figured out what had happened. Telltale signs that he hadn't noticed the night before were etched in the earth of the surrounding area: three sets of horses' hooves, the obvious outline of two men's footprints, and scuffle marks in the red soil.

Frank Calhoun had come for Annie, just as she had feared he would.

A white-hot fury rose in Eli. He spotted his horse grazing in the pasture nearby, turned, and strode purposefully toward the barn. He strapped on his gun belt, then checked the bullets in the chamber of his Peacemaker.

As he left the barn, the hate he'd carried for Garrett Buckley seemed trifling in comparison to his present feelings. He had wanted to see Garrett brought to justice lawfully. At the moment, he had an overpowering urge to kill Frank Calhoun on the spot, no questions asked.

Trying not to be too conspicuous, Annie twisted her chafed wrists in an attempt to free them from the rope wrapped tightly around the saddle horn.

From his own mount, Frank knew she was up to something. He kept a firm grip on her reins. Every now and then, he looked over his shoulder suspiciously.

She'd watched him carefully though. He hadn't seen her kick out her foot when they'd passed a bush or low-hanging branch or noticed that sometimes a snippet of her hem would get snagged and be left behind.

Buck had ridden ahead of them, setting a breakneck pace throughout the night. He had pushed the horses until they could run no more. Since the sun had come up, the poor animals were doing well just to saunter through the woods.

Annie leaned to one side to catch a glimpse of Billy. He rode double with Buck, situated in front of the outlaw. Buck had cuffed the boy's ear a while back when Billy had commenced struggling. The youngster had gone limp and hadn't made a peep since. Annie couldn't tell from where she sat whether the boy was truly hurt or merely frightened. She ached to hold him, tell him everything was all right—even though it wasn't.

Pressing her lips into a tight line, she set her mind to work. They would have to stop and rest the horses soon. Maybe she could think up some plan to distract Frank and Buck long enough for Billy to get away.

"You're aimin' on tryin' something, ain't ya, little sister? Hell, I can see it in your eyes."

Annie slid her gaze to Frank's and held it steady. "Just what in tarnation do you think I'm gonna do, Frank, with my hands calf-tied like this? Huh? You reckon maybe I might turn myself into a bird and fly off?''

''Girl, you've picked up a sassy mouth since you up and married that sheriff. Ya know that?'' He took a swing at her, but she reared back and he missed. ''You best not be usin' that sassy tone with me agin, ya hear?''

Annie simply lifted her chin and glared at him.

''Damn you, Annie. Don't you go gettin' uppity with me. I'll knock you from here t' high heaven, gir—''

''Shut up, Frank!'' Buck ordered, turning his horse to face them. ''We're not that far from the road. You want somebody to hear us?''

Annie searched Billy's pale features, and her heart constricted. Obviously terrified, the boy stared blankly. ''Buck . . . please,'' she said softly, her gaze never wavering from the youngster. ''Let the boy go. He's not well.''

Buck grinned. ''Aw, he's just fine now. Me and Billy-boy here just had to get a few things straight between us. Ain't that right, kid?'' He nudged the boy's shoulder, and Billy flinched. ''He ain't liable to cause no more trouble.''

Annie narrowed her eyes on the outlaw. ''I won't show you where the money is unless you turn Billy loose. Understand? I won't take you to it.''

Buck moved his horse in close to hers and grabbed the front of her dress, jerking her forward. ''Listen up, girl. You ain't in no position to bargain with me. You got that?''

Frank leaned sideways in his saddle. "You watch her, Buck. I tell ya, she's up t' something."

Buck glanced at his comrade, then looked at Annie, and raised an eyebrow. "Is that right? Hmm? You plannin' something, are ya, Annie?" He grinned slowly, then drew his gun and rubbed the barrel back and forth against her cheek. "Well, there's a little matter you ought to think about real hard before you make any sudden moves, darlin'. First off, I don't aim to part with Billy-boy anytime soon. Know why? Because it's plain as day you have a fondness for the kid." He transferred the barrel of his gun from Annie's cheek to Billy's temple. "But, ya see, I don't. I never did cotton much to youngsters. Pesty little critters, if you ask me."

Annie felt her heart sink to the pit of her stomach. She forced her gaze from Billy and focused on Buck's stone-cold features. In that instant, she knew that she and Billy didn't have a snowball's chance in hell of making it through this ordeal alive. As soon as Buck got what he wanted, he'd do them both in.

Surely Eli would come after them. She'd left him a trail. But it was highly unlikely that he could be close behind. They had half a night's head start on him, at least.

Annie squared her shoulders. It was up to her to see that no harm came to Billy. She resisted the urge to drop her gaze to the boy again, though she was certain he was frightened and could've used a reassuring wink.

Instead, she lowered her lashes a fraction

and smiled at Buck. "Aw now, Buck, ain't no need to go shootin' the boy to prove your point. Someone might hear the shot, you know. Besides, I get your meaning. And you're right about me being taken with the young'un. I'd have to be a fool to try and pull anything over on you."

The outlaw eyed her skeptically for a long, restless moment, then released the fabric of her bodice and holstered his gun. "Well now, missy, I take it we understand each other then?"

"I'd say we do."

"Then we'd best be on our way," he said, and turned his horse. "I'd like that money in hand by nightfall."

"Buck?" Annie risked taking the game a step further when he looked over his shoulder. "You mind if I ride alongside you for a spell? Frank here gets on my nerves with him yelling the way he does and all."

"I'll do worse than yell, you little—"

"Shut up, Frank." Buck slid his gaze down the length of Annie. "Give her the reins. She ain't going nowhere as long as I've got the boy." With a gesture of his head he motioned her to join him.

Annie moved her horse even with his. She had put on a cheerful expression, but felt sick inside at what she was doing. "How's the rest of the gang?" she asked while they rode on.

"All right, I suppose. What's left of them." Buck studied her intensely. "Will took a bullet in the belly a while back. Joe took off for Mexico."

Afraid he might guess her true thoughts, she set her gaze on something in the distance. "How about Deadeye?"

Buck shrugged. "Ain't worth much as far as I can see. He's gettin' rusty. Damned old codger needs to hang up his guns, if you ask me."

Annie bit her tongue and fought to keep her smile. She silently reminded herself that what happened from here on out might depend on how she acted now.

Looking directly at Buck, she forced the corners of her mouth higher. "I'm glad you came to fetch me when you did. I was fixin' to light out of there soon as the sheriff left for Tyler anyways."

Billy's head came up, but Annie was careful not to focus on the boy's face. "I don't mind tellin' you, I didn't much take to married life," she said. "Had me a hankering for wide open spaces, I did." She lowered her lashes coyly and cocked her head. "Say, Buck, these here ropes are rubbing me raw. Think you might be able to loosen them up a bit when we stop to rest the horses?"

Buck chuckled, then reached out and ran a finger along her jawline. "Annie, I don't trust you any further than I can spit. But I sure as hell like you better when you smile like that." He raked his gaze down the front of her dress. "You just keep on smilin' and remember little Billy-boy here, and you and me will get along just fine."

Chapter 23

⌒◯◯⌒

Eli knelt on one knee and ran his hand over the hoofprint in the dirt. Frank and the other riders were heading into the Territories, all right. They had stayed off the main roads and cut through the wooded areas, making tracking difficult. Eli had lost, then found their trail again three times already. Hunting for signs of them within the heavily timbered tracts had slowed him down considerably.

He straightened from his crouched position, hooked a thumb in his gun belt, then nudged the brim of his hat. Deep in thought, he scanned his surroundings. He'd narrowed Frank's destination down to two possibilities. Annie's brother was either taking her to the Calhouns' present hideout or to the spot where the bank money had disappeared.

Eli was fairly certain he could find his way back to the place where Annie's horse had thrown her. No more time would be wasted if he went directly there. But what if Frank was taking her to the hideout instead? Annie had once mentioned that the Calhoun gang moved from place to place every few days.

In that case, Eli had no choice but to continue tracking them.

A heaviness settled in his chest. He needed to make a decision, and needed to make it fast. He worried though, that if he headed in the wrong direction and had to backtrack, the mistake could cost him the two people he loved most in the world.

Annie had claimed that Frank had never killed anyone. But from what Eli knew, the Calhouns had left plenty of bodies behind in their lawless dealings.

He took a deep breath and searched the area once more for anything that might steer him the right way: a broken branch, crimped or missing leaves, a—

His gaze returned to a tiny spot of yellow in the distance that he'd formerly assumed was merely a blossom.

He walked forward slowly, almost afraid to set his hopes too high. But his heart lifted when he reached the bush and caught the bit of cloth between his forefinger and thumb.

"How much farther, darlin'?" Buck asked, a grin slanting across one side of his face.

"Just a little ways through these woods here." Annie shifted in her saddle, growing steadily more uncomfortable with the situation. She wasn't sure how much longer she could smile at Buck's crude remarks. This awful charade was taking every bit of strength she had.

Playing up to Buck had been a fool idea to begin with, she realized now. She didn't know the first thing about trifling with a man, and Buck had seen right through her ploy.

Nevertheless, she'd stayed on pleasant terms with him, hoping he'd let his guard slip. And in fact, he'd untied her hands when they'd stopped for water. But he'd kept Billy so close to him that Annie couldn't chance making a break for it.

She fiddled with the saddle horn as they neared the spot where she'd lost the money bag. She reckoned it didn't matter much whether she kept on smiling or not. Buck sure as hell wasn't going to be in a good mood when she turned up empty-handed.

Annie pulled back on her reins and glanced around the small, vaguely familiar clearing. Maybe, with a stroke of luck, she would be able to find the money. The bank bag *had* to be here somewhere. It had been near nightfall when Eli and his men had searched the area. The deputies might have overlooked the money.

"Is this the place?" Buck asked.

"I'm not sure." Annie wrinkled her nose and tried to work out another plan in case she couldn't find the bag. "There wasn't no leaves on the trees when last I was through here."

"She's stallin'," Frank said, circling her on his horse.

Buck moved in on Annie and caught her arm. His grin completely gone, he narrowed his eyes on her. "Look, girl, it's well into the afternoon. I been ridin' all day and half the night, and I ain't in no mood to play any more games with you. So you'd best get your butt off that horse and fetch me the money. Or else Billy-boy here ain't going to be nothing but a memory.''

Annie slipped from her horse. Her legs would hardly support her when her feet met the ground. "It's here," she whispered, more to herself than anyone else. "I know it's here . . . somewhere.''

"Get it," Buck ordered and climbed off his horse, hauling Billy with him. He held the boy in front of him with his forearm across the youngster's neck.

Annie went down on all fours and started scavenging through the decaying leaves. She searched a hollow log, dipping her hand into every crevice or cavity she came across. The bank bag had to be here. It *had* to be.

"I've had just about enough of this, Annie." Buck's voice was low and cold, and sent chills through her. She angled her head over her shoulder. Terror paralyzed her as he dragged a bowie knife from a sheath in his belt. "Maybe if I start carvin' on the boy, you might remember real quick-like where you hid the money. Huh? How about if I take off an ear first?''

"*No* . . . please, Buck." Annie scrambled to her feet, but thought better of making any sudden moves when the outlaw touched the blade to Billy's cheek.

She looked at her brother, who had dismounted and was wrapping the horses' reins around a low branch. He had paused in his task, and she could tell by his pale features that he didn't exactly approve of what Buck was doing.

"Frank, make him stop," she pleaded. "For God's sake, you gonna stand there and let him hurt a child?"

Her brother set his jaw and took a step forward. "Come on, Buck. There ain't no call to go and—"

"Shut up, Frank." Buck shot him a look that made Annie's half-brother drop his head. "You stay outa this. I know what I'm doin'."

Annie's heart sank. She had thought maybe just this once, her brother might stand up to Buck. But she knew as well as Frank did that the few who'd crossed the outlaw had ended up dead.

Tension stiffened her spine. Billy wouldn't look at her. The boy stared off at something no one else could see. "Buck . . . listen to me," she said in an easy, even tone. "The money's here. I know it is." Stretching her arms wide, she inched forward. "I lost it hereabouts when Ol' Blue threw me. The bank bag is here, I tell ya."

Buck grinned. "Sure do wish I could believe you, darlin'. Fact is, I don't." He pricked Billy's cheek with the tip of the blade, and a single drop of blood rolled down the side of the youngster's face.

A muffled sound caught in Annie's throat. She froze, not daring to take another step. Billy began to whimper in a soft, pitiful manner that made her ache. Tears blurred her vision as she focused on Buck's broad grin.

Her temples throbbed. Rage rose like a rearing horse inside her. Glancing about, she searched for some way of drawing Buck's attention away from the boy.

Her eyes settled on Frank, who stood a few feet behind Buck. An idea quickly formed in her brain, and she grabbed it.

"Frank, don't!" she yelled.

With lightning reflexes, Buck whirled and aimed his bowie at her brother.

Annie charged him, grabbing his wrist. With both her hands and all her might, she held the hand in which Buck clasped the knife high above her head.

Buck's attention came back to her immediately. The man claimed the devil's own eyes as he glowered down at her. In that moment, her confidence slipped, and she felt the strength leaving her body.

"Frank . . . help me." Her glaze flickered over her brother's stunned expression. "Damn it, Frank . . . for once in your life, do something honorable!"

Buck's low chuckle sent a shiver through Annie. Her arms began to quake against the downward pressure of his wrist. She stared up at the knife hovering above her head, saw the sun glint off the blade as it slowly, steadily descended.

"Sorry, Buck." Frank pressed the barrel of his gun under the outlaw's jaw, and Buck stilled the knife in midair. "Annie may not be much, but she's the only kin I got."

Annie slipped her fingers cautiously from the man's wrist, and looked at Frank in amazement. She attempted to smile at her brother, but her lips trembled in the process.

He winked at her, then returned his full attention to Buck. "Now, let the boy go," he said, cocking his gun. "Nice and easy-like."

Buck lifted his arm from Billy's neck, and Annie took the sobbing boy to her. Kneeling beside him, she hugged him tight. "Shh," she whispered, and kissed his injured cheek. "Don't cry."

"Annie, take the boy and get outa here." Frank shifted his weight and jerked his head to one side. "Go on. You get on back to the sheriff and make a decent life for yourself, ya hear?"

"Frank . . ." Annie fought the tightness in her throat. A tear trickled from the corner of her eye. "Frank . . . *thank you*," she blurted out, tugging the hard-to-say words from her heart.

Her brother smiled ever so slightly, then nodded. "Go on now," he said softly.

Annie took Billy's hand, but let her gaze linger on Frank a moment. She wanted to remember the gleam of pride he held in his eyes. She reckoned he was finding out how good it felt to do the right thing. "Bye, Frank," she said, starting to turn. But just then she saw a flash of motion out of the corner of her eye.

It all happened so fast. The knife Buck held frozen for so long swung down and sliced across Frank's face. The gun went off in the air.

"Run, Billy!" Annie set the boy away from

her, but he just stood there staring at her. "Dad-burn you, Billy, *run!*" She shoved him, and he stumbled. Then the youngster scrambled to his feet and took off through the woods.

By the time Annie returned her attention to the scuffle, her brother lay unmoving on the ground. Blood oozed around the knife protruding from his belly. Buck leaned over him, pulled his bowie from the body and wiped the blade on his pant leg.

Annie swayed. The world grew dim before her. She saw Buck grin as he began coming toward her, but she couldn't move. She couldn't think.

"Looks like it's just you and me now, darlin'." His voice was a hollow echo, it sounded as if it was coming from inside a train tunnel. "You wanna tussle with ol' Buck, do ya? Well, come on. You and me, darlin'. Just you and me."

Buck dealt her a blow that knocked her flat on her back. Before she could regain her senses, he sauntered over and stood sneering down at her.

For one endless moment, time stopped. She looked past him at the bright patches of sunlight peeking through the leaves above, trying to remove herself from what was happening.

"Get up," he said, nudging her with the toe of his boot.

Annie focused harder on something lodged in the fork of a branch. She could almost make out the writing on it. *F-i-r* . . . *N-a-t* . . . *B-a-n* . . . *B-a-r* . . .

"Get up, I said." Buck stooped, grabbed her arm, and jerked her to her knees.

Tilting her head, she widened her eyes at the object overhead. All of a sudden, the string of partially visible words made sense. "First National Bank of Bartlett Springs," she whispered.

"Won't do no good to start talkin' loco, girl. Ol' Buck can tell you're bluffin'."

"No, *look!*" Annie pointed to the money bag. "It must've been there all along."

Buck eyed her suspiciously, then dragged her to her feet. Grabbing both her hands, he held them behind her back before angling his gaze upward. A slow smile creased his lips. "Well, I'll be damned."

"That there is a fact," Annie murmured.

"Don't go shooting off your smart mouth when you got more important things to do." Buck shoved her toward the trunk of the tree. "Shinny on up there, darlin', and toss me down my money."

Annie started to protest, then it occurred to her that the farther away from Buck she could get, the better off she'd be. Finding a foothold, she pulled herself onto the lowest limb.

"Oh, and darlin'?" The outlaw waited until she looked at him, then he drew his gun and pointed it at her. "Don't try anything tricky."

She bit her tongue to keep from telling him to go to hell, and continued climbing. Her mind drifted while she scaled higher and higher. Billy had gotten away. That was all that mattered. Buck couldn't hurt the boy no more.

She had an inkling though, that the black-hearted devil below planned to shoot her as soon as she threw down the money bag.

Annie hadn't ever thought much about dying. She did now, and figured it must be sort of like going to sleep forever. The notion didn't seem so bad . . . except when she thought of never seeing Eli again, never holding or kissing him.

Her husband's face formed in her head, and her heart expanded. Eli had shown her a side of life she'd never known. He'd given her a home . . . a family. She had loved, and been loved. If her time to die came in the next few minutes, then at least she would die happy.

"Damn it, quit dallying, girl," Buck hollered.

Perched on the base of the branch that held the money, Annie glanced down at him. He stood directly underneath the holdup bag. The sack would probably plop right down on his head if she shook the limb. Of course, the money wasn't heavy enough to do him any real harm, and there was always the chance that he'd catch it. Still, it might catch him by surprise, giving her time to swing to the branch below, drop to the ground, and run for it. Maybe she could lose him in the woods.

Annie twisted her mouth to one side. It

wasn't much of a plan, but at the moment it was the only one she had. Bouncing up and down, she jiggled the branch as hard as she could. But it refused to give up its prize.

"I'm warnin' you," Buck yelled, and waved his gun in a dangerous manner. "Quit foolin' around! Scoot on out there and get the money!"

There was an edge to his voice that didn't set well with Annie. She sighed, relinquishing her last bit of hope, then wrapped her arms and legs around the limb. While she inchwormed forward, she prayed that God would forgive all her wrongdoings.

The branch bowed with her weight when she neared the money. She stretched her hand out, but could only touch the bag with her fingertips.

A shot cracked in the air. She flinched as a bullet whizzed past her ear.

"I'm gettin' a little impatient, darlin'," Buck called. "Next time, I won't miss."

"I can't reach it." Still shaken, Annie clung to the limb with her eyes squeezed shut. "I'm trying. My arms just aren't long enough."

"Well, they better grow longer real quick." He fired another shot. "Move out there further, girlie!"

"Stay where you are, Annie." Eli's voice was cool and commanding.

Annie blinked. She was almost afraid to look down. Afraid that if she did, she'd find the delivery of words were nothing more than an utterance of her own mind.

"Drop the gun, mister. Annie, get down. Annie?"

Certain this time that she wasn't imagining her husband's smooth, deep drawl, she peered below. She stared at the crown of the familiar Stetson, and her heart pounded. Eli held his Peacemaker on Buck. "Annie?" he repeated. "Are you all right?"

"I am now." She smiled and started to climb down.

"Hold it, darlin'." Buck steadied his aim on her, then slid his gaze to Eli. "Well, now sheriff, seems we got us a standoff here, wouldn't you say? Tell ya what. I'll make you a deal."

"Don't listen to him, Eli. He's a liar, and a cheat, and a low-down, murdering—"

"Shut up, girl! This is between me and the sheriff." Buck cocked his gun, and Annie closed her mouth. Apparently satisfied with her silence, he directed a grin Eli's way. "Just between us men, the only good female is one that's had her tongue cut out. They don't carry on so, ya know?

Nausea stirred in Eli's stomach. He'd faced down desperadoes more times than he could count. Something about this long-haired outlaw was vaguely familiar though—the way he moved, his voice, something. Yet Eli couldn't quite place him. The man hadn't been pictured in any of the wanted posters with Frank Calhoun.

"Well, now, sheriff, I can see that you're a lawman of few words, so ol' Buck will just tell ya how it's gonna be. You toss your gun over yonder on the ground. Little Annie can throw down the bank bag, and I'll ride outa here. Ain't no need for anybody to get hurt.''

"Don't you do it, Eli. He's the devil's own, he is. And there ain't no dealing with the devil.''

Eli stifled the urge to glance at Annie. He knew better than to take his eyes off the outlaw. He also knew better than to give up his gun.

"It's up to you, sheriff. You can stand there and deliberate the matter all you want.'' Buck flung his hair over his shoulder. "But you ought to know I'm itching to kill that girl. She's been a pain in the backside all damned day. So you see, it don't make no difference to me.'' He cocked his head, and his grin broadened. "But it does to you, don't it? I mean, if ya didn't care nothing for her, ya wouldn't have come traipsin' in here without a posse. Ain't nothin' quite like a woman to make a fool out of a man, now is there, sheriff?''

Eli kept his gun trained on the outlaw. He was fast. He could take him.

"I know what you're thinkin', lawman. I heard tell you were good with that Colt. But I'll wager you ain't good enough to cut me down before I shoot the girl dead. You willin' to take that bet?''

Cocking his gun, Eli laid his fingers against the cold steel trigger.

"All I want is the money, sheriff,'' Buck said. "That's all. Just the money. Then I'll ride out and you'll never see me again. What you gotta do now is ask yourself which means more to you, the bank bag or your darlin' wife.''

Chapter 24

$\sim\!\!\sim\!\!\infty\!\!\sim\!\!\sim$

Eli relaxed his grip on his gun. His confidence wavered. *Could* he get a shot off before a bullet hit Annie? Common sense told him to stand firm. But his emotions screamed something else.

"I swear on my mother's grave, sheriff, I'll leave here peaceably. No harm has to come to nobody. Just lay down your shootin' iron and back off. Now, I'm givin' ya till the count of five. One . . ."

Eli's heart pounded in his head. He scanned Frank Calhoun's body on the ground a few feet away. Then his gaze passed over the rabid look in Buck's eyes, and lifted to Annie. She was crouched in an awkward position in the tree. There was no way the outlaw could miss.

"Three . . . four . . ."

"All right, damn you." Eli tossed his gun aside swiftly, before he could change his mind, then spread his hands wide. "But I'm holding you to your word."

A slow smirk raised one corner of Buck's mouth. "Well now, that's a big mistake, sheriff. Ya see, I don't ever recall keeping my word." He veered his pistol from Annie and aimed it at Eli. "You ain't too smart for a lawman, are ya? Must be crazy in love. Is that right, sheriff?" Buck glanced at Annie, then snickered. "You know, your paw was the same, boy. Crazy in love with your mamma."

Something cold coursed through Eli's veins. "What do you know about my parents?" he asked in a deceptively calm tone.

"I know your daddy died on his knees. And that your mamma was *real* sweet. See here?" Buck held up his free hand and wiggled his little finger. The evening sun glinted off a small ruby ring. "I still wear her weddin' band just to remind me how special she was."

Hatred swelled in Eli's chest. Years had changed the outlaw's appearance, but the man's black soul should've given him away. A red haze coated Eli's vision. It was all so simple that he'd overlooked it. "Garrett Buckley," he said through his teeth, then took a step forward.

"Eli . . . no . . . don't move!" Annie's voice came from somewhere far away, then faded. He couldn't hear or see anything beyond Buck, couldn't feel anything but the raging urge to kill. The need for vengeance blotted out all caution when he looked down the barrel of the gun pointed at him. Pushed by one single thought, he made his move. He never even saw Annie leap from the tree and tackle Buck.

A shot exploded. The echo lingered in Eli's ears. Time stretched, distorting everything.

In a moment that seemed to last forever, Annie clutched at the front of Garrett Buckley's shirt, then slid slowly down the outlaw's leg.

Eli dove for his Peacemaker. He reached out across the bed of dried leaves and grasped the pearl handle.

Buck's boot pinned his wrist to the ground. "You're just like your paw, ain't you, sheriff? Neither one of you was quite quick enough for ol' Buck. Both of you had a weakness when it came to the ladies." Garrett Buckley grinned, then stooped and stuck the barrel of his gun to Eli's temple, pressing the side of his face into the dirt. "Don't you worry none about little Annie. She ain't dead . . . yet. Ol' Buck's gonna take real good care of her after you're gone. I just wanted you to know that." Buckley spat into the dust. "See you in hell, lawman."

"Hold it right there, Buck," called a deep, gruff voice from the distance.

Buck jerked upright, swinging his gun in the direction of the command. Before he could fire, another shot rang out.

Garrett Buckley stumbled backward. His eyes glazed over. When he fell, Eli saw the bullet hole in the center of his forehead.

Eli raised himself on his elbow. He looked at the body beside him, then scanned the thick line of trees surrounding the clearing. From the evening's purple shadows, a tall, stocky man carrying a smoking rifle walked toward him.

Eli stood and held his Colt ready. As the figure neared, the could make out a gray beard and a leather patch over the old man's left eye.

"How is she, Doc?" From his post in the hall, Eli peeked into Betsy's bedroom for a glimpse of Annie as Dr. Biddle stepped out and closed the door behind him.

"She's a strong, healthy young woman, sheriff," the doctor replied, stuffing his stethoscope into his black leather bag. "The bullet went clean through her thigh. I reckon she may have a little trouble with that leg whenever the weather changes, but other than that, I think she'll mend nicely. After a few days' rest, Mrs. Larson will be just fine." Frowning, Doc Biddle slid his spectacles part of the way down his nose and peered above the rims. "You, on the other hand, look like the devil. When was the last time you slept?"

Eli ran his fingers through his tousled hair and glanced at the closed door. "I can't sleep until I've seen Annie."

With a nod, Dr. Biddle patted Eli's shoulder. "She's been askin' for you. As soon as Betsy has bandaged the wound, you can go in. But mind you, just for a short spell, you hear? She needs her rest."

"Thanks, Doc." Eli gave the man a tired smile. "Would you care for a cup of coffee before you leave?"

"No, no. I can't stay. Need to get on out to the Moores' place. The missus is due to deliver any day, you know. Since I'm this far out, anyway, I'd best go by and check on her.

You get yourself some rest now. Doctor's orders."

Eli walked Doc Biddle to the front door, said good-bye to him, then went to relay the good news about Annie to Billy and Deadeye.

The two of them were seated at the kitchen table and looked at him expectantly when he entered the room. Billy's eyes widened inquiringly, and the old man squinted the one that wasn't covered by the black patch.

"Annie's going to be all right," he told them. "Doc says so."

Billy hopped up from his chair. "Can I go see her now? Huh? Can I, Eli? Please?"

"Not today," Eli said, moving forward and ruffling the boy's hair. It still amazed him how quickly Billy had recovered from the whole incident. "Maybe tomorrow, if she's feeling up to it."

"Aw, Eli." The youngster stuck out his lower lip and sank back into his chair.

Eli smiled down at him, glad to see Billy carrying on in his usual manner. The small nick on his cheek was a reminder of what the boy had been through. But at the moment, he looked nothing like the frightened child who'd had to be pried from his hiding place in the woods.

"You know what?" Eli asked, slipping an arm around his shoulder. "Betsy said she thought Prissy may have moved her litter of kittens into the Bruecks barn a couple of weeks ago. Said she'd been hearing cats mew out there. Of course, I'm sure it didn't have anything to do with the fact that you've been crawling under the porch pestering them daily, but I'd be obliged if you'd go out and check the hayloft and see if you can find them.''

Billy pressed his lips into a tight line. ''Well, I reckon I could do that. But you'll holler for me, won't ya, if Annie needs me to fetch her something?''

''I promise.''

Billy grinned, then dashed out the door and headed for the barn.

''That there is a fine young 'un, sheriff,'' Deadeye Pete commented. ''Is he yourn?''

Eli hesitated. He moved to the stove, poured himself some coffee, then walked over and refilled Deadeye's cup. ''I wish he were.''

The old man smiled, then ducked his head. ''I sorta know what you mean, sheriff. I've always looked upon Annie . . . well, like she was m' daughter.''

Eli pulled out a chair and sat down, placing the coffeepot on the trivet in the middle of the table. ''I don't know how to thank you for what you did yesterday,'' he said quietly.

Deadeye peered at him from under his bushy silver brows. ''Ain't no thanks needed, sheriff. What I done, I done for Annie. She's all I got, ya know.'' Straightening, he lifted his bearded chin and set both fists on the table. ''I came after her, I did. When I heard you had caught her, as soon as I was able to ride, I came after her. Then I got word that you'd up and married her, and I had to come see for m'self. I found your spread easy enough, stood on the ridge behind that line of trees, checkin' things out. Then Annie stepped out on the back stoop wearin' the prettiest yellow dress I ever seen." Deadeye swallowed and shook his head. "Well, sir, the sight brought tears to my eyes, it did."

Eli noted the present brightness in the old man's one good eye. "So you left without ever even talking to her?"

Deadeye nodded. "But I came back a few more times, just to keep a watch. I could see from a distance, I could, that Annie was farin' well with you. Don't mind tellin' ya, if I hadda thought you was doing her wrong I woulda done put a bullet in ya."

Eli scanned the outlaw's wrinkled face and felt a common bond. They both loved Annie—in different ways, but just as much.

It occurred to him that Annie had been right about Deadeye Pete. The old man was everything she'd said he was—honest, forthright . . . and honorable.

Eli ran a finger around the rim of his cup. "I still can't figure out how you knew Annie was in trouble yesterday. How did you find us, Pete?"

"Heard a couple of the boys talkin'. One of 'em said Frank and Buck had gone to fetch Annie back." Deadeye took a sip of his coffee, then sighed heavily. "I rode out for your place, but by the time I got there, the house was burned to the ground. I knew that had to be Buck's doing. He always was the meanest damned critter." He shook his head.

"Anyways, I was headed for the hideout when I heard shots. Took me a while to get my bearings, but I circled through the woods till I came upon Buck about to shoot your head off."

"I'm sure glad you got there when you did." Eli stared past the old man, and regret filled him. "I was a fool to lay down my gun."

"The way I see it, you didn't have no choice, son. In the same situation, I woulda done the same. Your paw woulda, too, ya know."

Eli furrowed his brows. "You knew my father?"

"Met him oncet in Abilene before the war. He was a deputy at the time." Deadeye scratched his beard. "Yep. It was a good while ago. Didn't know then I'd end up on the wrong side of the law. The wife and I were visitin' some of her kin, and I'd slipped down to the saloon. I was standing at the bar, mindin' my own business, when your paw walked in, sidled up next to me, and ordered a whiskey. Wasn't two seconds later, some yahoo who'd had too much to drink and apparently held some grudge against tin-stars, came up behind him with a knife." Dead-eye grimaced. "Never could abide backstabbers myself. I just reached out and grabbed the fella's wrist. He was so dead-drunk, wasn't no chore to take the knife from him."

Eli leaned forward. "You saved Paw's life?"

"Well, now I wouldn't go puttin' it that

away. I reckon anybody else in my place woulda done the same. Sam was obliged though, and asked if he could buy me a drink. Took us a bottle and moved over to a table. We jawed about this and that.'' The old man shook his head, then chuckled. ''Wasn't nobody ever believed me when I told 'em years down the line that I oncet sat across the table from Sam Larson. 'Course, back then, I didn't have no idea he would become the legend that he did. Never crossed my mind when we were sittin' there finishin' off that bottle that someday I'd be runnin' from 'im.'' Deadeye scratched his ear. ''You know what I remember most 'bout that whole conversation? Was something your paw said. Struck me as odd even at the time, but now, I ought to tell ya, we was both sailin' three sheets to the wind. Looked me straight in the face, he did, and claimed he hadn't never truly wanted to be a lawman. Said killin' hadn't never set well with 'im. Told me what he'd really wanted all along was to be a blacksmith. Can you imagine that? Sam Larson, a smithy?''

Eli stared blankly at the old outlaw, absorbing each word. He'd never suspected his father had wanted to be anything other than a lawman. The man had always seemed a little more than human. It occurred to Eli now that maybe his father *would've* understood if he had only stepped forward and told him that he wanted to be a schoolmaster. Maybe Sam Larson would've understood about a lot of things if Eli had chanced to approach him.

"Eli?" Betsy called from the kitchen door, jarring him from his thoughts. "Annie would like to see you."

Annie attempted to prop herself a mite higher on the pillows, but the movement sent a shooting pain down her leg. With the pain came a vision of her brother as she'd last seen him. She closed her eyes, willing the sight away, but it persisted along with memories of Buck and his cruelty.

The knock at the door rousted her. Eli's face replaced all the bad thoughts. She smiled at him, feeling her heart lift as he crossed the room and took the hand she offered.

When he settled in the chair beside the bed, she noted how weary and worn he looked. She traced his stubbled chin with a fingertip. "I've caused you a passel of grief, haven't I?" she asked. "Can't say I'd blame you if you sent me away now."

His pale green eyes held a soft glow. One corner of his mouth raised in a lazy smile. "Oh . . . I think I might just keep you," he said teasingly, and brushed a strand of hair from her cheek. His smile wavered slightly. "After all I've been through to bring you home, Mrs. Larson, I don't think I'll be able to let you out of my sight again."

Annie studied his features. She wanted to believe she'd heard sincerity in his joshing tone. "Honest?"

"Honest." Cupping her face with his hands, he pressed his lips to her forehead.

"You and me and Billy, Annie. That's how it's going to be."

Her throat swelled. She shuddered. Then her vision blurred. The puddles in her eyes spilled over and ran down her cheeks. "Eli," she blurted out, her breath coming in short rasps, "I'm . . . crying . . . and I . . . can't for the life of me . . . figure why."

He pulled back and looked at her, wiping his thumbs across her damp cheeks. "Do you suppose that could be because you're happy?"

Annie took a deep shaky breath. "Well . . . of course, I'm happy. But . . . it's plumb crazy to cr-cry when you're so happy, isn't it?"

"No, Annie, it's not." He folded her in his arms and held her dear. "Not when you're as happy as we are," he whispered into her ear.

She relaxed against him, letting his warmth calm her. She could barely believe it. She and Eli and Billy. That was how it was going to be. They were going to be a real family. She'd make a home out of Eli's place. A place filled with love and laughter and—

She stiffened suddenly. "Oh, Lord, Eli. The house. The house is gone, and it's all my fault. Buck never woulda done what he did if I hadn't been there."

"Don't worry about the house," he said, tightening his hold on her. "A house doesn't make a home. I believe sometimes things happen for a reason. Maybe it was time for a change. Time for us to make a whole new start."

Annie loved him so much in that moment that she thought she would surely burst. His words awoke the familiar feeling of sunshine deep inside her. "Eli?"

"Hmm?"

"Could you . . . can we . . . well, could we tangle? Right here, right now? We could latch the door and—"

Eli eased away from her, resting his hands on her shoulders. With a wide grin, he shook his head. "No. You are not going to talk me into it this time, Mrs. Larson." He lifted an eyebrow. "Not until your wound heals. Understand?"

"But it only hurts a bit, and we could be care—"

"Annie." He cocked his head. His expression plainly stated he was taking a stand here.

Annie twisted her mouth to one side. She figured there wasn't much use in pursuing the matter. She could always try again later on. Dropping her gaze, she fiddled with the blanket. "Did I hear Deadeye out there a while ago?"

"You sure did."

She looked at Eli in surprise. "How come he ain't locked up?"

Eli closed his hand over hers, stilling her nervous fingers. "Because he taught me a very valuable lesson. Sometimes the law and justice are two different things."

Annie nodded. "So you're letting him go?"

"Yes. But he wanted to tell you good-bye before he left."

Annie jerked her gaze to his. "Left?"

"He's going to Mexico."

"What in tarnation is he going to do a fool thing like that for?" she asked with a frown.

Eli shook his head. "I suppose you'll have to ask him that question."

"Get him in here and I'll do just that."

Eli stood and crossed the room. Opening the door, he called for the old outlaw.

Within moments, Deadeye appeared in the doorway, holding his battered hat against his chest. When Eli started to leave the room, the old man caught his arm. "You stay, son. What I have to say ain't gonna take long."

He curled the brim of his hat as he moved forward to stand at Annie's bedside. A slow grin spread over his face. "How you doin', girl? You hurt much?"

"Nah." Annie returned his smile. "I reckon I'll live long enough to give you hell. What's this I hear about you headin' out for Mexico?"

He glanced down at his hat. "Yeah, well, I'm gettin' on in years, Annie. Had a little *señorita* sweet on me down south of the border once. Thought I might look her up and see if she's gotten herself hitched yet. Besides, it's time to leave my lawless ways behind. Ain't much good at it no more, anyhow."

"I wouldn't say that." She reached out and

caught the edge of his worn coat between her fingertips. "You were good enough to take Buck."

"Lucky shot, that's all." His grin faded, and he lowered his gaze. "I'm sorry about Frank. He wasn't all bad, ya know."

"I know that, Deadeye. You woulda been proud of him at the end. He was trying to help me." Annie stared at the old man's gray beard. "I hope—" She raised her gaze to his, then bit her bottom lip. "I mean, you didn't bury him next to Buck, did you?"

Deadeye shook his head. "Laid him to rest in a nice peaceful spot under a shady elm."

"I'm much obliged," she said softly.

"Wasn't no trouble." He glanced around the room, appearing flustered, then focused on Annie again. He looked at her for a long, quiet moment.

She watched a mistiness grow in his one good eye, and in that instant, knew that he was truly leaving. She swallowed hard and tried to smile, but her lips quivered with the effort.

"I come to say good-bye, Annie." His voice cracked as he spoke. "I couldn't go without tellin' ya—" He sniffed, then cleared his throat. "Dad-blame it. You know I've always thought of you as my own. I'll let you know where I am after I get settled. If you ever need me . . . if you need anything a'tall . . . you can . . . well, you know that I . . . that I . . ." His chin quaked.

"I know, Deadeye." Annie patted his arm. "I love you, too."

He nodded, rubbed his nose, then strode to the door. Squinting at Eli, he set his hat on his head. "You be good to her, son, ya hear?"

"Yes, sir. You can count on that."

Deadeye glanced from one to the other. "I expect y'all to get word to me when ya have your firstborn. Maybe I'll mosey up for a visit."

"We'd be glad to have you, sir." Eli grasped the old man's hand and shook it firmly.

Deadeye's gaze flickered to Annie once more. "Be happy, girl," he said, then stepped out the door.

Eli walked to the bed, braced his hip on the edge, and slipped an arm around Annie. She snuggled against him, pressing her cheek to his chest. "If our first is a boy, would you mind too much if we called him Pete?" she asked.

"Peter Larson." Eli rubbed his jaw across the top of her head. "I think that's a fine name, Annie."

She closed her eyes, sinking into the peacefulness of resting in her husband's arms. "I want to be with you when you tell Billy about us staying together," she murmured. "I want to tell him right away."

"You get some sleep. We'll tell him the good news after you wake up." He ran a fingertip along her hairline, then kissed her earlobe and whispered, "Have I ever told you how much I love you?"

Annie opened her eyes and cocked them

his way. "No. As a matter of fact, you haven't. But you know, I kinda figured you did all along. Leastways, I had a powerful inkling that you liked me. It was just like Deadeye said it would be, too. Sometimes, it just sneaks up on you and grabs you, don't it?"

"Annie, has anyone ever told you that you talk too much?"

"Well, as a matter of fact, there was the barber in Dregg's Flat who commented on that very thing a time or two. Then Deadeye, well he always did say that I—"

Turning her to face him, Eli pressed a finger to her lips. "Shh," he whispered, then covered her mouth with his.

Annie's heart was so full that she barely had room for the notion that she and Eli would be together forever. She wrapped her arms tightly around his neck, meeting the challenge of his kiss—the challenge of a new life—and plumb forgot whatever it was she'd been about to say.

Epilogue

April 22, 1889

Anxiously awaiting the return of her husband, Annie shifted her weight on the wagon seat and viewed the crowded border of the unassigned lands of Indian Territory.

Though a strong breeze blew from the south, it was a beautiful, cloudless day.

Excitement crackled in the air. Folks from all walks of life, Annie reckoned, lined the horizon for as far as the eye could see. They came in covered wagons, much like the one in which she now sat. They came in rigs, buggies, and buckboards. Some rode horses. Some were even afoot. But they all held one common dream. They were all seeking a new beginning.

Leaning forward, Annie peered past four other families and raised her hand to catch Betsy's attention. Betsy smiled that beautiful smile of hers and waved back, then nudged her new husband. Delbert turned and greeted Annie with a salute.

While Annie looked on, Delbert said something to Betsy, and the young woman regarded him with an expression of tender devotion. Annie settled back, knowing the two were lost to everyone but each other for the moment. She was happy for her friends, glad that they had decided to take a chance in the opening territory after Betsy's paw had passed on.

Of course, Ida Phipps hadn't been too pleased to hear the news. The woman had dang near had a conniption when the pair had married. Annie smiled every time she thought of the way Delbert had stood up to his ma. Ida had left the church complaining she "hadn't never" again, but Annie had already come to the conclusion that Ida surely must have at one point or another.

Recalling the day she'd spoken her own vows, Annie lovingly observed the wedding band on her finger. Eli had said he figured his mother would've wanted her to have it. He had worried, though, that the ring might cause bad memories. But Annie never thought of Buck when she looked at the small ruby set in gold. Instead, the ring served to remind her that she was a Larson. And she aimed to do the name proud.

She raised her gaze and scanned the green grassy prairies and the hillsides covered with wildflowers of every color. They were calling this land Oklahoma. Annie and Eli would soon call it home.

With the money from the sale of the spread in Bartlett Springs, they would build a school. Eli had come up with the notion of housing homeless Indian children, as well as any other orphans in the area. Annie intended to labor hard by her husband's side to make his dream come true. It was a good idea, she told herself now as she looked past the line of blue-uniformed cavalrymen and surveyed the countryside. And it would work. Reverend Perry had already offered to take up a special collection from time to time to help keep the school functioning. The Women's Circle of Bartlett Springs planned on having a bake sale to raise money for books.

The wagon wobbled, and Annie glanced sideways as Eli climbed onto the set beside her.

"Well, we're all set," he said, taking up the reins. "I've told Billy to round up the dogs and get them settled in back, and to make sure Priss and her kittens are all in their basket. It's almost noon. They should be firing the cannon any minute, and we'll be on our way." His smile dimmed as he searched her pensive expression. "Hey, you aren't having second thoughts about this, are you?"

"Nary a one," she said, then placed a hand on the side of his face. "I want this as much as you do, Eli."

"Ain't it time t' go yet?" Billy asked, bounding into the back of the covered wagon with the dogs at his heels.

"Almost," Eli replied over his shoulder, but kept his gaze on his wife. "Annie, do you remember the first time I—" He lowered his voice so that Billy couldn't possibly hear. "Do you remember the first time I kissed you?"

"Out by the corral?"

"Yes."

Annie cocked her eyes to the side and put a finger to her chin. "Well, let me see. Hmm. As I recall, it was *me* who kissed *you*."

"Yes, well, I don't suppose it really matters who kissed who." Tugging down the brim of his Stetson, he set his attention on something in the distance. "Do you remember what you were wishing for that night?"

"I sure do." Annie's lips curved slightly upward. "That particular wish was for a baby."

"Yeah." Eli nodded, then cleared his throat. "Well, the way I got it figured, we ought to stake our claim somewhere with a good clear view of the North Star." He took her hand, and his eyes met hers with a sweet, soft seriousness. "I think the first thing we should do once we're settled is make that wish again."

Annie's smile grew. She bent forward slightly and kissed him. "Eli," she whispered against his lips, "I had planned to wait till the land run was over before I told you, but since you brought it up . . . well, I sorta have an inkling that particular wish has done been taken care of."